The child of psychologists, Mary Mandolin's inquiry into the human psyche began at a young age and grew with her into adulthood. She seeks to understand a person's deepest pain: When did it happen? What did they learn from it? Who did they become as a result?

When called to write, Mary's first foray was to solve the riddle *What manner of love is strong enough to overcome an unforgivable act?* This question slung her into the romance genre, where she's been unraveling the answers ever since.

After living in Mexico, Great Britain, her Volkswagen van, and a smattering of US states, Mary has come home to a remote plot of land in California where she writes with permission from her two children, cats, and dogs, and with the support of her husband.

AIA PUBLISHING

MARY MANDOLIN

Whiteout

Mary Mandolin

Copyright © 2022

Published by AIA Publishing, Australia

ABN: 32736122056

http://www.aiapublishing.com

ISBN: 978-1-922329-30-1

*To the friends, family, editors, reviewers, and supporters
who helped bring this book to light.*

PROLOGUE

External nature is only internal nature writ large.
Swami Vivekananda

Grant rubbed his temples as the last two hours swirled in his mind—the crackling fire, the semi-nude woman curled in his arms, the near-death experience that confused her into kissing him. That kiss would have been a slam dunk except everything about it was horribly wrong.

Grant's skin crawled at the memory of Melinda's body twisted in the snow, that damned rotten branch tangled in her hair. He shook off the image and shoved more wood into the stove. The snowstorm had raged all afternoon since their return and tonight would be hard—harder than the one before.

His distraction failed; his movement stilled. The flashback of their hour in front of the fireplace played like an erotic movie in his mind. She'd made it difficult on him and snuggled into his embrace while he'd tried to keep his distance.

"This is an interesting way to save me," she said, pressing her breasts into his chest. *Mind over matter*, he told himself. Exactly how many snowflakes were there in a typical snowstorm?

"You were on your way to hypothermia," he replied stiffly. "This was to save your life."

"Well then," she breathed. "Would it throw a wrench in your chivalry if I said how much I'm enjoying being rescued?"

Grant had no idea what to say. He'd gone from mild flirtation to sprinting through a blizzard with an unconscious woman in his arms, and now he was struggling to stay on his white horse. Was that her foot inching up his leg? Those were definitely her fingers teasing the hair on his chest.

"You need to rest," he said weakly.

"I need to get warm," she whispered, and kissed him.

Oh, hell.

Being kissed by her was like alighting from a tornado. There was noise and panic and whirling energy, then suddenly there was stillness. Softness. Melinda's lips brushed his and drew him further from the storm.

CHAPTER ONE

*In a day when you don't come across any problems, you can
be sure that you are traveling in a wrong path.*
Swami Vivekananda

The Embraer 175's wings dipped to reveal the Rocky Mountains'
whitewashed peaks as the plane bumped east toward Denver.
Snow clouds hung heavy in the Colorado sky, muting the fading
sunset and reducing the landscape to gunmetal gray. Feathers of
ice stroked Melinda Sen's window and she wrapped her green-
and-gold dupatta more tightly around herself. It was December
and she was almost home.

Gauzy, gray-white curtains of snow hovered over the Front
Range, visible on her left. Melinda's eyes traced the frozen
world below as she worried the gold Chandi goddess pendant
at her sternum. Forecasters predicted nasty weather tonight,
even threatening blizzard conditions in parts of the foothills.
Fortunately, her condo was at the base of the mountains near
Golden, so she shouldn't be cut off from civilization. Still,
she was eager to collect her car from the Park & Ride and get
home safely.

Melinda shivered beneath her layers and rubbed her calves together. *Note to self: don't cuddle the fuselage next time.*

The plane sank and the pilot announced their imminent arrival. Plane landings reminded Melinda of the giddy, weightless feeling of a descending elevator, and her jacket hid her smile as she resisted the urge to jump in the aisle. Then, as usual, she wondered, *Could I blog about that?* Was there a parallel with food in there somewhere? What in the kitchen could possibly correlate to the childhood game of achieving a split second of weightlessness in an elevator by jumping as it reached its destination? And then, by extension, by jumping in a plane as it descended from the sky?

Obviously there'd be sprinkles. Melinda giggled out loud. The man in the aisle seat next to her hiked his eyebrows at his *Reader's Digest.*

"Sprinkles," she whispered, conspirator to conspirator.

Nope. *Digest* man spared her a sidelong glance, then pointedly continued reading, and Melinda glared at him before returning to the growing darkness outside her window. *Sorry you have no imagination, Magazine Man.*

Her wandering train of thought chugged along. *No, not sprinkles. Wasabi. Intensity followed by a lift—perfect.* Melinda sighed and sat back in her seat, food parallel achieved, and just in time.

The cabin lights flickered and dimmed, flight attendants collected stray cups and coffee sticks, and the captain wrestled more turbulence. Melinda dug her thumb into the nickel-sized metal button controlling her seat's angle and her seatback lurched forward. Sprinkles indeed.

They dropped lower.

Denver International Airport's peaked tents filled her window for a split second, then the plane angled into the wind and the

4

airport vanished. Melinda sized up the clouds lying in wait over the Front Range. Heavy, gray, looming. Not comforting, as adjectives went. *Hold off for another hour, could you?*

The natural light was almost gone and the earth grew closer and closer, larger and larger. The landscape blurred into shadow and indistinguishable shapes raced below her window. Runway lights flashed into view. The plane hit the ground with a force that jerked her head back. As they taxied to the gate, Melinda breathed a sigh of relief, despite how far from home she still was. Somewhere in her future were a glass of wine, a pair of clean pajamas, and hopefully a cooking show where contestants made cakes in the shapes of Michelangelo's *David* or double-decker buses. She wriggled her toes in her boots.

The quick weekend trip hadn't warranted checked luggage, so when her turn came, Melinda shouldered her black leather duffel bag and deplaned, bound for ground transportation. As an amorphous herd, the passengers tromped up the gangway and through Terminal C until a restroom beckoned, and she and a few others broke off. Melinda used the bathroom, took a quick sink bath, and rejoined foot traffic toward the underground train.

Tired faces droned past hers as she reviewed the conference that had taken her to Salt Lake City, an event so jam-packed she'd not showered for the two and a half days. She'd gone to the food blogging mega-expo because the organizers embraced weird and unusual subject matter. Her blog, *A Wing and A Prayer Kitchen*, was more of a cooking adventure blog, and it lacked the socially sexy *perfect meal in under thirty minutes* concept. Instead, Melinda tackled projects like "It's 5 p.m. And Your Fridge Is Empty, What Do You Do—WHAT DO YOU DO?"

She contributed a monthly column in Denver's lifestyle rag, *Mile High Home Magazine*, and a weekly experiment in her own kitchen landed on her blog. Her motto was "Let go and let it get good." As mottos went, it was a bit optimistic but somewhat truthful. Her concoctions were unplanned, undirected, and unsophisticated. She enjoyed highlighting issues her readers faced on a daily basis, like lack of time, lack of equipment, lack of essential ingredients, and turning them into success stories. Or humorous failures, she freely admitted. No matter what, it was a niche angle, it was her social outlet, and monetizing it paid the bills.

Melinda took her place on the moving walkway. Food bloggers were a funny bunch. Obsessed, enthusiastic, at times relentless—that was the world of food blogging. Crazy about finding the next big trend and cultivating an ever-growing following. Melinda boarded the train and contemplated semicolons. The right way to use them, the wrong way to use them, their relevance, or not, in five-hundred-word-maximum blogs that used words like "spicetastic" and "zingalicious." She gripped the train's support post as thousands of small propellers in the *Kinetic Light Air Curtain* installation spun in time with her mind.

She sighed. Semicolons weren't the conference's real takeaway. Neither were the quick coffee dates with the other bloggers, though it had been fun to put faces to the screen names.

Melinda had seen the writing on the wall, and it wasn't pretty.

Her work was cold. Forced. Heartless, even.

How was that even possible? Melinda stomped her foot and turned away from the surprised faces of fellow passengers. Despite aiming so artfully for laissez-faire breeziness, the conference speakers had shown her, through their own passion, that she was phoning it in. *So irritating!* Weren't her quirky approach and punchy language enough?

Apparently not.

Apparently she was closed off. Skilled but forgettable.

Pretending to be happy but patently fake. Trying to sparkle as she fell flat.

She may or may not have audibly growled. The woman to her left took a slow step backward.

Melinda forced her mind back to the conference. What did they know, anyway? She enjoyed what she did! Didn't she? Inspiring non-cooks to pick up a spatula interested and challenged her. Why did someone hate cooking one minute, then tackle *pasta fagioli* the next? That brave, uncertain moment in someone's day, or week, or life piqued her curiosity.

Did she obsess just a little about what they thought of her? Maybe. But a business owner should engage with her clients. So what if she didn't have that many friends outside of her blog? Hearing from readers was very rewarding. And if she worked late enough into the night she could almost pretend she had a social life.

Melinda was proud that she managed her own social media platforms, all stinking day long, and she celebrated her readers' attempts to cook along with her. She cared about their process. She enjoyed her readers. That should count for something. She grimaced. But did she care too much? What if she was codependent with her readers?

And a warm welcome back, Doctor Sen. Her therapist mother's parlance reared its unwelcome head. Melinda hadn't spoken with her mother in two years, yet never failed to recall Katrina's pedantic pearls of wisdom when life got complicated. *Insipid word, "codependent."*

Besides, Melinda wasn't one to avoid responsibility, and responsibilities had to be met. A social life was an indulgence she couldn't afford.

She stared past the flash of cement walls outside the train.

Fine. She might lack heart, but her writing kept her fed and housed. That should be enough. That was more than enough.

Melinda squared her shoulders and stepped from the train into a sea of people shuffling urgently but resignedly toward the escalator. She leaned on the escalator's black rubber handrail. What was "urgent but resigned" in the world of food? TV dinners, maybe? Potato chips? As she reached the top, she realized resigned food would have to wait until she had coordinated the last leg of her journey.

Melinda debated the Light Rail. It was more economical by miles. *But wine. And Michelangelo.*

Melinda turned away from baggage claim and liberated her smartphone from her duffel. One percent battery. *Stay with me and get me a car. Don't make me take the train.* She opened the Kaar app, requested a car, and watched the spinning dial indicate its progress. The screen registered success and she set off to meet Gerald in his luxurious navy sedan.

A Mercedes Maybach screamed "felony" at airport pickup but there was nothing to be done about it now. Grant Samson hunched over the wheel of the black four-door and scanned DIA's Arrivals loop for the woman whose picture illuminated his cell phone. Melisa Moorehouse was dark-haired and dark-eyed. Beautiful, if reserved-looking.

She had arrived from Phoenix at 5:17 p.m. and would request a Kaar. All Grant had to do was intercept her path to the real Kaar.

Fuck. Why not just steal the Crown Jewels? Grant rubbed his calloused hands together. Worn work gloves waited on the seat next to him for when he and Melisa reached the mountains. For now, the luxury vehicle's heating system was adequate. But not for nerves.

Nearby vehicles collected passengers as Grant inched forward, the corner of one eye trained on the parking sharks. He'd already circled the airport twice. *What the hell kind of favor is this?*

There. Acid flared high in his stomach as Melisa strode through the glass sliders. *At least Paul "Moneybags" DiMario can afford my bail.* His foot crept off the brake.

Melisa was taller than he'd expected, half a head above the average female travelers around her. Grant watched her shrink into her coat, then scan the line of cars and settle on his. Her eyes sought the Kaar sticker taped to the inside of his windshield, and she pulled her phone from her pocket.

Melisa closed her eyes and appeared to think for a long moment. Presumably, miraculously, the color of the car sent to meet her matched his own vehicle well enough and she shoved the phone into her bag as she walked toward him.

What are the odds. DiMario, you lucky son of a bitch.

Grant tracked Melisa as she crossed the sidewalk, dodging luggage and antsy children. She moved fluidly but carefully. There was a deliberateness to her steps, as if she anticipated the unexpected.

Grant eased the car forward to meet her and rolled down the passenger window as she approached. He breathed deep to soften the stress from his face. She reached his car and leaned down to peer at him.

Her large, dark eyes met his directly, without hesitation or coyness. Oh, hell. The phone picture had done nothing for her. Grant inhaled as a veil of glossy black hair obscured Melisa's face momentarily as she twisted to give a luggage cart clearance behind her. She turned to face him again and the ground dropped away.

Against his will, Grant's eyes fell to her mouth, wide, softly sculpted, a muted mauve that wore no augment. Grant felt his own lips part in anticipation of—*What the hell?* his mind interrupted. *Get it together.*

Paul had never mentioned that she was Indian. She was Indian, wasn't she? At least half. *That mouth.* His mind scrambled for traction. Where was he? What was he doing? *Shut the hell up!* he yelled silently. This was Paul's woman. His girlfriend, and probably very shortly his fiancée, if Grant's guess was correct. *Get your mind out of the gutter, Samson.*

Because it was there. The gutter. The delicate, feminine gutter. He imagined brushing her hair from the nape of her neck and leaning down to kiss—*Dammit.*

This was going to be difficult.

"Mel—" he began.

"Gerald?" she asked, breathless from the cold, and smiled as he nodded. "Great. My phone froze but I thought this was you." Her voice was honey. Tempered by the frigid air, but honey nonetheless.

Gerald. I guess that's my name. And you'll be Gorgeous, Gorgeous.

"I aim to please," Grant said. He left the engine running and rounded the car's nose to stand before her. His fingers twitched. *Steady, now.* He kept his gaze level and reached for the strap on her shoulder. Melisa jerked her face to his.

"I can keep it with me," she said, reflexively grabbing at her bag. A black luggage tag embossed with a gyroscope-like design bobbed with the movement.

"I know." He held the bag between them like a monster. *I know?* his mind parroted. *Smooth, Don Juan.* "Or . . . I can stash your stuff up here with me. Get it out of your way?" Grant's nerves flailed and spun along with the bag's ID tag. This was not

10

typical Kaar driver behavior.

Melisa eyed her bag as it dangled from his fist.

"That's okay," she said slowly. "You don't want my bag cluttering up your front seat. Plus, I don't like to be more than a few inches from my phone at all times." A wry smile played on her lips and he laughed, but he knew he had lost.

"We're all hooked on them, aren't we?" He struggled to bring his smile up to his eyes. "Sometimes I leave mine where I can't reach it so I can feel like a human being again." What the hell was he saying? There was no way to force her hand without being completely obvious.

"Actually, I forgot my charger where I was staying," she said. "Do you have one?"

"No," he lied. "Sorry about that. I left mine at my house. Rookie mistake." He hated himself. *Stop flirting with Paul's girlfriend.* Why was he making this situation worse?

Because Grant wasn't in the mood to hear her talk nice with her perfect boyfriend, that's why. Not with himself a foot away. And if the real Kaar driver contacted her before Grant was ready to spring the surprise, Melisa would think she was actually being kidnapped. Not exactly a romantic Christmas gift.

He kept the smile as he slipped a hand past her hips to release the rear door handle. Melisa stood clear and Grant swung the door wide.

Melinda paused at the door Gerald held for her and scanned him from toe to top. Worn jeans overlapped work boots and a brown-and-green plaid flannel peeked above the collar of his brown suede jacket. She surveyed his face and found it to be an honest one. Attractive—ruggedly so. Laugh lines at the eyes, smile lines around the mouth, a little salt in the stubble. Somewhere around forty, she would guess.

His hazel eyes fixed her brown ones with an expression she couldn't read. Professional distance? Attraction? Guilt? The skin at the nape of her neck prickled. Was something off? Maybe. There was a tension about him. Then again, airport traffic was a nightmare.

Melinda heard her mother's voice telling her to walk away, sit down, take a break, feel it out. "If something's not right, trust the feeling." *Easier preached than done, Kitty Kat.* Katrina Sen, broken marriage and family therapist. What good was advice from a defeated soul? None, which was why Melinda had stopped taking it when she was thirteen. Also why she took Kaars, lived alone, worked alone, and didn't expect to get married. Was she a little too vehement about thumbing her nose at the rules? Maybe. Had things turned out all right so far? *Yes.* She thought of her faltering career and solitary existence. *Mostly.*

Confidence emanated from Gerald like a pied piper's tune. He wasn't hurried and he wasn't worried. He knew she'd get in the car. There was no socially acceptable reason she shouldn't.

Why did he deserve confidence while she didn't? His above-average height and tree-trunk legs? The shoulders like a bull in the stocks as it waited to break free? A bull with sexy eye crinkles and tousled brown hair, she amended. He stood patiently as her mind dallied with his physique.

Stop staring and get in the car. Melinda gave up her analysis and settled into the rear seat. Gerald waited as she buckled her seatbelt, then handed in her bag and closed the door with a controlled *click*.

Electric heat warmed her legs and back and Melinda moaned in spite of herself. Maybe Gerald could drive her to her next conference. She shifted her seatbelt to remove her jacket. *If I survive this ride, Gerald's getting a good review.* She chuckled quietly. *Who am I kidding. If I survive this ride I'm ordering a Kaar every day of the week and hoping to get Mr. Mountain Man again.*

"Do you know where the Park & Ride off Ward is?" Melinda asked as Gerald dropped into his seat. His scent flooded the car and she inhaled automatically. Was it cologne? Or just cleanliness plus the smell of the cold? "I know it's in the app," she continued, as if all her senses weren't on fire, "but there's construction there so I wanted to check."

"Been there twice today already," Gerald replied with a quick one-sided smile in the rearview mirror, and she relaxed, marginally. Hopefully he was too yummy to be a serial killer.

She snorted silently. What the hell did that even mean? She immediately answered herself. *It means he's hot, Melinda. Subtly, darkly, confusingly hot. Like a boozy bread pudding that's not too sweet and makes you slow down to eat it, but then you eat the whole thing. And you're too satisfied afterward to hate yourself.*

Great. Now she was in food fantasy *and* man fantasy mode. Melinda's fingers snaked to her goddess pendant. *You there?* she asked Chandi, hater of evil-doers, slayer of demons. Her idol hadn't glowed red or shot lasers at Gerald on sight, so hopefully the drive would be uneventful.

A Kaar wasn't worth the expense, given that the train would have taken her directly to her car. But after the emotional turmoil of the weekend, plus the packed overwhelm of the flight, she wanted to be alone with her thoughts before she had to be in charge of a moving vehicle. And her life. Melinda saw the flash of what must have been Gerald's phone as he checked directions. Then he buckled his seatbelt, put the car in drive, and pulled into the steady flow of Arrivals traffic.

13

Got her.

Grant sent the text, secured his cell phone in the dashboard holster, and followed the stream of cars out of the covered pick-up zone.

The first flakes of the night's storm hit the windshield and Grant turned the wipers on low and the defrost on medium. He checked the rearview mirror. Whatever whizzed past them captivated Melisa's attention. *Damn.* No, not damn, damn was wrong. Melisa was one hundred percent not available. Which meant that being in the car with her was all that he was going to get.

Except he sensed her body in the seat behind him. He heard the fabric of her jeans over the hum of the engine as she crossed her legs. Heard her sigh and felt his body tighten. *She's taller than I expected.* His mind idled. *Almost to my nose. How tall is my nose if I'm six foot three? Did she have boots with heels?* Grant couldn't remember. He cursed under his breath. It was hard to undress her with his mind if he couldn't remember what she wore.

"Warm enough?" Grant asked. *Pathetic. What's next?* Grant's mind taunted. *Maybe she's got deep thoughts on weather patterns?*

"Yes, thanks," Melisa replied. "This heated seat is amazing. That plane was made of cardboard and duct tape." He laughed. Her voice was warm. Contented.

Okay, buddy. Get it together. Tonight, he was a Kaar driver. And the woman he lusted after was in love with his friend.

"Work trip?"

"Yes," Melisa said. "I'm a writer. A blogger, if you must know." She laughed lightly at herself, and it was all he could do to stay on the road. Who laughed and it sounded like sex?

Grant stared at the taillights of the car in front of them, puzzled. Paul had made it sound like Melisa was a massage therapist, not a writer. But he figured that these days everyone needed a few jobs to make ends meet.

"Why the laugh?" Grant struggled to compose himself. "Blogging counts as writing." He needed the honeyed voice to continue. Desperately, no matter how wrong it was. Maybe a laugh or two—if she spaced them out so he wouldn't crash the car.

"Thanks," she said, a smile in her voice. "I like the connections I make with people, the emails I get from them saying they tried something I suggested and it woke up their palates." She recrossed her legs and leaned forward, and Grant gripped the wheel. "But the truth is that when you get us all together, we're like gerbils who've found a stash of Gummy Bears."

She laughed at herself again, low and husky, and his foot twitched on the gas pedal.

Keep it in your pants. "Why?" he managed.

"Because we're all amped up about menial stuff." Something soured in her tone. "We run around stuffing our faces with vendor food and discussing the best way to build a following or photograph an eggplant in July. It's frantic and funny and relatively meaningless." She shifted and for a moment her hair shone in the rearview mirror. "There are good times too. Like, a mom wrote me recently. She'd gotten brave and tried some of my recipes because she wanted to fall in love with food. She wants her *daughter* to love food. There's something real there. That part feels good." She sighed. "At least that part feels good."

Grant nodded. "I get it. I know what it feels like when I contribute and when I don't. It makes a difference."

"Yeah," she said quietly. Then she seemed to shake herself.

"What kind of car is this?" she asked brightly. "I've never been in such a nice Kaar before."

Way to blend in, Paul. Grant scrambled for a suitable reply. "Yeah it's a little above and beyond, but boys and their toys, right?"

Melisa laughed. "And does this toy have snow tires? Are we going to make it to my car?"

"Nothing but the best for this baby. You'll get to where you're headed, no problem." Grant forced his voice to be calmer than he felt and waited. Was a little lighthearted chauvinism enough? Lit by oncoming traffic, Melisa's cheek flexed in the outline of a smile and Grant released the breath he held.

That's enough talking for now.

It felt good to talk to Gerald about her weekend. *It always feels good to get down on some bread pudding, especially when it smells this amazing.* Melinda inhaled. Was there pine, too? Yes, plus spice. And . . . Motor oil? She was enjoying herself. What was the food parallel for a sexy-smelling man? Did there need to be a parallel? A good-smelling man was delectable on his own.

City lights brightened beyond the tinted windows. Gerald's car changed highways and industrial complexes made way for stadiums and high-rises. Snow fell faster, and the windshield wipers whirred steadily. The engine's hum soothed her, and before long a sign predicted the Ward Road Park & Ride. He'd taken her to her car. Not a serial killer.

Point, Melinda.

Not that she'd wanted her internal parent to be right. And not that Melinda didn't trust her own sense of unease. She'd honed her instincts over the twenty years since adolescence; it was a requirement of being a woman. "Is he looking at me?" "Is there anyone else around?" "Was that innuendo?" "Did anyone else see that?" The list of questions in the playbook of Sexual Harassment and Assault Prevention was long, not to mention infuriating.

She waited for Gerald to signal and move to the right lane, almost sad that their chemically charged time together was ending.

Gerald's signal stayed silent. The car stayed left.

Oh, he knows another route. Melinda pushed against the tinge of worry. She peered around Gerald's seat to check his GPS. Instead of the illuminated map mounted to the dashboard that she expected, she saw a phone with a darkened screen. Melinda's stomach tightened. Why wasn't Gerald following a map?

Well obviously it was because he knew of another exit. *Stop being dramatic. He's been here twice today; he's avoiding construction.*

"This is the exit," she said, her voice intentionally light, as if she were simply reminding him and not speculating on his likelihood of being a psychopath.

"Tonight's the night, Melisa," said Gerald. He angled his head toward her and smiled. "Congratulations."

The smile was off, and Melinda's stomach clenched harder. No eye crinkles this time.

"Wait, what?" The hairs on her arms stood high.

Melinda flattened her palms against her thighs and forced air into her lungs.

What had he said? He thought her name was Melisa. A simple mistake—he hadn't read her name correctly.

Or she was in the wrong Kaar. It probably happened all the time. Soon he'd pull over and they'd figure out what went wrong.

Gerald's eyes flicked to hers in the rearview mirror.

"Paul set it up for Sunday night because he wanted it to be a surprise. He said it's normally over a weekend, but he knows how you like surprises. So here we are." He smiled the empty smile again. "*Variety*. Hope you enjoy yourself."

A cold fist gripped her heart and Melinda shivered against the warm seat.

"*My name is not Melisa*," she said, emphasizing each word and leaning forward to try to meet his eyes. "You got the wrong person. You need to pull over. *Please*." Where was her phone? Maybe it had enough life for an emergency call. She patted the seat next to her and sought the zipper on her bag.

Gerald's eyes narrowed in the rearview mirror. "He didn't say anything about you acting like this." He sounded annoyed and Melinda's pulse picked up. "Is that part of the thrill? Do me a favor, save the act for Paul. I have to concentrate on getting us to the mountains."

The mountains? Melinda's skin crawled. *He's angry—why are psychopaths always angry?* Was he insane and pinning some ex-lover's betrayal on her? Or was he genuinely mistaken about who she was? And was he saying this Melisa person expected to be kidnapped? Melinda unzipped her bag and dug through dirty clothes. Shouldn't cell phones come on command by now? Why the hell hadn't someone invented the Cell Phone Clapper?

She tried to reason with him. "Gerald, I don't know who Paul is. Please, please could you please stop?" Melinda found her wallet and flipped it open to her license. "Check my ID. My name isn't Melisa, it's Mel*inda*. Please, Gerald, please?" He had to be insane. No honest man would keep driving after learning he had the wrong passenger.

Gerald glared at her in the rearview mirror but made no move to take her ID.

"Is this how you get turned on?" he growled. "This is messed

18

up. I'm just trying to do a favor." He barked out a laugh. "*A favor.*
You guys are sick. I knew this was a mistake. Where's the favor
in kidnapping someone and hauling them to some mountain
cabin? Especially with weather coming. I'll be lucky to make it
to my place after I take you to him."

Kidnapping? Cabin? Melinda's mind sputtered and spun.
"Gerald, please, listen," she said. "I don't know any Paul. I don't
know who Melisa is. You picked up the wrong person. Won't
Paul be upset if I show up and he really wants Melisa?"

Finally. She found her phone wedged beneath her bag on
the seat. Would the sudden brightness of the screen alert him
and make him become violent?

No—because it was well and truly dead.

Grant's stomach churned. Paul hadn't said anything about
Melisa playacting that she was anything but willing. Happy,
even. His hands tightened on the wheel and his foot depressed
the accelerator. Shouldn't she be happy right now?

"I didn't sign up for the drama, lady, and I'd appreciate it if
you'd knock it off. Paul gave me your picture. I know it's you.
Quit the role-playing, for all our sakes," he said. He hit the
button to raise the partition between the front and back seats.

"Gerald!" She clawed at the wall he erected.

"Calm down, lady. Give me a break!" Grant's blood pressure
had to be in the four hundreds, if that was even possible.

"Please! Please, I'm not who you think I am!"

Grant's seat shook as her fists beat the partition and he ground
his teeth together. No way was he lowering the partition again.
This chick is crazy. Who the hell got turned on by pretending to

be held hostage by a stranger?

DiMario had said it would be easy. A bizarre favor, but a favor nonetheless, to pretend to kidnap his girlfriend of three years and whisk her through the foothills to his cabin for who-knows-what. Grant's lip curled. Apparently something wild, if Melisa's behavior was any indication.

This night couldn't be over soon enough.

Paul had loaned Grant his loaded Mercedes for the evening and explained that Melisa would want to call Paul once she realized their annual rendezvous was happening. With a slight cough, Paul had suggested raising the partition in case the phone call got "personal." The partition, typically for private business meetings when he was being chauffeured, was the perfect solution.

"You'll be able to hear her if she yells," Paul had said as he showed Grant the button for the automated barrier. "But not if she speaks at a normal level. So give her a little privacy when she asks for it and expect her to call for you when she's ready for small talk."

Nothing awkward about chit-chatting with my buddy's girlfriend after they have phone sex. But to each their own. Grant somewhat admired Paul and Melisa for keeping their romance alive.

"Won't she recognize the car?" Grant had asked. "Are you sure you want to trust me with this? It's worth more than my fleet put together." As a snowplow driver, Grant was used to the snow, but airport traffic could get cutthroat and he wasn't responsible for other drivers' states of inebriation or idiocy.

"She's never seen it," Paul said. "I use my Land Cruiser after work so that's what she knows. She doesn't care for flash."

"You have too much money." Grant laughed.

"Don't scratch it." Paul tossed him the keys.

The timing had been perfect, since Grant needed a lift from

the airport to his own property, ten miles from Paul's cabin in Silverthorne. Grant had visited his brother's family in North Dakota for a week after the birth of his second niece and hadn't had a spare rig to leave at airport parking during snow season. Paul had snapped his fingers and someone met Grant's flight that afternoon with the Mercedes. Up until Melisa started the waterworks, it had seemed like an okay plan.

Grant found a classic rock station and twisted the volume to an uncomfortable level to drown out Melisa's hollering. Surely she'd get bored soon and call Paul. He squirmed in his seat, conscious of growing abdominal pains. *What the hell? This isn't keeping the romance alive, this is giving me an ulcer.*

Melinda was crying. Again. She'd cried, stopped crying, yelled, kicked the doors, hit the partition, screamed for help. She'd tried and failed to roll down the windows, tried and failed to squeeze into the trunk space and kick out the taillights. She'd beat on the windows and waved frantically. But with the late hour and tinted windows, no one saw inside her luxurious mobile prison.

Now she cried tears of incredulity. This wasn't what was supposed to happen to her. She deserved better than this B movie terror. She cried tears of remorse that she hadn't trusted the voice of fear, that her gut sense about Gerald had been wrong—that she had been attracted to him for even a moment. She cried the tears of giving up, of realizing that this was when bad things happened.

Where would he take her? What would he do to her? Was Paul some made-up persona that Gerald would become after they arrived at their destination? Or was there really a Paul?

Would there be two of them? Two men—and her?

Melinda's elbows dug into her thighs, fingers caging her face and fingernails biting her scalp. Her throat ached. Her head ached. Her pride ached.

Outside, wind pelted the car with snow. She looked at her phone accusingly. Why the hell had she forgotten her charger at the hotel? She could have charged her phone on the way. Somewhere. Anywhere.

If her dumb phone had had any juice left, she'd be in a police car right now giving them a play-by-play as another car took her kidnapper straight to hell. *Or jail. Jail, hell, whatever— hopefully they're the same thing for him.*

If her phone hadn't died she could have at least texted someone. Made herself anything other than completely helpless. Melinda pushed back her hair and stared out the window with raw eyes. She laughed, a hollow sound that rang in her own ears. Oh yeah? Who could she have texted? Her editor? Remy wouldn't have known what to do—the woman was a mouse. And certainly not her useless brother, Max. This was too inconceivable. He would have laughed. "Figure it out, Sen," he'd say. What he always said when she needed him. Then he'd hang up, crack a beer, and watch a movie.

Melinda shuddered and hiccuped, and then her tears ceased like a dried-up spring. She was surprised tears had come at all. She worked hard to keep the drama of life, and its emotions, at bay. The last time she'd cried was at her maternal grandmother's funeral, in her senior year of college.

Who would worry that she hadn't checked in after arriving home? No one, that's who. There was absolutely no one. And she had liked it that way, for so long. No one to shame her for wearing the wrong thing, the way friends did. No one to tell her what to do, what to think, the way boyfriends did. No one to abandon her, the way family did. She was independent. She was free.

A fat lot of good that freedom was doing her now.

Melinda twisted in her seat. Her readers thought she was so brave, so adventurous. She could handle anything life threw at her. Even when she failed, she laughed it off and kept trying—that's what made her relatable! Authentic! Too bad she was a total fraud who controlled everything, so nothing and no one could control her. And what she couldn't control, she slept through, a somnambulist in daredevil's clothing. Well, this was one hell of a wake-up, wasn't it?

They'd been driving for so long. They were well into the foothills now. She recognized I-70, Genesee, Idaho Springs, Loveland Ski Area. *Oh God, we're going through the tunnel.* The road noise intensified and was simultaneously muffled. Where the hell was he taking her? Melinda's throat clenched and she struggled to swallow. The car chugged along and emerged at the top of the ten-mile slope above Dillon and Silverthorne. And then it slid sideways.

I-70 twisted and turned through the foothills to higher and higher slopes. Shoulders hiked to his ears, Grant counted the minutes and gripped the wheel. Swirling snowfall blurred the high-mast lighting at the highway's edge and dampened their yellow beams to an ominous amber fog. Trees that Grant knew lined the highway morphed into a legion of murky black shadows witnessing his crime.

Melisa had stopped yelling a while ago, before the snow had gotten bad and the car had lost traction. Whether she was dozing or relishing her performance, Grant didn't care to speculate. Either way, it was about time she shut up and let him drive. He'd lowered the volume of the music earlier so she could call Paul if she wanted, and now it was his turn. One hand on the wheel, Grant snagged his phone from the passenger seat and pressed its command button, enunciating "Call Paul DiMario" at the robotic voice's prompt. Then he cursed. No cell service. Of course.

By the time they made it through the Eisenhower tunnel, the Maybach was cruising at an exhilarating five miles an hour. The car's wipers slapped frenetically at the windshield in a vain attempt to mitigate the dumping snow. Despite the car's chunky tires, they were slipping all over the ten-mile, two thousand-foot descent between Loveland Ski Area and Silverthorne. Grant's shoulders burned with strain.

A hundred bucks said they were shutting down the tunnel at that very moment. The blizzard had added over an hour to their journey, and Grant noted the time as he took the exit for Silverthorne. 9:24 p.m. How the hell was he going to get home? The last place he wanted to be was ringside at Paul and Melisa's celebration. Grant turned right, veered left, passed avenues, drives, and circles, and snaked closer to Paul's cabin.

"You'd better be here, Moneybags," Grant growled as, at last, he guided the car from the paved public lane to Paul's roughshod road.

With one last turn, the sedan's tires met Paul's gravel driveway and Grant's neck flushed with relief. He urged the vehicle forward and parked on the detached garage's concrete pad where he rolled his shoulders and flexed his cramped fingers. The relief was short-lived, however, as Paul's Land Cruiser was conspicuously absent.

"Shit." *What now?*

His phone connected to Paul's Wi-Fi, and the phone service that had eluded him for the last hour and a half returned in a flurry of text messages. Grant's eyebrows lifted. The power was still on. That meant he could crank up the heat when they got inside. Finally, something would go right tonight.

Messages chimed one after the next and Paul's name flashed repeatedly across his phone's screen.

Easy there, fella. He opened Paul's chat stream and the blood drained from his face.

> *How's it going? All go according to plan? You must be out of range so I'll see you in a bit. Was Mel surprised or did she guess?*
> *Got held up, leaving now.*
> *Oh shit.*
> *You got the wrong chick.*
> *Grant where the fuck are you? Mel just got here with me. She took a real Kaar home. I'm going to be sick. Who's in that car?*
> *Damnit, where are you?*
> *This is a train wreck. They closed the tunnel and Mel and I are stuck at a hotel in Georgetown. We're going to jail. If you make it to my place, call me.*

Grant waited for the buzzing in his ears to stop. He waited for the nausea to abate. Neither happened.

Grant dropped his phone on the passenger seat. He pushed open the door and dragged himself to his feet without feeling the tornado of snow that slammed into him. He reached for the door handle to face Melinda—because that was her name, apparently—and couldn't think of a thing he'd dreaded more in his life.

25

CHAPTER TWO

Comfort is no test of truth.
Truth is often far from being comfortable.
Swami Vivekananda

Melinda's tears were long gone, voided like a physiological need. Before tonight she'd been proud of how she resisted emotion, but now no form of release remained. Now she was numb with tension, with exhaustion and stone-cold fear. She wished she could cry again. Or scream. Or vomit. Anything to break this oppressive confinement.

She'd thought they'd reached the cabin when Gerald had suddenly slowed the car near to stopping. Then the car slid at a sickening angle, and she understood that he was saving their necks. They swerved, fishtailed, and gently slid across four lanes of traffic a dozen times before Melinda decided it was better not to count. Why did she have to get kidnapped during a blizzard? *Because this is a nightmare. And in nightmares even nature pits herself against you.*

It had been a while since they had slid and Melinda stared at the partition with eyes hot and dry. The cruel humor of being an

Indian American woman separated by a literal partition was not lost on her, but she'd already indulged in one ironic laugh. She hooked two fingers through the chain of her necklace. Where the bloody hell was Chandi? This officially constituted an evil act, which the goddess loathed.

Et tu, Chandi?

Melinda's shoulders heaved and trembled, but no tears came. Why hadn't she called her mother on her birthday this year? Even if she had hoped to reach voicemail, Melinda still should have tried. She wished she called her brother more, or at all. She wished she responded to her father's endless forwarded emails. She was online enough. There was no excuse. Instead, the blog got all of her attention, and all of her heart, empty vessel that it was.

Melinda clutched her knees to her chest and stared into the dark night.

Slowly, then more strongly, the colored lights of restaurants and storefronts flashed across her window, and Melinda realized they'd left the highway. *No. No, not yet, not yet.* She wrapped her arms around herself, scoring her arms with her fingernails. She whimpered, the sound hoarse and keening as the car plodded on.

Then the car slowed, turned, and crunched the gravel of what was obviously a driveway. *Oh God oh God oh God oh God.* Her mind chanted its funeral dirge, her body nearly vibrating with fear. They had to be there. But where exactly was "there"? *A broken-down kill shack in the woods,* her ever-helpful mind supplied.

The car stopped.

The engine died.

Melinda whimpered again and searched the soulless windows for any sign of hope.

The car heaved as Gerald's weight left the vehicle. His door slammed shut.

Melinda pressed her body hard against the door and clutched her duffel bag like a shield. Frigid wind struck her like a blow as the door across from her jerked open, and she immediately began to shiver.

The car's dome light splashed across Gerald's hulking form as he leaned down to glower at her. Low lighting hollowed out his eyes and sculpted shadows beneath his cheekbones.

"Who the hell are you?" he yelled.

Melinda didn't answer, didn't dare move from where she was trying to disappear into the car, didn't peel her eyes from his. Already, snow blanketed Gerald's hair and shoulders.

"Hell!" He shouted to be heard above the shrieking wind. "This is a disaster. I know you're the wrong person. I'm sorry. Dammit." He hammered the roof with a fist and she flinched. "*Dammit.* I know sorry's not good enough." He squatted on his haunches and balanced a hand on the seat where her bag had lain for the last three hours. He raked snow-covered hair from his forehead only for it to blow forward again.

"Look, I don't know who you are, but I believe you that your name is Melinda," Gerald enunciated. He pinched the bridge of his nose with his thumb and forefinger. "How the hell did this happen? What the hell are we going to do?"

Melinda blinked. *Seriously?* What sort of short-straw irony was this? To get kidnapped by the village idiot? Was he not going to kill her? Or would he simply know her real name as he did? *Comforting.*

"What are we going to do?" she repeated, cold and biting and livid. "I'm going to call the police and drive right back to civilization. You're going to give me the keys, get the hell away from the car, and wait for the cops to come."

Gerald made no move to stand, but his eyebrows slanted

in apology.

"Melis—*inda* . . ." He grimaced. "This storm is way too strong. Didn't you feel us skidding on the way here? It took me an hour longer to get here than it should've. We can't leave. We barely made it. And if you want to make it through the night, you need to come inside with me." Melinda started and Gerald rubbed his hand roughly across his face. Looked like it was Option B: he would know her real name as she died.

"Dammit, that came out wrong. But the cops aren't coming. A hundred to one says they're completely occupied with pulling grandmas out of snowdrifts. As much as I know you want to be away from me, you can't stay out here. You'll get hypothermia. Can't you feel how cold it is? My shoes are freezing to the ground as we speak. Put on your coat. You're shaking."

Melinda's eyes bulged. "What are you talking about?" Her voice rose, thick with the strain of being heard above the storm. "You think I'm going into some stranger's lair with you? Are you insane? You think I don't watch the news? 'Never let someone take you to an alternate location.' That's the moral of every kidnapping story. Well, this bloody well counts as an alternate location!"

She yanked her coat over herself like a blanket. Fear was transmuting into fury, and it felt good, felt something close to powerful. A spark of hope scraped to flame inside her. If she could get angry, she could get her power back. Get free. Or die fighting.

"Now give me the keys and get the hell away from me!" Melinda yelled. With one fist, she pounded the evil wall he'd erected between them. With the other, she smacked her own seat.

Gerald's face twisted in emotions she couldn't read. Jaw tight, he stared at her. "Please believe me, I would love nothing more than to help you set the cops on me. I'm sick at the thought of forcing you into this house. But it's not safe out here. You have to trust me. I do this for a living." He winced and made to speak.

"You do this for a living?" she screamed. "You abduct people and drag them to kill rooms in God-knows-where for a living? And you're telling me to *trust* you?"

Again, Gerald pushed speckled hair off his forehead.

"Melinda," he shouted above the wind. "You begged me to stop earlier and I didn't listen to you. I'm sorry. I'm so sorry. I wish I could do everything differently. But now I need you to listen to me so you can understand. My buddy Paul and his girlfriend have this weird anniversary ritual where he gets a different friend to pretend to kidnap her and they go have a romantic getaway." He held up his hand as she started to speak. "Please, let me explain. The thing is, you look just like her. It's crazy. None of it makes any sense to me, so when you started going on about being the wrong person, I thought you—that is, Melisa—were just getting into the scene. I got freaked out so I put up the partition. I really thought you were her. This was all a horrible mistake. It's unforgivable and I deserve everything you throw at me, including the law." Gerald's eyes were pained. "But right now we have to go inside. Now *I'm* begging *you*. I plow snow for a living. I know weather, I know these mountains. My cabin's ten miles from here. This storm is coming in hard and it won't let up until tomorrow or the next day, if we're lucky. We have to get inside."

As if to illustrate his point, snow blasted through the car and spattered her jacket with white.

Melinda's hands shook in her lap. The air was below freezing. She had no idea if he was telling the truth about his friend or his job, but she knew he wasn't lying about the weather. She'd hired a Kaar not just for the solitude but also because she wanted to be thirty minutes ahead of the weather. Now she was at its mercy.

"Go to hell!" she yelled through chattering teeth. "You drove me hours into the woods while I screamed, and you're calling it a mistake? If you're so worried about me, then leave the keys and go jump off a cliff!"

Gerald's exasperated breath hovered like a cloud between them. "Do you really think I could leave you out here? You'll freeze to death. People die from exposure all the time!"

"Do I think you could leave me?" Her voice vibrated with cold and fury. "Because you're such an upstanding citizen? *Yes.* Yes, Gerald, I believe you could leave me." She stopped short as she recognized her error. "Gerald. That's not your name, is it." It wasn't a question because she knew the answer. "I was the one who said your name before. You just agreed. You're not a Kaar driver. You're a kidnapper. What an idiot I am! What's your name?" She spat his question back at him. "Who the hell are *you?*"

Not-Gerald's mouth flattened into a tight line.

"My name is Grant Samson," he said. "I live over that ridge." He gestured at the dark behind him. "I drive a plow, and I know Paul DiMario—who definitely won't be making it here tonight, by the way, not in this storm—from ice hockey. Plowing is my business. I have a damn website, okay? I have weather advisories plugged in from the news. Go on your phone, and you'll see we need to get the hell inside."

At his mention of her phone, his face fell and both hands gripped the rear seat. His head hung and behind him swirled a tsunami of snow. "Your phone died, didn't it?" he said finally. "Dammit to hell. I'm a monster. You must have been out of your skull. You said your phone was almost dead when I picked you up, and I . . . Dammit, I was relieved. I had a stupid charger and I lied to you, do you know that? I lied to you. Paul said Melisa—"

He stopped and looked directly into her eyes. There was that flash of pain again.

"He said Melisa would want to call him after she realized their date was happening. And I didn't want to hear the pillow talk." His jaw flexed and nostrils flared, and her mouth dropped partway open at his attempt at empathy. *He's ashamed.* Melinda blinked. *Well, he should be.*

"Why would you care if they talked on the phone? They're together! You had your *partition*," she yelled with as much venom as she could muster with a frozen face.

Grant, if that was even his real name, shoved his hair back from his face yet again and returned his hand to its chokehold on the seat.

"Because I thought you were the most beautiful woman I'd ever seen and I couldn't bear to know you were back here, uh . . . talking with him. I couldn't bear it."

Melinda's mouth dropped open entirely. She blinked several times. *Shouldn't the screaming have tipped him off? Oh right. Village idiot.* Her mouth closed, tried to form words, dropped open again.

"So please, Melinda whoever you are, please come inside. *Please.* I've told you all the truth I have. I'll walk away from the car." He gestured behind him. "I'll stay by the trees over there until you're inside and you say I can come in. I'll tell you where Paul keeps his gun. The house key is here." He stood and bent into the driver's door to retrieve the keys, as well as his phone and gloves, she saw. "There's just the car key and the house key." He laid them on the seat.

"Please," he said. And then Gerald-turned-Grant shut the door and left her. She felt him watching her, though. Even as she squinted through the windows at violent veils of snow, she felt his eyes on her and shivered.

32

The car went black and Melinda jumped. *Oh.* The door had been open for a while, she realized, and even the dome light abandoned her. There must have been an exterior light, though, because light from somewhere spotlighted the snowfall near the house.

Melinda marinated in indecision for a full sixty seconds before she slid her arms through the sleeves of her coat and zipped it. There were no options. Grant was right, as awful as it was to admit. To drive in this was impossible at best and deadly at worst. Staying in the car was a countdown to frostbite.

She gave herself a mental shake. *Right, then.* Out of the ice chest, into the igloo. *If I survive the cabin, I'll write him a good review.*

Melinda hoisted her duffel bag onto her shoulder, collected the keys, and opened the rear passenger door. Ever an opportunist, the wind exploded in her face like a bomb. Force and fury snarled her hair and snow blew down her collar. Melinda sat in shock on the edge of her seat, bruised with cold humiliation.

That was unnecessary.

She steeled herself and tried again, tightening her scarf and assuring herself that Grant still waited by the nearly invisible trees. Melinda chanted a mantra in time with her choppy footsteps: *keep moving, keep moving, keep moving.*

The looming edifice of Paul's cabin interrupted her self-hypnosis and she froze. *Cabin?* Surely "chalet" would be a better word for it, since "cabin" implied something less prestigious. Whatever it was, the building's dark, stately door terminated the fifteen-foot planked walkway, bordered on the right by the stone-faced house and on the left by a solid wood railing.

The ground must be steep to warrant a railing. Maybe there's a stream. Mountain properties are so cush.

Melinda chastised herself for getting fanciful while

33

being kidnapped.

The door and doormat were black and speckled by angry snowflake welts. *Welcoming, in a murdery sort of way.* Melinda giggled to herself. *Uh oh, the stress is getting to me.*

No! I'm fine. I'm fine. I'm a strong independent woman with a condo on the hill.

Melinda giggled again. She held the metal key aloft and aimed it at the lock. Warmth was just inside this door. Safety, not so much, but warmth, yes. She could open a door, no problem. She did it all the time. She'd do it now, in fact.

The key bounced back.

Melinda's eyes tracked her hand as she aimed again.

It wouldn't fit. Why wouldn't it fit? What the hell was wrong with this stupid murderer's stupid key? She tried again but the bloody thing wouldn't work.

"I can't do it." Her voice cracked. "It won't freaking work." Harder and harder, she bashed the key and her useless fingers against the lock.

Nothing. What now? Now she needed the kidnapper's help, that's what. She turned and realized he had started away from the trees. Grant reached the car and grabbed a bag that she'd not seen until now. He shut the doors and strode down the walkway. The crunch of his boots danced in her ears and she blinked at him in confusion. Why was he being so loud? Was he always so oafish?

"May I try?" he asked. Centered. Without condemnation.

Too little, too late, Kidnapper. You're a mean mean meanie and I'm going to make sure everyone knows it.

Melinda hesitated but nodded.

Grant's hand floated in slow motion toward her and drew the key from her petulant fingers. The key slid effortlessly into the lock and turned in an easy, fluid motion. Melinda blinked at the key. *Traitor.*

Grant pushed open the door and, running one hand along the interior wall, withdrew another key.

"Gotta put the car in," he said. "Wait here. Keep your eyes on me." Grant stepped back and gestured for her to walk inside, out of the storm. The phone charger dangled from his gloved hand alongside his Army-green backpack. *Kidnappers wear gloves, Grant.* She glared at him. *No matter how you spin it, that's what you are: a big, mean kidnapper.*

Melinda stood in the doorway and watched as Grant left his belongings and walked both sets of keys toward the car. Even inside the house, Melinda's hair blew across her face and caught on her cracked lips and in her eyelashes. She thought distantly about tucking it back but that was too much effort.

Was this a dream? Was she sleepwalking? That made sense. More sense than the present reality. Grant disappeared around the corner of the house. "Eyes on me," indeed. Typical kidnapper lies.

She imagined him wrestling the garage door open and up. *Wait, no, a millionaire mastermind would have a mechanized garage door, wouldn't he? Masterminds are fancy.* The car's faint purr reached her where she stood frozen and tires crunched over snow. A muffled slam echoed down the walkway. *Okay, not mechanized. Too slammy to be automated.*

Suddenly the kidnapper was back, whitewashed with ruddy cheeks. He stopped before the house.

"Time to get the gun," he said, ice crystals woven between his stubble. "Open the closet to your left and search on the shelf above the coat rack. It's a Smith & Wesson revolver. A Chief's Special. It'll be in a shoebox. Take the lid off the box and take the gun out with your right hand. Are you right-handed?" She blinked and nodded. "With your right hand, then."

Such a bossy kidnapper man. Why was he giving her a gun? Village idiot kidnapper.

Melinda palmed the closet doors but turned to him and cocked her head.

"Why shouldn't I just shoot you?" It was part threat and part question. She truly wanted to know why she shouldn't end all her problems by, at the very least, locking him out of the house. Dammit, he had the keys. Okay, fine. By shooting him.

Grant stood his ground.

"You don't know where the food or water or firewood are. This place is one of those cookie-cutter models with shit insulation. It's going to feel like it's made of paper until we turn on the heat. If you shoot me you'll have to deal with the body and the cops. But I wouldn't blame you."

Hmph. At least there's a reason. Satisfied, she opened the closet door.

"Do you know guns?" he asked.

"No."

"Then keep your finger along the barrel, never on the trigger unless you're prepared to shoot. Imagine every place that you point that gun has a bullet hole that you made. Point it away from your feet, legs, anything you want to keep whole."

Are all kidnappings this ludicrous? Melinda patted the shelf for the shoebox. She found and extracted the gun, angled the weapon toward the floor and away from her feet, and closed the closet door.

"Okay," she said.

"Okay." He walked inside.

Melinda's beautiful face was empty. She was lucid but the fatigue, fear, and physical intensity of the storm were taking their toll. Grant's jaw clenched. The revolver had been the only thing he could think of to make her feel in control. He was pretty sure Paul had said Melisa didn't let him keep it loaded, but hell, maybe he'd get lucky and Melinda'd shoot him dead. Then he wouldn't have to face this sickening guilt. He just hoped she did so in the morning, so he could help her survive the night.

Who the hell ignores a terrified woman pleading with him to stop? Fuck! His conscience was outraged, and with good reason. *Murderers and rapists, that's who.* He slowly approached her. Snowflakes were melting in her hair.

"Melinda, we need to close the door," he said, gently but firmly. She didn't answer but turned and walked farther into Paul's dark cabin. Her scent trailed behind her like a lifeline. Grant gritted his teeth. "I'm going to shut the door behind me, then I'm going past you to the right, into the kitchen," he told her. "And then I'm going to turn on a light. Follow me and keep me in sight. I'm going to Paul's bedroom and I'm going to turn on the heat for you. Stay in the kitchen. I need to text Paul before we lose Wi-Fi."

She stiffened at the word "bedroom" but didn't pull the trigger, so that counted as a win. Grant did as promised and removed his phone from his jacket pocket in the stark kitchen light. He brought up Paul's messages and replied, rapid-fire.

What the hell? This lady looks just like Melisa and she walked right to my car. What are the damned odds?
I'll put her in your room and take the couch. We're going to lose power so I won't have Wi-Fi.
It's pretty bad up here. We'll have to melt snow and keep a fire going constantly.

We'll be ready for whatever when you guys come, including the cops. Bring one of my rigs with a plow. It'll be two days before you can reach us. Get Bryan to cover my routes and let my dad know I'm back in town.
Her name is Melinda.

Grant closed his eyes and rolled his shoulders. It felt important to tell Paul that the woman they'd stolen had a name. A name and probably a loving family and a boyfriend or husband. *Dammit!* He was such an ass.

"Okay." He straightened. "That's done."

Grant switched on Paul's bedside light and cranked the thermostat as high as possible, willing the vents to produce heat. Pausing in the doorway, he caught Melinda's eye and saw stale fear. Shame twisted in his gut.

"I'm not going to hurt you." He watched her face for any sign of awareness. "I know you can't believe me. I get it. But I'm not going to attack you. You can point that at me if you need to." He nodded at the gun in her hand. Her chin trembled as she followed his gesture and saw the revolver. "You don't have to," he added quickly. "Just keep holding it like you're doing. You're doing a great job." He waited for the trembling to stop and rubbed a hand across his face.

"What is it?" Melinda asked. She was present enough to be sensitive to his stress, and Grant felt a twinge of pride.

He grimaced. "We're going to lose power tonight. I'm surprised we haven't already. I want this place as warm as possible before the heat shuts off. I'll build a fire, but that's in the den. We need to load you up with blankets in here, but if you get too cold, you need to wake me up and sleep in front of the fire. I'll take the floor. It's no problem. You can keep the gun handy."

"When will they get the power back on?" she asked, her voice small, and Grant's chest constricted.

"Could be a couple days." He watched her face fall. Might as well get the bad news over with. "Also, Paul's on a well out here, so we'll have to get creative with water and the bathroom. The good news is that if we could find anything to cook, the stove is propane and there are matches. Before I start a fire, I'm going to fill up all the pots with water so we have something to drink. I'll melt snow for flushing water." He tried a smile. She stared at the floor. He let the smile drop.

"Can I use your phone?"

Hell again.

"Of course. Sorry, I didn't think of that. You need to call your boyfriend?" Was it possible for his mind to shake its head in disgust? Possibly. Phone outstretched, he stepped toward her and the house went dark.

Grant froze. "Shit. Shit, shit, *shit*." *What now, Samson? The house is barely one degree warmer than that blizzard.*

"Flashlights," he answered himself. "Melinda, I'm going to walk toward you now. You can stand in that corner back there, by the coffee maker, with the island between us."

"Okay," she said quietly. Then even more quietly, "It's fine. I've got no one to call, really." The emptiness in her voice gutted him.

Where had Paul kept the camping lanterns when they'd lost power during the thunderstorm last July? The closet by the front door. With the batteries and snack bars. Grant jerked into motion and winced at Melinda's swift intake of breath. He stopped as quickly as he'd started.

"Sorry. Sorry. I remembered where Paul keeps the flashlights. They're in the closet where we got the gun. Want to walk with me, or stay here while I go get them?"

"I'll go." Her voice wasn't angry, wasn't scared. It wasn't even irritated. It was dull. Lifeless. And it hit Grant like a fist. *She's shutting down as I fuck around. Get it together!*

They shuffled in blind tandem from the kitchen to the closet. He patted at the shoulders of coats, found the shelf, then hunted among the boxes for the plastic hulls of Paul's LED lanterns.

"Found them," he said, relief and victory puffing his chest. He clicked on a lantern, washing their surroundings in eerie bluish-white. Grant's eyes went straight to her face. Exhaustion deepened her eyes in their sockets, strain hunching her shoulders. *Dammit.* He grabbed a second and third lantern by their square plastic handles.

"You good to follow me?"

Melinda nodded and followed him, stopping when he did at the end of the sofa, laden with both duffel bag and firearm. Both seemed out of place—one was an instrument of leisure, the other an instrument of destruction. *Which this might very well be.*

"This is where I'll sleep tonight." He dropped his bag to the floor. "You get the room. I need to make a fire and then we'll search for food. Then we're going to sleep. It's late. You need to get warm as soon as possible. And feel safe," he added lamely. Grant searched her face for a response but of course, there was none. She was barely keeping up with the task of breathing in and out.

Grant squatted in front of the cream-colored wood stove with its white marble fireplace and white tiled hearth, all blue-gray in the light of the lanterns. He crushed sheets of newspaper into baseball-sized bunches and stacked them at the center of the stove. Grabbing split wood kindling from the nearby fireside sling, he propped pieces against the newspaper in a precarious pyramid. Matches lived on the mantel and he grabbed the box

40

to shake one free and strike it against the gritted strip. Flame burst from the tip, and Grant leaned carefully forward so the tiny fire could catch paper.

After the kindling caught, he leaned close and blew the flames alive. Slowly. Deliberately. This was an easy place for a man to kill his progress. Rush in too eager, kill the mood. He blew again. When the kindling was burning to Grant's satisfaction, he grabbed four large pieces of wood from the rack and created a blocky teepee of split wood.

Then he cracked the door to allow oxygen to circulate and spied on Melinda from the corner of his eye.

Who knew that guns were so heavy? Melinda stared at the burnished metal paperweight in her hand. *It takes a lot of strength to be a mercenary.* And while she was here, what was the food equivalent to a gun? Hmm. It was a big responsibility. It could kill her and other people. She thought a moment.

A deep-fried turkey. Found it.

Melinda longed to experiment with deep-frying a Thanksgiving bird, but she didn't have a fryer large enough. And truth be told, she was more than a little nervous about replicating one with a trash can and an alarming amount of vegetable oil, despite the advice of enthusiastic homesteaders.

Okay. She checked her wandering mind. *My brain is officially Jell-O and I'm holding a cowboy gun. It's time to straighten up.* But how? Maybe Grant could tell her. He seemed to be done with his inferno.

"So. I'm in shock, right? How do I get out of shock?" Her voice was dull and mechanical, even to her.

"We get you warm. We get you fed," the kidnapper answered. He pivoted sideways to look at her after slowly closing the stove and adjusting the flue. "Do you have warm clothes in your bag? Something not covered in snow?"

Melinda looked at her jeans, wet to the thigh from their trek through the storm, and at her down jacket, deflated and dripping. *Oh.*

"I'll change," she said. "Can I have a lantern?"

Melinda retraced her steps to the bedroom, dropped her duffel bag on the queen-sized bed, and stationed the lantern on the adjoining table. Beside the lantern, she placed the gun. It was so heavy. Likely to do more harm than good in her hands. A liability. She felt the same about that impulse-buy spaghetti maker.

Melinda didn't know Grant had followed her until she heard the door close behind her.

Ohmygod it's happening this is it ohmygod. Heart in her throat, she lunged for the gun and whirled to face him.

"Change into pajamas if you have them," Grant called. From the other side of the door.

Oh. Melinda gingerly returned the revolver to the bedside table.

He was outside. He'd shut himself out of the room with her inside it.

"You'll want to sleep as soundly as you can after this messed up night, and wet jeans will wake you up. Put on a sweater if you've got one. The room'll take ages to warm up."

He was outside the room and was offering fashion advice.

So he was an attentive kidnapper. *Lucky me.*

Melinda paused to collect herself before riffling through her bag. Her navy flannel pajamas were wrinkled, but changing into them, she realized he was right. Despite her environment they hugged her skin with soft familiarity. *Thank God.*

Melinda layered a sweater beneath her wet coat, doubled up her socks, and exhaled. Still cold enough to see her breath. Sleep should be relaxing. Melinda snorted.

The comfort of dry clothes against her skin reminded her of other bodily needs, and she realized she was dying for the bathroom. Armed with lantern and gun, she used the toilet and returned the lit lantern to the side table. *How to decorate your igloo, by Melinda Sen.*

Melinda bit her lip. She couldn't hide there all night inventing blogs. She wasn't hungry, but that must be the shock talking. Plus, she had a gun. Melinda eyed it dispassionately in the cold light. *I don't know how to use one, but I've got one.* She laughed once. At the very least, she could club him with it. What was a parallel food made useless by the inexperience of the operator?

A duck. Obviously. Duck prepared well was crispy and indulgent, a glorious, ethereal experience. Bad duck was fatty and limp, a culinary tragedy. *I sure as hell don't know how to prepare one. But I could club him with it.*

Bolstered by mental gibberish, Melinda squared her shoulders and faced the door. The kidnapper was on the other side. She could feel him. Waiting. Breathing. Looming.

He was a strange kidnapper. First he flashed his eye crinkles at her and tricked her into getting into his car. Then he locked her in the back of said car and hauled her deep into the mountains while she screamed. Then he yelled at her, told her she was beautiful, and gave her a gun and her own room in a millionaire mastermind's chalet. To complicate matters, he was as handsome as he was confusing, and he was currently devoted to her every physical and psychological need.

What the freaking hell?

Melinda cleared her throat. "I'm coming out."

43

"Okay." The kidnapper's footsteps receded. "I'll hunt for food."

With the gun trembling only slightly in her grip, Melinda cracked the door to the darkened kitchen and found jeans and a plaid shirt protruding from a pantry to her left. Lantern light deepened the creases of Grant's clothing and he looked very much the rugged woodsman. Did that make her Snow White, led innocently to her doom? She gulped.

"There's not much that's easy to prepare for tonight," he said, chagrined, emerging moments later. "It's box after box of packaged food that you have to cook. Speaking of useless, I didn't have time to save drinking water, so I'll be melting snow. How do you feel about crackers and olives?" He placed a box and a jar of each on the countertop.

"Dandy," she said, dry as day-old toast.

Grant gestured her toward a round table with a single tulip-style pedestal stationed to the right of the stove. "Have a seat. I'll make you a plate."

Melinda floated through the kitchen, her cheeks prickling with a familiar sensation—warmth, she realized. The fire was spreading heat slowly through the frosted house, though the bedroom remained an icebox. She dropped into the leather chair, laid the gun carefully on the table, and waited as Grant assembled their meal. In a moment he slid a plate in front of her—a clumsy yin-yang of seed-studded crackers and oily black olives. Firearm at her elbow, Melinda nibbled an olive and immediately felt ten percent more human. She ate another, then another. *Thank God they're pitted.* The last thing she needed now was to be responsible for excavating anything from her food.

The kidnapper ate standing at the counter, twisting a can from a six-pack and holding it aloft. "Can I interest you in a sparkling beverage with"—he eyed the label—"'Real fruit and no preservatives?'"

"Sure," Melinda puffed through an unladylike mouthful of crackers. He pushed a can illustrated with dancing raspberries toward her and took the chair opposite her. Melinda cracked her beverage and sipped gingerly.

"God bless carbs," she murmured aloud, and took another sip. Grant turned and she jerked her eyes to her plate. Was she getting chummy with a psychopath? Well, they were sharing a meal together . . . *What next, compare hobbies?*

"What's your blog called?" he asked, on cue.

"Not a chance, *Grant*," she countered and swallowed. "Tell me again why Paul kidnaps his girlfriend and why she's into it."

Apparently she was. She *was* getting chummy with a psychopath. But what the hell? If he was going to murder her, surely he wouldn't fatten her up first. Perhaps they had combined fairy tales and were about to follow a trail of delectable breadcrumbs and meet a ravenous witch.

Melinda reached for a cracker. *Ugh.* Anyway, she didn't want to befriend the guy, but she did get the sense that he was telling the truth. The insane, implausible, near-impossible truth.

Also, was this tabletop real marble? She stroked the surface with her palm. *It is. It's freaking marble. Stay humble, Mastermind Murderer.*

Grant sighed and tossed olives into his mouth. "I don't know all the details. A few years ago, she actually did get kidnapped and it was a pretty rough deal. As part of the process, either she or her shrink thought it'd be beneficial if she relived the kidnapping and fought her way out of it successfully. In the real deal, she got rescued, and that made her feel incapable or something. Gave her nightmares. Paul fake-kidnapped her the first time. The next time he got someone else to do it, and the time after that. The first time really helped her, and after that, it became a thing between them. It's been three years, I think."

Melinda stared at him, cracker suspended midair.

"That's crazy." She chewed and swallowed. "Clearly his wealth has rotted his brain if this is his idea of fun."

Grant nodded and crunched crackers. "Safe to say it's never gone wrong like this before."

"I guess it's kind of cool, though."

Grant's eyes widened. "You think?"

What the hell was she saying? Did Stockholm Syndrome kick in that fast? Melinda stared at the table's gray veining and said nothing. No way could she defend that wild thought.

"Well," he said, "I told him we're here and need help. Said I didn't know what you'd want to do but that whatever it was, we're behind it one hundred percent. In terms of calling the cops," he added. All that remained of his crackers were crumbs. "Melisa's with him. She got a Kaar, a real one, went to their house, and scared the hell out of Paul. They tried to come up, but the storm got bad and the tunnel closed. They're at a hotel in Georgetown."

How cozy. "I'm ready to go to bed," she blurted. She was as empty as her plate and had no energy to spare.

Grant didn't answer but stood and walked behind her chair to pull it out for her. *Oh, now he's chivalrous. Thanks, Dr. Jekyll.* He waited as she carried her pet firearm into the bedroom, then spoke from outside the door.

"I need to get you extra blankets and show you how to lock the door," he said. "Can I come in for a minute?" Melinda nodded, surprised that she didn't feel wary. She was on her way to trusting him, she realized. *How's that for a sucker. Fool me once, shame on you, fool me twice, abduct me and feed me crackers.* As unlikely as his story was, he was sticking to it and he wasn't abusing her. He seemed to be doing everything in his power to make her feel safe. Plus she could hit him over the head with her duck if she wanted to.

Grant fairly tiptoed inside and veered left to open a small linen closet.

"Could you bring the lantern over here?"

Melinda held the lantern and Grant tugged out two extra blankets followed by a man's black quilted jacket with a fur-lined hood.

"Sleep in this," he said. "I'd have put you in the den to be close to the fire, but I want you to have the bed. And the door."

Grant laid blankets on the bed, then grabbed a straight-backed chair from the corner of the room, the uprights like matchsticks in his broad hands. "Have you used a chair this way before?"

Melinda blinked at him. "Sat in one?"

"I'll take that as a no. After I leave, jam this chair under the door handle," he said. "There's no actual lock on the door, but this will do the trick. The only bathroom is in your room, but you don't have to worry about me. I'll go outside when I need to. Mountain man tricks." A smile curved his lips, and then immediately disappeared. Good. She needed to lie down before she fell down, not get distracted by sultry smiles and eye crinkles.

Grant wedged the chair's back underneath the handle, trapping the door closed, and for a tenuous moment they were locked in the bedroom together, driver and passenger, culprit and victim. Kidnapper and kidnappee.

Melinda's breath stilled. He, too, must have felt the charged air because he made no eye contact with her while he worked. A millisecond later he freed the chair, left the room, and closed the door. Melinda stared after him.

"Lock the door, Melinda," he said quietly, and waited until she'd placed the gun heavily on the bedside table and slipped the chair into position before his footsteps retreated.

Melinda used the bathroom but skipped brushing her teeth. Her kidnapper hadn't mentioned the curative effects of dental hygiene, and she was bloody exhausted. She awkwardly removed her bra, replaced her wet coat with the black quilted jacket, and crawled into bed. Then she switched off the lantern and collapsed onto the pillow and into sleep.

The light beneath Melinda's door vanished and Grant breathed more deeply than he had in the last five hours. He allowed himself a moment to grip the kitchen countertop and lean his forehead against the cool, unforgiving cabinet above. *What the stupid hell. How're you going to navigate out of this one, Samson?*

Grant sighed and opened the kitchen taps into a saucepan to capture any remaining water. How much was there? Paul hadn't visited the mountains for a month. What remained in the gravity-fed tank? Grant deliberately avoided looking at the thermometer, which whispered his name outside the kitchen window, a sadistic siren yearning to reveal its frigid temperature and taunt him with how cold it would soon become.

DiMario, if we survive this, you owe me big. Halfway to the pot's rim, the water sputtered and died, and Grant lifted the pot from the sink to the counter. Beyond big. His-own-desert-island big.

Grant pawed through cabinets and moved as many saucepans, stockpots, vases, and pitchers as he could find to the kitchen island. He donned hat, gloves, and boots, zipped up his brown Carhartt coat, and carted the empty vessels to the end of the walkway. Patternless gusts of snow slapped his face, pummeled his back, and crept inside his jacket. Grant dropped to one knee and tipped the first saucepan into a snowdrift. It was a cold but relatively easy process, and within minutes he was inside again, stomping snow off his boots and shaking snowflakes from his hair.

Back in the kitchen, he struck matches and coaxed the stovetop to life. Each burner received a snow-filled pot, and each pot's contents were melted and boiled. Before long Grant was resting saucepans on cookbooks and dish towels to cool.

By the time he left it, the kitchen looked like intrepid pioneers had dealt with a leaky roof during a monsoon. It also looked colder—he'd finally caved and seen that the temperature outside was negative seven. Ignoring this damning information, he headed to the den.

The sheepskin rug in front of the marble-faced fireplace was gratuitous, but Grant admitted that it added to the look. If you were into that sort of thing. The charcoal-gray couch appeared too modern to be comfortable. Grant crossed to it and sat.

Wow. Grant conceded that it offered a level of comfort. *We'll see how it sleeps.*

Tucked beyond the den was Paul's small lounge area, too close for Grant's comfort to a sliding glass door leading to a back deck. That damned slider. Might as well have left a hole in the wall, for all the good it was doing. He walked to the back of the room and was surprised that, while it was degrees cooler than in front of the fire, it wasn't that much worse.

"Hmph," he snorted. That was what you got with two-thousand-dollar curtains to compensate for a five-thousand-dollar slider. He grabbed a hank of curtain and noted its heft. Okay, probably worth it. Grant laughed quietly. Only Paul would prioritize swanky curtains over insulation and a damn generator.

At least they had the wood stove. The lifesaver. Efficient, and of course, posh. A cordless, motorless fan adorned the stove's top, its only power the heat rising from the stove below it. As the stove heated, the blades turned, and hot air circulated throughout the room. *Not bad, City Boy.* The hearth's gold-looking firewood rack sported a tower of dried, split wood, and Grant knew there was at least a face cord of split logs stacked under a tarp outside.

He rubbed his hand across his jaw. They were going to need that wood. They were going to burn up a forest making it through the storm. He added two more logs to the fire. Grant guessed he'd sleep poorly enough to not miss adding more wood, but just in case, he set his phone alarm for two hours. While he was at it, he set it on battery-saving mode.

Two hours later Grant was sliding logs into the stove as the phone's alarm sounded. He silenced it, stood, and tiptoed to Melinda's door. He put one hand against the wood. Was she all right? Could she sleep? Probably best not to break in and check, especially since he'd coached her to shoot him on sight. He sighed. He crept back to the den and reached for his own backpack. He extracted Melinda's wallet, which he'd collected from the floor of the Maybach.

Grant stared at the zippered enclosures.

Don't do it.

In the end he didn't have to because instead of his invading her privacy, the wallet slipped from his hands. Not every pocket exploded its contents, but at least one did, and guilt coursed side-by-side with excitement through his veins. Coins, receipts, and several magenta-and-orange business cards spilled onto the floor.

Her name? Hope shoved aside guilt.

"Melinda Aahana Sen," he saw embossed in gold script, "A Wing and a Prayer Kitchen" below it. Was that her phone number at the bottom? His pulse quickened. It had to be. He stared at the number, trying to memorize it. No dice. He tucked a card into his back pocket, a child in a candy store who'd scored a two-for-one treat. Anyway, he'd need someone to call from prison. The rest of the items he tucked back into their pouch, then deposited the wallet on the coffee table.

First kidnapping, now theft. What have I become?

Inadvertent robbery complete, Grant lay down on the couch for what was sure to be a sleepless night.

CHAPTER THREE

Never think there is anything impossible for the soul.
It is the greatest heresy to think so. If there is sin, this is the only
sin; to say that you are weak, or others are weak.
Swami Vivekananda

Melinda chatted with Grant from the back seat as he drove. She knew he was Grant and that he smelled good. Laughed deeply. Watched her. She knew, very distantly, that she was dreaming.

"Where should we go?" he asked.

Excitement thrilled her spine. "A drink?" she suggested.

He exited the highway. Bright lights pulsed like fireworks past her window. Suddenly they were tucked in a cozy alcove in a bar. Grant's drink rested on their table, a dark concoction in a pint glass. Wine floated in a wineglass suspended by her fingers. Butterflies danced in her chest though she wasn't nervous.

Instead she hummed. She anticipated. She hardly breathed.

"Why did you choose me?" she asked.

"It was you who chose me." Grant's eyes darkened as he tugged her across the red leather bench seat and onto his lap.

Melinda closed her eyes and reveled in his strength. And then he kissed her. His mouth brushed against hers like velvet, his tongue patient and coaxing. Melinda moaned and slid her fingers past his temples to bury themselves in his hair. Grant's arms wrapped around them both like fibers so that she was bound to him, shoulders to shoulders, hips to hips. His face was like satin against hers and she marveled at it. How could a mountain man have such soft skin?

Melinda nuzzled her pillowcase and dallied with consciousness. To her sadness, the kisses receded and the reality of Utah intruded. The conference organizers had really outdone themselves. Not all hotels cared this much about their bedding. But something must be wrong with the heater—the room hadn't been this cold the night before.

Her eyes flew open. This wasn't a bar. This wasn't Utah. This wasn't the conference. This was the kill house and there was a kidnapper in the living room. There was a blizzard and a dead phone. There was no power, no running water. No hope.

She sat up and immediately lay back down and yanked the blankets to her chin.

"Whoo." The outburst hung in the air, an icy reminder that there'd be no heat. It had to be forty degrees in here, at most. Melinda extended a jacketed arm and switched on the lantern.

Mercifully, her duffel bag was on the bed from last night. She tugged her jeans over her pajama bottoms, despite feeling both uncomfortable and idiotic—warmer was better. She changed from her pajama top into her bra and her long-sleeved black blouse, subtly covered in dark gray *alpana* patterns, and felt thankful she had splurged on the silk. She wrapped her black thigh-length sweater around herself and topped it all with a black fleece hat and the Mastermind's jacket. She eyed her thickened form. *I look like I've been working out.*

She snagged the lantern and went to the bathroom. The bowl emptied and Melinda remembered belatedly that the tank wouldn't refill without the electric pump. What had he said? *I'll melt snow.* She needed melted snow. Thank goodness they had lost power with an abundance of frozen water outside. Melinda nearly groaned at the thought of brushing her teeth and drinking a cup of hot tea.

She left the lantern in the bathroom and liberated the chair from beneath the bedroom door handle. Gun in hand, she opened the door to the kitchen. Startling daylight ricocheted through the room. Clearly it was later than she'd imagined. Melinda huffed out a breath. No cloud—the bedroom was freezing but the kitchen was just cold.

Melinda tiptoed to the den and spotted the wood stove. *Ah.* With no fireplace in the bedroom, the den would be the warmest room in the house and the bedroom like a meat locker. From her place on the free side of the prison glass, she'd suggest to the Mastermind that he remedy the situation.

Melinda snuck forward to check on the kidnapper. Was he asleep? Was he awake? Had he fled in the middle of the night? No, there he was: asleep, flannel-clad chest too broad to fit on the couch, legs too long, sock-covered feet balanced on the armrest. He looked for all the world like Snow White's woodsman asleep on a doll's bed. Huge. Out of place. Scruffy and appetizing. *Seriously?* It wasn't fair. Despite their predicament, he looked sexy as hell. Melinda glared at him.

She pressed a palm to her breastbone. *What am I feeling?* Oh. That was it: mourning. She was mourning something. What was it?

Her mother would be doing backflips at her self-inquiry. *Ugh.*

The illusion. The fantasy, she realized. She'd enjoyed a cozy fantasy about Gerald, his huge hands, muscular thighs, impossibly broad chest. She'd reveled in the timbre of his voice and the sexual hum of his low chuckles. And then last night had exploded, good and proper, and Grant had emerged from the rubble in all his questionable glory.

Tiny flames flickered through the stove's smoke-stained window, and Melinda realized he'd kept the fire going all night long. He had known this was going to happen. The lack of power, the lack of water, the lack of everything. He was keeping them alive.

That gave her pause. Who was this guy, really? Who in his right mind wouldn't have pulled over the car when she'd asked him to stop? She knew the partition hadn't eliminated all of her racket. He'd blasted nineties rock for half of their hellish ride. Could he have had any legitimate reason to ignore her, to traumatize her, to scare her into thinking she was going to be assaulted, murdered, and disposed of?

Melinda eyed the gun in her hand. She looked at Grant's face, slack with sleep, throw pillow bunched beneath his head, breath light and steady. He'd apologized, pleaded with her to come indoors. He'd fed her, given her a gun, locked her *in* and him *out* of her room. She didn't know what to think. Hold up, yes she did. She thought he was a monster. *But is he a monster with a conscience?* Again, she gritted her teeth.

Why couldn't he have just been a yummy Kaar driver?

She wrested her eyes from the conundrum that was her kidnapper and turned her attention to the den. A cream-colored lounge chair oozed bohemian chic to her left, complementing the Midcentury Modern liquor cabinet and bookshelf—presumably full of books about how to abduct people—and a brown leather recliner. The recliner looked nice, but it definitely wasn't new. *Is that a bit of personality squeaking out, Paul? Or worse, sentimentality?* Maybe Paul's girlfriend had decorated the place and allowed him one personal item. The fireplace was marble. The kitchen table was marble. *I bet the toilet's marble too. We get it, Mastermind. You're rich.*

Her eyes circled back to the sleeping lumberjack. "Snacks from An Unwitting Monster," she would title the blog she'd pen. "Tales of An Unwitting Kidnapper." No, he was a witting kidnapper, he just had the wrong victim. Her jaw clenched.

A confused kidnapper, then.

No, an attentive kidnapper and a confused victim.

Melinda shoved her hair behind her ears. Why was she still standing there? Because she couldn't walk away from him, that's why. Her eyes traced the length of him where he lay, following the line of his arm to the floor, the floor to his backpack, the backpack to the coffee table. To her wallet, on the coffee table. Her wallet?

Anger flooded her senses, flared her nostrils, incited her feet to stomp to his side and kick him awake. Why the hell did he have her wallet? When had she last had it? Melinda drew air deep into her lungs, expelled it, breathed again. *Calm down, calm down.*

She'd probably left it in the car. He'd found it and brought it inside. *Still, he didn't need to cuddle it all night long.* She tiptoed forward and lifted it straight up, her arm like a crane to avoid any hint of a noise.

Poised to return to the kitchen, her glance trickled down to his backpack. *His phone.* Where had he put his phone? She scanned the couch, the side table, the coffee table. Nothing. It had to be in the pack. She tucked her wallet under her arm. Then, breath held, she bent in slow-motion to draw up the pack by its coarse woven strap.

She retreated to the bedroom and stopped at the foot of the bed. Too many things, not enough hands. And the gun was heavy. She laid it on the bedside table, relieved yet naked, and turned to the kidnapper's arsenal. The zipper growled as she opened the smaller compartment but she was rewarded with a shiny, black corner of technology.

Hope whirled in her chest. *Please please please please—oh.* The phone was password protected. Of course it was. Melinda pressed buttons. Held buttons. Spoke at the phone, into the phone. Gave instructions. No service. No signal. *No fair.*

She searched for a signal in the bathroom. No luck. She tried all four corners of the room. Eyes locked on the screen, she headed for the kitchen. Nothing. *Maybe by a window?* Big fat no. She held the phone high in the air. Nope. Failure washed through her, draining her into the floor.

Melinda shoved the phone resentfully into its pocket and jerked the zipper closed. *Stupid, bloody service in the stupid, bloody mountains.* Her footfalls didn't bother her now, and she clomped to the den and dropped the bag by the kidnapper's head. He flinched in his sleep. *Good. I hope you're dreaming of dying in an avalanche.*

She needed a cup of tea. She turned on her heel and stalked into the kitchen. Then she stopped short as she noticed what she'd been blind to before.

A motley collection of water vessels decorated the countertops, table, and kitchen island. He'd kept the fire going all night long *and* melted snow for them. She sighed. *Fine. Point, Mountain Man.* A rogue thought sprinted through her mind. *For a kidnapper, he could be worse.* She paused indignantly. If he had really wanted to be nice, he should have listened to her when she was begging for help. That, and his freaking phone should freaking work.

Negative one-hundred points, Kidnapper Man.

That felt better. And now she had tea to make. Melinda

moved a small saucepan full of melted snow onto the stove, shook a match from a carton on the counter and lit the burner. It was time for something warm to drink. "Self-Care, Hostage Style." These blogs were writing themselves.

Melinda searched the collection and found a large, precariously full stoneware bowl of water. She hauled it to the bathroom to fill the toilet, then dug toothbrush and toothpaste from her bag and scrubbed eighteen hours of tortuous travel from her mouth.

Melinda slid her tongue over deliciously clean teeth and held the lantern high to take in more of her surroundings. Restrained opulence reigned supreme. The countertop and skirted toilet were white ceramic, cabinets painted a bright white. She wiggled her socked feet on the floor and noted that, while the gray slate was elegant, it was a terrible surface in winter. The thin Turkish-style rug helped not a bit.

Melinda caught her reflection in the circular mirror. Oh, good, she looked like cold, haggard hell. Fitting, since she felt like dog dookie.

Empty bowl in hand, Melinda returned to the bedroom and continued her tour, morbidly charmed that she'd been hijacked by an interior decorator. Or was Paul so loaded that he'd hire someone to decorate his home away from home? Inquiring minds wanted to know. How had she noticed none of this last night? *Oh yeah, 'cause I thought I was going to die screaming.*

She pulled back the curtain from a window and sucked in a breath at the instant drop in temperature. Condensation on the glass made it impossible to see outside, but there still seemed to be plenty of flurries. The light fixture caught her attention, a modern-looking contraption resembling a jumble of gold pickup sticks with clear globe lights at the ends.

Why the hell was she so distracted by the interior design?

58

She knew why. It was the same reason she loved cooking shows on TV—it was a pretty distraction from a less than wonderful reality. Not that complex of a coping strategy, really. Katrina Sen applauded silently in her mind. Of course, *now* her mother was there for her, as a figment of her imagination. Soon enough she'd imagine her hopping on her high horse and riding away. Art reflected life.

The water had to be boiling by now; time to medicate with caffeine. She froze. What if Paul didn't have tea? *Kidnapping's one thing, but caffeine deprivation will add ten years to your sentence.*

Melinda walked to the stove and turned off the burner. Now, where did Paul keep the tea? She doubled back and ducked into the pantry, confident that Paul would have several high-class teas available. *Aha!* She emerged victorious. Organic Assam Black bags in a fancy tin canister. If only he had Bengal Spice. She dropped two tea bags into the steaming saucepan and placed the lid on top.

Pain flashed through her abdomen and she stared at her stomach. Oh, she was hungry.

Ow.

Beyond hungry. At least that was something she could control. The tea was steeping, her mouth was a field of wintergreen . . . It was time to push up her sleeves and make breakfast.

"Oh, for crying out loud," she muttered as she failed to shove the thick layers of shirts, sweater, and jacket past her wrist. Here she was, trapped in an icy hellhole, and she couldn't even roll up her sleeves for effect.

Blizzard, one, Melinda, zero.

Okay, forget sleeves. Time to open all the cupboards and take stock.

In her first pass, Melinda pulled out boxed cereal and three types of granola, but these were a tease to her yawning

59

pit of a stomach. Stewed tomatoes, cream of mushroom soup, dehydrated milk, a box of stuffing mix, and can after can of beans came next. There was more food here than Grant thought. But she hadn't found It yet. *It*, the right combo, the Holy Grail of food combinations that would make her feel safe, even for a few savory moments.

Ten minutes later Melinda perused her findings and felt the stir of excitement that accompanied one of her cooking adventures, when she was pitted against a particularly difficult task. She twisted her hair at the nape of her neck and reached for the diced tomatoes.

Something was shuffling. Something was making quick movements and then stopping, then starting again. Something was clinking. Where was his Glock? Or was he hunting? Grant's eyes blinked open, saw white vaulted ceilings. No, not hunting. Definitely no Glock. The "something" was a captive woman named Melinda, and by the sound of it, she was awake before he was. *Damn.*

From the couch, Grant swiveled his head and sought flames or hot coals through the stove's darkened glass door. Neither presented themselves, though the room was above freezing. Not great. Could be worse. Grant rolled into a seated position and muffled a groan so as not to alarm his hostage. And love interest. No, too soon, too soon. Lust interest. He groaned again.

Grant crawled around the coffee table and cranked open the stove to add wood to the coals. He breathed a sigh of relief that they were still hot and he didn't need to start from scratch. He revived the fire and gently closed the door to track down his sweater.

Grant checked his phone. Seventy-nine percent battery and 8:21 a.m. Not bad on both counts. Now that they had another hour's worth of heat, it was time to check on Melinda. Get her to trust him. Sure, that seemed probable. He rubbed a hand across his tight jaw.

Grant walked quietly toward the kitchen and saw Melinda. When he'd seen her at the airport there had been something strong about her, but also something—he searched for the words—on alert. Or fearful. Not fearful of something specific. A wisp of something akin to condemnation veiled her like mist. But in the kitchen, she moved with ease, even through Paul's thick jacket. The more she stacked, opened, and drummed her fingers, the more she gained momentum until she looked as if she might take flight in a swirl of sparrows. He wanted to say something, to tell her she looked like an angel, but he didn't want to make her self-conscious. Instead, he tried very hard to blend into the archway.

Melinda stopped for a moment, her face turned away from him, stock-still as if she were thinking. Suddenly, she spun around, saw him lurking, and shrieked.

"Sorry!" Grant said quickly, hands splayed in front of him, beseeching. "So sorry. You were deep in reorganizing Paul's cupboards and I didn't want to bother you. Or scare you," he added with chagrin. "So I didn't say anything."

She withered him with a look. "I am not *reorganizing*, I'm gathering ingredients. I'm starving. Olives and crackers aren't going to cut it this morning. What time is it?"

"Eight thirty," he replied. "You been up long?"

She shook her head.

"Good," he said. "We slept a long time, which is great. How do you feel? And how can I help?"

61

She gestured to supplies on the butcher block. "You okay with mushrooms?" At his confused acquiescence, she continued. "I'm cooking for both of us. I don't want to have to listen to you eating crackers. Plus, all that are left are gluten-free saltines, and that's just insulting." She pointed at the bowl and container. "Put a cup of dried mushrooms and one and a half cups of water into the bowl. I promise to be judicious with it." She passed him a glass of water. "But I'm not eating dry grits and dehydrated mushrooms for breakfast."

"Paul has grits?" Grant's stomach rumbled and he laughed. Melinda did not.

"Paul has more food than you gave him credit for," she said, brows arched. *Oops.* He'd failed the manly hunter test and she was now in angry gatherer mode. Grant decided it safer to not answer. Instead, he sat at the kitchen table and did as he was told, pouring first dried mushrooms and then water into the bowl, eyes on her. Snowfall continued outside, but even the diffused light of day turned her hair to silk and her skin to tawny satin. The light caught her lashes and he saw they were longer than he'd thought. Her shoulders were broad, wider than her hips, but even through a jacket, her waist dipped above her hip bones for a feminine hourglass.

"Are you stirring?" she asked, and he jumped. She'd nearly caught him checking out her ass.

"Stirring!" he said abruptly and whisked too quickly with the fork she'd supplied.

"Good. Then you're ready to open." Melinda handed him a jar of tomatoes and cylindrical shakers of garlic powder, oregano, and celery salt. "Pour the tomatoes into this," she said, passing him another bowl and a small wooden measuring spoon. "Add two spoonfuls of each seasoning and mix them together. We're going to let that infuse for a little while."

"I confess I've never infused before." He eyed her askance to see if she would play.

What the hell was he doing? She was a prisoner.

Yes, but she's strong, he thought. And achingly beautiful. And there was something about her.

"Well then, this experience might have a silver lining," Melinda said sternly, "if you learn a thing or two about infusing."

He watched her realize she was almost joking and then shut down her face. Even so, he crowed silently in triumph and allowed his smile to turn smug.

Grant opened his mouth to speak, but she'd turned away. She hefted a cast-iron sauté pan onto the range. "Do you know where more matches are?" She riffled through the drawers beside the stove.

"Try the dish in that lazy Susan."

"Thanks."

Grant combined the tomatoes and seasonings, then held them out for inspection.

"Do these pass muster?" he asked.

Melinda glanced at the bowl he held and took it from him with a nod.

"They're fine."

Grant held back a sigh. It wasn't exactly a "screw you," but it was close.

Melinda pushed back her hair for the umpteenth time and lit a burner on the stove. She added a generous spoonful of salt to the water, then covered the pan. In a separate saucepan, she heated water for more tea. Being snowbound meant more tea.

Lots more tea. All the tea she could brew.

Plus, Grant was being too nice to her. Polite, attentive, making jokes, respecting her space. *What the bloody hell?* The man's good-versus-evil balance was completely out of whack. If he were evil, he would have forced himself on her, right? She'd be dead or wishing she was. Melinda stilled. Cold seeped through the window above the stove and caressed her face as the heat from the flame warmed her midsection.

What was his attitude? Melinda bit at her lip. It was beyond politeness, short of ingratiating. It was kindness, yes, but there was something more. *Familiarity? Care?* Yes, something like that. But there was also a spark. A level of intimacy.

Melinda sighed. The word she was looking for was *chemistry*. The chemistry they'd exchanged last night couldn't be dampened, even by this deranged setting. He had accepted it and was engaging with it—engaging with her. He was tracking her, monitoring her, keeping pace with her feelings, making sure she had what she needed. What the hell was she supposed to do with that?

Melinda stiffened her spine and got on with making breakfast. The tea water was boiling, so she added a couple bags of Assam and replaced the lid. The cast-iron pan was hot, so she added olive oil, onion flakes, and cardamom and stirred gently. She tested the mushrooms and added them to the fragrant pan, their sizzle curling her toes.

The grits water was also boiling so she emptied half the bag of minced grain into the pan. If she ignored the fact that she was cooking in a jacket, things almost felt okay. Melinda closed her eyes. She inhaled the sultry scent of cardamom and was transported home. Powdered, freshly ground, sautéed, in its pod, it didn't matter. One whiff and she was in her kitchen, about to embark on a new journey. Or even farther back than that, at home in Bellingham learning to make and fry *chanar jalebi* for Durga Puja with her father.

Okay, what else, what else? Melinda strummed her fingers on the countertop. How to complement her meal? Her eyes closed. *What's missing from "Snowbound Breakfast 101?" We've got creamy and salty with the grits.* To complement that she'd need butter. No chance there. The fridge was bare. *I bet he'll have coconut oil!* Melinda darted to the cabinet where she'd seen oils and vinegars and to her joy found a jar of ghee. She set the jar down by the stove for later. *We've got savory, garlicky, oniony, herbed . . . What else do we need?*

She laughed aloud. What they needed was wine.

"And why doesn't he have a single vegetable?" she muttered.

"He never knows when he's coming up here next," Grant replied behind her. She jumped. He smiled an apologetic half-smile. "Sorry I startled you again." He continued, "You learn not to buy produce if you're not going to eat it while you're in the mountains. The freezer can't be trusted in winter since the power goes out intermittently. But I think I saw a sad bag of frozen spinach in there last night. You want it? Even if it's been thawed and frozen a few times?"

"Why not? Let's go for broke. Actually, I was tempted to pair breakfast with a glass of wine, if you must know. My standards are a little skewed at the moment."

Grant didn't miss a beat. "Red or white?"

Melinda's eyes widened.

"Why not?" He stood from the table. "No one's coming for us in this weather. I'm in favor of liquid reinforcements."

"White." She turned her back to him. Why not indeed. Apparently she had decided to trust this kidnapping mountain man, despite the ominous proclamation that they wouldn't be rescued today. "We'll save the red for dessert."

This is a terrible idea, Grant's mind chastised as he peered into the wine fridge in Paul's bedroom closet. *Your priorities—not to mention your boundaries—are way out of line.* Getting drunk before 9:00 a.m. was not on the road to good decisions.

"Hush," he said aloud. It had to be quarter after by now.

"Actually, is there a rosé?" Melinda called from the kitchen.

Grant checked the bottles. "Yes. Do you care what the winery is?"

"Not a whit," she answered.

"Then I have your bottle, madam." He rejoined her.

She paused in the act of stirring decrepit-looking spinach into the tomato slurry on the stove and took the bottle.

"This is good." She evaluated the label. "I like the rosés from the Paso Robles area."

Relief pricked Grant's skin and he grimaced at his need for her approval. Could he not play it cool at all? He leaned on the kitchen island and hiked an eyebrow at her. "Oh yeah. Me too. Because I know what that means. I'm a connoisseur like that."

Nope. Playing it cool was not a skill he possessed.

Melinda coughed as she set the bottle on the counter—but was it a real cough, or a laugh? She returned to tending the food. She didn't cough again. It had to have been a laugh. Grant was doing an invisible happy dance when she spoke again.

"Do you like your wine extra chilled? I can pop it into the deep freeze for a few moments, if you'd like." She gestured to the wintry landscape beyond the kitchen window. She smiled, then seemed to realize she was fraternizing with the enemy and flattened her mouth into a line.

"That would be preferable." He grinned and rocked back on his heels. "I hate drinking anything without actual ice crystals in it."

Was she done? Or would she play more?

This time her laugh was a bark but his pulse skipped.

"Can I do anything?" Grant's hands itched to slide around her waist.

"Sure," she said. "This is about ready. Will you pass me two plates and then pour the wine?"

Grant handed her two of Paul's white stoneware plates, then passed her mugs for tea. He searched for two glasses that were breakfast-wine appropriate. Not lunch wine or dinner wine. He was looking for a wineglass that said, "This is a great way to start your day!"

"How about another mug?" he asked.

"Fitting." She slid two steaming plates plus gold-looking flatware onto the table and sat down opposite him.

Grant filled the wine mugs halfway—that was the classy way, right?—and brought them to the table.

"This looks incredible! You found all this stuff in Paul's deadbeat kitchen?"

"I like a challenge," she said. "Actually, Paul's pantry was all right. I thought we'd have to use olive oil for the grits, but he had ghee! Clarified butter."

"Ah," Grant said, then kicked himself for his lackluster answer. But then he forked a bite of grits into his mouth and everything became irrelevant. "Ehmeged."

She swallowed. "Pardon?"

"Oh my God," he tried again. "This is delicious."

"I can't really take credit for the grits," she said after a bite for herself. "But they're good, aren't they?"

He went for a larger bite this time and nodded his agreement.

"Grits are inherently delicious. They're like that expression about pizza—even when you have bad pizza, it's still pizza," she laughed and then quieted it with another bite. Grant had heard that expression only in reference to sex.

Grant liked her mind on food and he liked her mind on sex. His mind was on both right now, too. He tried the sautéed vegetables.

"I know these are all from a can," he said, "but they still taste out of this world. What did you say you do again?"

Melinda chewed and swallowed. "I'm a food writer who likes to experiment with culinary roadblocks. I dare myself a lot to cook, well, kind of like this. Like, 'What would I do if I had a fancy dinner party and no fresh food?' or 'All I can cook are green foods—Go!' I get bored pretending to know everything, so I make up games for myself that I feel replicate what people go through when they have to make a meal."

She toyed with her spoon. "But it's been made clear to me recently that I've got to change my approach. I think . . . All my gimmicks are just gimmicks. I might not be reaching people at all." She took a sip of wine and closed her eyes.

Melinda's eyes rolled back in her head before she closed them, Grant noted. His to-do list immediately changed from splitting enough wood to keep them alive to making her eyes roll back in her head with his own body. *Shut it down*, he warned himself. *Your job is keeping her alive, period. You can try anything you want after we're out of here.*

Her eyes opened. "What did you say before? *Ehmeged?* This wine is perfect with the creaminess of the grits and the tang of the tomato. Did you notice how meaty the mushrooms got? They're a great meat substitute if you don't want animal protein."

"Is this how you think all the time?" he asked through his food.

Melinda burst out laughing and Grant froze, pierced by a stab of desire. Her laugh sounded like sex and cognac and a bubbling stream all at once.

"This and worse," she replied. "Count yourself lucky that we have a limited number of meals together."

She forked another heap of grits into her mouth and he felt an overwhelming urge to kiss her. He wanted to tell her they'd have more meals together, that he'd make sure of it, but it was too fast. Last night she'd thought he was a nice guy named Gerald and this morning he was getting her drunk in a blizzard and plotting her seduction. Almost of its own accord, Grant's hand rose to stroke her cheek. At the last moment, he realized what he was doing and shoved a lock of hair behind her ear. She turned to him, eyes wide. *Smooth. Real smooth*, he thought, and dropped his hand to the table.

"Your hair was going to get in your food," he said limply.

They both turned their attention to their breakfast and wine and held off on speaking further. He had seconds of both dishes and she switched from rosé to tea.

Grant tried again. "I think if we left the food in the blazing sun on the counter it would still stay fresh in this cold kitchen." Bland, but friendly enough.

"First you'd have to find the blazing sun," Melinda replied as she peered out the window at the heaving snowfall. She looped her hair behind her head and Grant kicked himself for highlighting their uncertain circumstances.

"We're going to be okay, Melinda," he said. She dragged her gaze across the table to meet his. "I'm going to do everything in my power to make sure you're okay. Paul and Melisa know we're here. They're coming for us as soon as they can. Paul can drive one of my trucks up here and we will get out." His eyes searched hers. "It'll be a couple days, though." The shame of it twisted his gut.

Her eyes tightened but she managed a small smile. "I know," she said. "Maybe just one more mug of wine."

CHAPTER FOUR

Take risks in your life. If you win, you can lead.
If you lose, you can guide.
Swami Vivekananda

Melinda struck a match. One at a time, the stove's burners sparked into life beneath four snow-filled saucepans. The dishes would take a while since they had to melt more snow, but hopefully it would clear her head.

She reduced the flames to medium and wandered to the pantry while she waited for warm water. Had she seen dried beans when she was rooting around earlier? She had! Pinto, cannellini, flageolet, and mung. *Mung beans?* Her father had cooked with mung beans when she was a child! Simmered into *dal*, spiced into curry, mashed into flatbreads—the pellet-shaped legumes were a culinary chameleon. There had to be something she could make with them that would count as comfort food. *For me, at least*, she conceded. *Probably not for the mountain man.* She snorted. But did she care? Not in the slightest. This wasn't a five-star resort.

Melinda peeked at the stove. Tiny bubbles simmered at

the pots' edges. She pulled the two-quart flip-top Ball jar from the shelf.

"And today we'll learn how to measure under duress . . ." she mused. Melinda measured two cups of the green-tea–colored beans into a bowl, then poured barely melted water from a saucepan over them to submerge them by three inches. Was that enough beans? Of course it was. They'd be rescued soon. Probably. Hopefully. She recalled her mother's expression: *Belief is a powerful spice. A little goes a long way.*

Melinda grimaced.

The remaining saucepans steamed. Time to wash dishes. Melinda hoisted a pan of warm water in each hand and made her way to the sink: one for washing, one for rinsing.

It was just like camping.

In a million-dollar cabin.

With a sexy lumberjack whom she might shoot if he got too frisky.

Yeah sure, exactly like camping.

In a short while, pans, bowls, dishes, and cutlery were stacked high in the dish drainer. *Speaking of washing* . . . Melinda eyed the remaining pan of warm water. No one liked to think of their undergarments as gamey but facts were facts.

Melinda carried the pan into the bathroom and collected her small mesh bag of dirty underwear and socks along the way. After a bare-bones wash in the vanity's sink, she hung her underthings to dry on the bathtub's faucets, shower nozzle, and curtain rod. If only she could leave them to dry in the den. They were likely to become panticicles back here in the bathroom. But no. No knickers on display for her kidnapper.

Boundaries, man.

Washing pots and panties had sobered her, and now she longed to walk outside, to feel free even for a short while. Melinda returned to the kitchen and peered out the window over the sink. Miraculously, the storm was taking a break. Heavy clouds hovered overhead and occasional snowflakes meandered toward the ground, but the raging whiteout had ceased for the moment.

A slow, rhythmic thumping sound interrupted her thoughts and Melinda's neck prickled. Rescuers? How long had it been going on?

"Grant?" Melinda called to where he'd been stacking firewood by the hearth. No answer.

"Grant?" She checked the den, found his jacket on a chair, but no Grant. She sought the closet immediately next to the front door. She knew he wouldn't be in the coat closet but she couldn't help opening it, as if he were lying in wait for her and she'd surprise him first. She didn't find him, but she learned that Paul was a bit of a Prepper—someone who liked to stock up for the worst-case scenario. *You have a tub of zip ties and a hundred of every battery known to man, but you don't have a fireplace in your bedroom? Great job.*

Melinda paused. Her duffle bag could use a little reinforcement. She slipped two zip ties and four batteries into her jeans pocket. Paul owed her. And she chose to be paid in double As.

Melinda didn't know where to continue her search for Grant beyond the three rooms. The remaining option was outside, so she grabbed her hat and gloves from her room and slid her feet into her boots, deliciously dry after twelve hours on the not-so-useless-after-all boot dryer by the fireplace. Keys on a nail by the door caught her eye but she left them be; heaven forbid she go for a stroll and drop them in a snowdrift.

Snuggled as tightly as possible into the Mastermind's jacket, Melinda cracked the front door open an inch. Not terrible. She pulled harder and icy air sucked the breath from her lips.

"Holy crap," she choked out. Undaunted, she shouldered her way outside and noted that the walkway was shoveled clear.

A *whoosh!* Followed by a *thwack!* caught her off-guard. *What are the odds a pinstripe-suited guy is assaulting my kidnapper with a violin case?* Because that was exactly how it sounded.

Whoosh! Thwack! Melinda clutched the handrail to keep from slipping her way to the driveway. Step, step, *thwack!* Step, step, *thwack!* Louder and louder.

Melinda peered around the house and froze. Definitely not a mob hit.

Grant swung an axe overhead and drove the blade deep into the chunk of wood at his feet.

Whoosh! Thwack!, then a rending twist as he ripped one piece free from the another. *Ah.* The noises made sense now. So did his back muscles.

Melinda retreated until she was mostly concealed by the corner of the house and watched. The man was an ox. Each movement was fierce, fluid, animal grace. First came his deep inhale, followed by the explosion of an exhale as his torso contracted and the axe flew to cleave the wood in two. Each piece that caved to his will sailed to a pile by the house. The next victim came from a small stacked row of round logs. Its tarp lay crumpled beside it. A larger row of already-split logs, also partially covered with a tarp as well as a thick layer of snow, rested on a rack between the house and the garage.

The garage.

The car.

How's about we stay warm by lighting it on fire? She shook her head to clear the morbid image and Grant turned suddenly and followed her eyes to the garage.

"Shit." A short puff of air accompanied the expletive.

Melinda stared at him.

"I never want to see that damned car again." His breath heaved.

"I have to agree with you," she said, unable to tear her gaze from his. He dropped the head of the axe to the ground with a thump.

"I'm trying, Melinda," he said, the words hard from exertion. "All I can do now is keep you safe. Keep you comfortable until they come. That's the best I can do."

She blinked.

He was pleading.

Not for himself, she realized. *What for?* She cocked her head. Not for his safety. What was it, then? Ah. For her forgiveness. He was asking her to understand that he was trying to right the wrongs he'd committed.

What on earth did she do with that? Because . . . she kind of liked it.

Excuse me, what the hell? her mind inquired. *This guy might not be a murderer, but he's not a decent human being.*

Grant's eyes smoldered. Could hazel eyes smolder?

Heat curled through Melinda's chest and her lips parted.

Back off, her mind warned. *This is neither the time nor the place. It doesn't matter how chivalrous he is today. Where was that attitude yesterday? Yesterday! Have you forgotten yesterday? Does the phrase "Please, Gerald, please" ring any bells?*

Melinda sidestepped her conscience. "It's stopped snowing for a minute. I'd like to go for a walk. Will you take me?" She blushed at her choice of words as the testosterone wafted off him like steam. Her lashes veiled her eyes as she gauged his reaction.

Grant leaned his axe against the un-split wood and moved toward her.

"I would love . . ."

A step.

". . . to take you . . ."

Another step.

" . . . on a walk," he finished, toe-to-toe with her now, his chest slowing as he regained his breath.

She froze.

Did he really just say that?

He did.

Did he mean what she thought he meant?

Um, he really did.

What the hell was he thinking?

Chemistry, that's what he was thinking.

And so was she.

Melinda closed her eyes as Grant brushed a snowflake from her cheek. When she opened them he was still there, still staring at her like she was lunch. Her stomach flipped.

"So which way . . ." Her voice faltered and she cleared her throat. "Which way do we go?"

For as thick as it was, the air took a millisecond to clear.

He grinned at her. "Let me stash this wood and grab my coat." He hoisted the wood into his arms and carefully placed it atop the existing row of stacked wood, then replaced the tarp. To Melinda's surprise he walked to the other end of the long row of split wood, uncovered it, and gathered a bundle of wood in his arms. He tucked the axe under his arm and clomped down the walkway and into the cabin. He made three more trips until at last he shrugged into his coat and joined her at the end of the walkway.

She scrambled for acceptable small talk. "Why the do-si-do with the wood?"

Grant smiled. "That pile is freshly cut. If we burned that, it would take longer to catch because it's still green. Even though that wood, that wall of about four by eight feet right there, has been partially exposed to the snow, it's still going to burn better.

It's been split. It's had wind drying it out. And also, I know this isn't a vacation or anything, but splitting wood is a good way to keep warm, and it makes me feel good to replace what we use up here."

He chuckled. "Don't know if that made sense at all."

"I get it," she said. "I didn't see the axe in the house."

"Gorg—Melinda, that was a *maul*"—he grinned wider— "and it was in the closet below the guns, next to the thirty yards of rope and military rations." He laughed out loud. "Paul has to have every tool. But hey, turns out he's right. Pretty much everything's been useful so far."

Melinda's head spun. Had he said her name aloud before? Maybe just once, the night before. Something about his bass gliding over the syllables awakened her senses like so much frigid air.

"What's down there, beyond the cabin?"

"Paul's property curves back a ways. In the summer it's a really nice meadow with conifers and aspens all around it. We can walk through the clearing a bit. We just need to come back before too long so the snow doesn't start on us. And we won't walk under the trees."

She shot him a confused look. "Aren't we going for a walk in the woods?"

"Near them but not under them," Grant said. "At this point in the snowfall we need to stay out from under the branches. They get so laden with snow that they'll dump their load on us, which I don't recommend. Or they can completely break off and kill you."

Melinda's eyes widened.

"It's not a nice way to go. Have you been hearing the branches snap?"

She shook her head. Actually, she'd been day drinking and

flinging her undergarments around a stranger's house. She hadn't paid much attention to the warning sounds of nature.

"The weaker branches are feeling it today. Some are giving way. We'll have to be careful."

She stared at the hand he offered her. She looked at the fifteen-foot slope in front of them. Odds were she'd eat snow if she didn't hold on to something.

Snap out of it, you patsy.

"That's okay." Her chin lifted. "I'm fine." And for the first three feet, she was. Then her heel hit ice and she skidded down the hill, legs splayed, until a rock halted her slide and she stopped, entire body hinged on the pebble beneath her right foot. Arms outstretched, legs trembling, Melinda held her breath for fear any movement would catapult her again into a one-woman landslide.

"Still okay?" Grant's voice floated down from the top of the slope, tone almost neutral. Melinda's cheeks could have melted glaciers.

Melinda said nothing but extended a wobbly hand toward him. After sidestepping halfway down the hill with a minimum of awkwardness, Grant wrapped a gloved hand around hers. Layers of wool and fleece couldn't dull the thrill of being held by his strength. *Don't romanticize static electricity! It's dry mountain weather.*

Grant wrapped an arm around her waist and lifted her above the snow. Melinda squeaked as he held her airborne, then lowered her again into the ocean of white.

"Okay?" he asked with a straight face and a small twinkle in his eye. He was laughing at her, but just a little. She could deal with a little.

"Okay," she answered, resentful to find herself breathless.

Even as she regained her footing, he didn't let go of her

hand, and clumsily, clunkily, they found a rhythm and made their way down the hill. Knee-high snow slowed their descent as they inched their way down the embankment. With every step, Grant planted his feet to anchor her as she slid and pivoted past him, arms rigid, back outstretched.

Soon enough the absurdity of the situation overtook her embarrassment and by the time they reached the meadow, Melinda was degrees warmer and laughing. The hand Grant held tingled from their contact and she dropped his as soon as possible. She glared at her fingers. Traitors. She focused on her surroundings and found a snowy lagoon surrounded by a forest of greenery that resembled white-cloaked wizards more than Christmas trees.

"Wow," she breathed, entranced, and immediately tripped and landed up to her armpits in snow.

"You okay?" He reached for her and she nodded, face hot.

"Let's just keep going," she muttered.

"Going" was a slow process. The storm had raged for more than twelve hours, and Melinda had to lift each foot high for every snow-logged step. Drifts of snow resisted her steps and cold air bit her nose and lungs. They both breathed heavily as they stomped forward.

Yesterday she had been trapped in a hotel, trapped in a plane, trapped in a car, trapped in a cabin. She snorted. This morning she was trapped in limbo. But this moment was better. Outside was better.

If you must be kidnapped, be sure it's in a winter wonderland, she advised her readers in her next mental blog. What was the food parallel to a winter wonderland? Cotton candy? Not cold enough. Sno Cone? Not fancy enough. She stopped to close her eyes. Something with meringue.

Baked Alaska.

79

Success burst from her lungs in a huff and bloomed into a grin. She'd put it in the blog if she made it home alive.

To their left, a muffled snapping echoed through the trees, and Grant caught her eye. Melinda nodded her understanding. They trudged on. The snow-covered meadow extended further than she'd supposed. After about a quarter-mile, Grant stopped.

"We shouldn't go too much further . . . When was the last time you built a snowman?" His smile was wide and open, his chest lifted with exertion.

In spite of herself, Melinda burst out laughing, and the sound rang through the quiet. "Probably two or three decades ago," she admitted.

Dark eyebrows climbed Grant's brow. "Well then, you're way overdue," he said. "Let's get rolling." He bent at the waist to clap handfuls of snow together into a ball, which he delicately and artfully rolled into a larger and larger sphere. "Get a move on, Blogger." Grant jutted his chin at the snow between them. "I'll make the legs but the stomach won't paunch itself." Melinda laughed again and did as she was told.

"You know when I last built a snowman?" Melinda packed snow into an approximation of a belly and Grant looked up from sculpting. "I had to have been around eight. It was with my dad. We got into a fight because I wanted to make a snow*woman* and he refused." She smiled ruefully. "He didn't want to mess with the anatomy. What upstanding accountant wants to make snowboobs for all the suburbs to see?"

It had bothered her for years afterward, though. What father wouldn't support his daughter in such an innocent way? What kind of man was so scared of keeping up appearances that he squashed his child's innocent dream? *A weak one. One who lets his family fall apart.* Melinda pounded her section of snowman. Too hard, it would seem, as a chunk gave way and crumbled to the ground. *Weak!* she shouted silently.

Unaware of the bitter pain in Melinda's chest, Grant laughed and patted more snow on the sphere in front of him. Twenty minutes later a passable snowman stood between them.

"So where are we going to find a carrot?" she asked. "And what about poor Stanley's buttons and hat?"

Grant paused in the act of smoothing the base.

"*Stanley?*" Mock indignance widened his eyes. "I think you mean *Fergus*. And Fergus's outfit is going to have to wait, unfortunately. The snow's starting again." The eye crinkles were in effect but this time they came with a furrowed brow. Melinda followed his eyes to the sky, which was beginning to fall around them.

She grimaced. "Don't be a quitter. He doesn't even have arms. I see some twigs sticking out of the ground over there. I'll grab a couple." The denied child within would get her snowman arms, darn it. Otherwise Stanley was just a precarious pyramid.

Grant looked uneasy. "You never know if those are attached. Come on, let's go back and finish Stanley later." He held out a hand, but she was already halfway to the sticks she'd spied and she sure wasn't giving up now. Melinda gave the twigs a yank, but they were caught on a rock.

"Come on," she coaxed, and braced her foot against the tree to yank again.

"Melinda, I don't like this. That tree looks pretty dead," Grant called. She heard the crunch of his footsteps as he started toward her. "The wind is kicking up. You're cranking on that tree, which is a bad idea with all the snow it's carrying. Could you please—Mel!" he yelled, then everything went black.

Snow sucked at Grant's shoes like quicksand, every step made heavier with the weight of his burden. Blinding wind whipped his face as if the storm had never broken. Melinda's head sagged against his shoulder and his own ragged breathing abraded his ears. He longed to run, but knew he'd twist an ankle and then they'd both be dead.

How could he let this happen? Grant clutched Melinda's limp body more tightly to his chest and silently begged her forgiveness.

He was lucky they'd stopped when they did. Visibility was no more than ten feet and he could still barely trace their footprints back to the cabin. He'd taken her on a pleasure cruise in the eye of a hurricane.

Just when she was starting to trust me. Could I be any more stupid? Thank God she was still breathing. He'd checked for a pulse. There was hope.

Snowflakes pasted themselves to his eyelashes, stringing frozen curtains across his vision. Had they really been laughing together mere minutes ago? Grant lengthened his strides, his feet slamming through the snow to reach the ground, clouds of snow crystals exploding around him. He was a Clydesdale in a testosterone-driven commercial selling beer, only much less graceful and infinitely more desperate.

There! The back of the cabin phased into view like a lighthouse in a sea of fog. Grant veered left, past the raised deck at the back, to avoid the slippery slope. He tightened his arms around Melinda and ducked under tree limbs, skirted the low wall of stacked logs, and hustled past the garage. Numb fingers twisted the handle and pushed the front door wide. Warm air hit him square in the face and he offered thanks to whatever deity was looking out for them. The firewood he'd collected earlier waited by the fire, another saving grace.

Grant kicked the door shut and made straight for the couch. He lowered Melinda as gently as he could and propped her head on cushions. He checked her breathing again: shallow but steady. He brushed snow from her body onto the floor, ignored her boots, and yanked blankets across her motionless form. Outside, the wind howled, angry to have lost its prey.

It made him sick to leave her, but they needed heat. The coals had cooled while they'd been outside. *Careless!* his mind yelled. He flung his gloves to the ground.

Building a fire with frozen fingers was an exercise in idiocy. The newspaper wouldn't compact, kindling spilled from his hands, splinters scored his skin. His hands were ungainly puppets. At last it was time to light the mess. He dumped matches on the floor and grabbed at one, staring it down.

"Don't be cruel."

It only took him three tries to light the match and he thanked his lucky stars. His thick hands enclosed the tiny flame and he let it lick the newspaper's edges.

"Thank God," Grant whispered and blew gently on the flames. Slowly, slowly the kindling caught. As soon as he felt it safe, he turned back to Melinda and his heart clenched at what he saw. So lifeless, so pale.

"Dammit," he bit out, crawling to her. He worked his fingers through her hair and found the rising lump, but minimal blood, considering.

"Thank God," he said again. Then he shoved aside the coffee table and stripped off his clothes.

Pain wrapped Melinda in a mummy's prison. Her hands and fingers ached with arthritis she didn't know she had. Her toes, feet, and legs were blocks of ice. Her head twirled on a spike. She moaned against the hurt but couldn't figure out how to open her eyes.

Time passed.

When she woke again she was held fast in a bear's embrace. Unforgiving arms trapped her like a vice and rough legs pinned her to the ground. Her whole body hurt, and somehow her face was sunburned. Melinda moaned and pushed against the bear's grip.

"Mel?" the bear said, and she blinked back to reality, sort of.

Not a bear. Grant. Grant the kidnapper, Grant the wood-splitter, Grant who gave her wine for breakfast.

Well, this was interesting.

Melinda lay on the floor of the Mastermind's cabin with Grant tucked against her backside. Blankets swathed them both and a fire blazed a few feet in front of her face. That explained the sunburn. But why did she not remember earning the hangover?

And where on earth were her clothes?

Where were *his* clothes?

"What are you doing?" she croaked.

"A dead branch fell on you." Grant's words were gentle against her head. "Clobbered you pretty good. You went down like a ton of bricks. I got you back here 'bout a half hour ago and I've been trying to get you warm. The snow went all down your jacket. Your body was like ice—"

Tension that she didn't understand emanated from the

masculine form behind her. Was he angry at her for being so foolish? She was no delicate waif. How had he managed?

"You carried me? All that way?" Why would he carry her if he were mad at her? Nothing made sense. Was he mad *because* he'd carried her? She scrunched her eyes shut against the cloud of questions.

"Of course I did," he replied curtly.

"Well, wow," she said, incapable of anything more eloquent. "You're, like, really strong, aren't you?" she asked, and then giggled at how ditzy she sounded. The giggling was a bad idea on many levels she realized quickly, and she groaned. "My head hurts . . . Stupid snow in the stupid trees." That was wrong. It wasn't the tree's fault. The trees had been so pretty. "No, stupid me for not listening. I did just what you said not to do." That much was crystal clear.

"I was the one who took you for a walk in the middle of a storm," Grant replied gruffly. "Stupid *me* in the stupid trees." His voice reverberated like a low engine against her flesh. His warm breath caressed her neck, rough stubble scratching her cheek. His chest was hard and massive against her back. He was so close. So safe. Her tension eased and his great bear arms tightened around her.

"Thank you," she said quietly. "For saving me."

"Melinda . . . of course."

This bear might be a knight in shining armor.

She shouldn't play with fire. But he was so strong. So selfless. So unlike the men she'd known. The men in her family, who let her brave the world alone, who taught her that to love someone was to need them, and to need them was to be denied.

Melinda twisted onto her back, then closed her eyes hard against the ensuing wave of pain.

"Bad idea," she groaned, then sucked in a breath and shifted again. She wanted to see him face-to-face. To apologize and thank him with sincerity. It was the nice thing to do. It was also the wrong thing to do.

"For Pete's sake, keep still," he said as he tried to hold her in place.

"I want . . . to see you," she said, catching her breath as the pain in her head peaked and subsided. "There." She exhaled. "See? Totally worth it." She smiled at him, tugging her tangled necklace away from her throat. It was a goofy smile, she could tell, and maybe her eyes crossed a little, but it was a smile just the same.

His brief struggle for words was ample reward.

"Foolish," he sputtered. "You could have a concussion. You should lie still for the rest of the day." He pulled back as he spoke but she wasn't having it. At her imitation of a shiver he drew instantly close, wrapped her in his huge arms and pressed the planes of his abdomen against her curves. She couldn't help the sigh that escaped.

"Better? Warmer?" His eyes searched hers.

She kept her nod small so as to not upset her skull.

He exhaled. "You gave me a hell of a scare." He drew her closer and rubbed his hand across his brow.

"Better," she sighed, tucked against his chest and smiling like the cat who'd got the cream.

Grant rubbed his temples as the last two hours swirled in his mind—the crackling fire, the semi-nude woman curled in his arms, the near-death experience that confused her into kissing him. That kiss would have been a slam dunk except everything about it was horribly wrong.

Grant's skin crawled at the memory of Melinda's body twisted in the snow, that damned rotten branch tangled in her hair. He shook off the image and shoved more wood into the stove. The snowstorm had raged all afternoon since their return and tonight would be harder than the one before.

His distraction failed; his movement stilled. The flashback of their hour in front of the fireplace played like an erotic movie in his mind. She'd made it difficult on him, snuggling into his embrace while he'd tried to keep his distance.

"This is an interesting way to save me," she'd said, pressing her breasts into his chest. *Mind over matter.* Exactly how many snowflakes were there in a typical snowstorm?

"You were on your way to hypothermia," he replied stiffly. "This was to save your life."

"Well then," she breathed. "Would it throw a wrench in your chivalry if I said how much I'm enjoying being rescued?"

Grant had had no idea what to say. He'd gone from mild flirtation to sprinting through a blizzard with an unconscious woman in his arms, and now he was struggling to stay on his white horse. Was that her foot inching up his leg? Those were definitely her fingers teasing the hair on his chest.

"You need to rest," he said weakly, cringing. *Pathetic.*

"I need to get warm," she whispered, and kissed him.

Oh, hell.

Kissing her was like alighting from a tornado. There was noise and panic and whirling energy, then suddenly there was stillness. Softness. Melinda's lips brushed his and drew him further from the storm. *Don't just lie there, dummy. Did the branch hit her or you?* Fortunately Grant had remembered how to move his arms and had come alive. Taking delicate control of the kiss, he'd shifted his lower arm to cradle her head in his hand. His other arm snaked down her torso to press his palm into the small of her back. She moaned into his mouth, and his hips pressed into hers involuntarily.

He couldn't lose control. Nobody liked a debaucher dressed like a hero. Angling his head over hers he slowly turned her onto her back, careful to support his weight while caressing her face. She was less inhibited. When she'd kissed him, her hands had been against his chest, but now they were everywhere. Wound around the nape of his neck, buried deep in his hair, stroking the length of his back.

"Melinda," he tore out, propping himself above her to stare at her glorious skin in the firelight. "Melinda, this can't happen. You have to rest. And I have to get us ready for tonight. We're losing light."

It was an excuse, but it was true, even though it couldn't have been later than three thirty. That was winter in the mountains. He had to get away from her. He had to keep them both alive. Her beautiful eyes opened lazily and refocused on him. If she kissed him again he'd be lost.

"Please, let me go," he begged, his forehead a hair's breadth from hers. "You have to rest. I'll get you some dry clothes and help you to the couch. If for no one else, rest for me, because I'm worried about you."

After a long moment she acquiesced. She smiled shyly and wrapped her arms around his shoulders.

"Carry me to your couch castle, if you must." Grant grinned and complied.

He called to her several times as he raided Paul's closet for dry clothes to make sure she was still conscious in the other room. Then he checked her pupils and allowed her to sleep.

Melinda was propped by pillows, wrapped in blankets, drinking endless hot tea. She was achy. She was groggy. She was confused. The mountain man was stomping somewhere, chopping something, missing in action but at least giving her time to think.

She felt better in some ways and worse in others. Better for having rested. Better for the heating pad around her neck. Better for not being left to freeze to death. *Thank you, Kidnapping Mountain Man Grant, whatever you are.* Worse because the swelling in her head was mind-numbing, and her neck and shoulders throbbed down to the bone. Worse because she'd been off her rocker earlier and had kissed him.

Melinda sipped her tea and watched the flames.

Grant had refused to leave the bedroom while she'd used the toilet—after he'd disallowed her walking and had carried her there himself. No man had attempted it before and Melinda wasn't quite sure how she felt about it.

Curious, she thought, sipping again. *Curiouser and curiouser.*

On the plus side, while trapped in the bathroom with her audience of one, Melinda had put on fresh underwear. It might've been cold and damp from its bath in the sink, but it was cleaner than a pair of two-day-old airplane knickers. Then she slipped into Paul's bulky but blessedly dry long underwear, plus his shirt, pants, socks, and jacket.

Grant had returned her to the couch and scrounged up some salves and anti-inflammatories for her. She'd fallen asleep, he'd sliced and diced a few trees, and she'd awoken again to find a cup of tea on the table, no less. He helped her get situated before disappearing again, and now she was alone and ruminating.

Grant's good-versus-evil balance was tipping in his favor. Wasn't that interesting? Fool her three times and she'd make out with a liar in front of a fire. If she didn't have such a crushing headache, she'd give herself a significant facepalm. Melinda clinked down her mug and adjusted the makeshift heating pad.

Cold air shocked the room as Grant slipped through the door with an armful of logs.

"What's your blog about, again?" he asked, booting the door closed. "And by that I mean, how'd you know how to rig a heating pad out of a pillowcase and a bag of rice? Are you a MacGyver groupie?" He crossed to the fireplace and deposited the latest bundle of wood on the hearth, then stacked it piece by piece in the rack.

Melinda laughed lightly. "Well, hello to you, too. Are you suggesting I call my column *Mel*Gyver?"

"Hold up, is it a column or a blog?" Grant asked over his shoulder.

"It's both," she said. "I started with a blog, *A Wing and A Prayer Kitchen*, and a couple years later *Mile High Home Magazine* contacted me and asked me to morph it into a monthly column for them. So I did, and now I do both. I try stuff in my kitchen all week long, then I blog about the funniest disasters or the unexpected success stories. Once a month I write an article that describes the most interesting experiment. I write pieces for larger publications, but that's less consistent."

Grant turned to face her. His eyes found her mouth and she felt a surge of warmth.

"What makes the cut?" He brushed wood chips from the tops of his knees.

"Well . . . I love the accidents, the awkward stuff." Melinda twisted her mug in her hands. "I love the real moments of cooking where you mess up a recipe and end up with three cups

90

of chives that were supposed to be the garnish but only three tablespoons of broccoli for your side dish. And you have to figure out what to do before the guests arrive. I like to highlight my own mistakes to show people that cooking is about the feeling you get when you're in the kitchen just as much as it's about the finished product. And I want people to feel alive . . . and confident, even if they screwed up." She laughed. "Which is not to say that if you've used salt instead of sugar you shouldn't throw it out because anything like that will be *vile.*"

"And the homemade heating pad?" He gestured with a piece of kindling at the object in question slung around her shoulders.

"Well, I read a lot of home-ec websites and mommy blogs. There are some badass women out there getting it done, and I'm not afraid to learn from them. I read one about a lady who sewed rice inside fabric and microwaved it, and voilà, a heating pad was born. So here we are with fifty pounds of emergency rice but no sewing machine, a wood stove but no microwave, and we need a cloth receptacle. My choices are a sock—no, thank you—or a pillowcase. Easy." She peeled the knotted pillowcase away from her shoulders and made to pass it to him.

"Would you put this back on the stove for a minute?" She smiled at him.

"Happy to." He laid the pillowcase into the roasting dish he'd placed on the stovetop. "Want your ice pack again?"

Melinda grimaced and flexed her head from side to side, exploring the stiffness in her neck.

"Yes, please. And for the record, the irony of having to use an ice pack in the middle of a snowstorm is insulting." She winced. Grant passed her the ice pack that of course Paul had in the closet of wonders, and she laid it atop her bruised head. "How's it look?"

His laugh rumbled low in his chest.

"Becoming." His smile slipped and the pain tightened his eyes. "Dammit, Melinda, I'm so sor—"

"No chance, Mountain Man, this wasn't your fault," she interrupted, surprised at her own sincerity. "You told me the stakes and I chose not to listen. Maybe I'll learn my lesson." She sank back and let the couch support her.

His eyes narrowed and she knew he wanted to say more, but all he said was "Want more drugs?"

"No but yes." She half-smiled. "I don't want the inflammation to get ahead of me. You don't want to piss off the brain, right?"

"Yeah, I think I've done that enough for one trip." He walked into the kitchen. Melinda heard him crack open a cabinet door and take out the bottle of pills. She heard the rattle as he released the lid and the shiver of tablets as he shook some into his palm. She closed her eyes, heard the lid snap again, the bottle slide into the cabinet, the cabinet thump closed.

What was the food parallel for a life-and-death nightmare? *Too easy. Soufflé.*

Grant's stomach, jaw, and heart ached. Every time he caught sight of Melinda's features pinched with pain, the face she made when she thought he wasn't looking, his gut clenched. He handed her two tablets and a glass of water and watched her swallow them down.

"Got enough food in your belly to take those?" He grabbed the warmed rice-filled pillowcase.

"Never." She gave him the flirtatious half-smile he was starting to crave and took the makeshift heating pad from him.

"Well, that won't do," he said. "Could I perhaps interest the lady in a light snack before she retires?"

"Am I retiring so soon?" She pouted delicately, then moaned as she eased the heating pad onto her neck and shoulders. Grant paused.

What had she said?

"It'll take a while for the chef to scrounge together something edible," he said. "For the record, it won't be nearly as good as your entrée this morning. And yes, you sure as hell are retiring soon, because you need your rest if you're going to survive this insanity."

She cocked her head at him. Then came the raised eyebrow.

"You seem pretty worked up."

Dear God in Heaven.

"Stop flirting with me, woman, I've got to make you a meal and build up the fire."

Melinda eyed the fireplace. Orange flames licked the stove's window and the fan churned out a steady stream of hot air.

"Seems pretty stoked to me," she deadpanned, going for a rise. Trouble was, she was getting one.

Grant turned on his heel and stalked into the kitchen, grumbling to himself about head wounds and the need for seriousness at a time like this. Her low chuckle taunted him like perfume.

"You're incorrigible," he called.

"You like me," she called back.

That shut him up quick. Grant squatted at the doorway of the pantry to root through dry goods. How the hell had she turned this boxed graveyard into food? It would serve her right if he gave her a peanut butter and cream of mushroom soup sandwich for dinner. He paused. Maybe he was onto something. Everyone liked PB&J, right? He scanned the shelves for bread. There it was. Gluten-free, of course. Paul was a health nut, just

93

like Grant's dad. How did he have two of these people in his life?

"Hey, Mel?"

"Yes?"

"Peanut butter and jelly?"

A cross between a moan and a groan reached him in the kitchen.

"Does that mean yes?" He laughed, then braced one arm against the door frame and dropped to one knee.

"Yesssss," came the reply. A beat later she added, "I want three."

Grant's head shot up.

"Three?"

"There's no such thing as too much peanut butter and jelly, Grant, and anyone who says different doesn't want you to be happy," she called. "Plus we didn't have lunch," she added. He laughed.

"Well, forget *that* guy," he called back. He transferred supplies from the pantry to the butcher block. "Three sandwiches *au peanut*—uh, no, *au almond butter et jelly* coming right up."

Fifteen minutes later he had ten sandwiches in front of him. What next? Chips? Pickles? Both, of course. He ducked into the pantry again. He grabbed two bottles of sparkling water by the neck, snagged both barbecue and sea-salt-and-vinegar chips, and added a jar of classic dills. Organic emergency rations. Naturally.

With two hourglass-shaped glasses trapped between his index and middle fingers, Grant made his way into the den to find Melinda asleep on the couch.

"Good idea, Gorgeous," he said quietly, resting the glasses on the coffee table. He left one lantern illuminating the kitchen and returned to the den to assemble their dinner, babysit the fire, and stare at Melinda.

The windows were rattling when Melinda woke. The wind whistled, whooshed, walloped. Something nearby crackled and popped. She blinked blurry eyes. Right, the fire. A gargoyle hunched in front of the fireplace, tilting a glass to its lips with a brawny, sweater-covered arm. Gargoyles wore sweaters? No, mountain men wore sweaters. Mountain men in cabins. Right, cabins. The Mastermind's cabin. Why did every wake-up feel like she'd been dropped into Wonderland? On her head? And she, the achy Alice, too big, too small, too brash, too cold, too heartless, too vulnerable. She shut her eyes against the cascade of thoughts.

Apart from the fire's glow, the cabin was dark. The day was gone.

"Grant?" she croaked. Great. She was a frog again.

The gargoyle swiveled its shaggy head and dark eyes zeroed in on hers. She saw concern. And from the way her head was pounding, the concern might be warranted.

"Head hurt?"

"Yeah." Now the frog was gone but her voice faltered and she hated it. This wasn't how she'd imagined their evening together. Why the hell had she ignored his warning in the snow? Why had she wanted to go for a walk at all—who went for a walk in a blizzard? A self-proclaimed adventurer. She was disgusted with herself. Adventures didn't always end well. Real adventurers knew this. More evidence that she was a fraud. Failure was a lot easier to take when it was in the kitchen and she could spin it as unimportant or fun. Buy a replacement quiche at the store for the photo.

She ran her fingers through her hair, over her scalp. Even places that weren't injured hurt. Gingerly, she turned her head side to side. *Ow.* No, not a good idea yet.

"Is it time for another round of Advil?"

"I doubt it," Melinda said with regret. She didn't like the way he looked at her: pity, compassion. *Don't waste your sympathy on me.* Not after the foolish mistake she'd made. But she'd be damned if she was going to act the martyr. "Where's my sandwich, you big bully?" She cocked her head to the side, smile faltering only a millisecond as she flinched.

His jaw tightened, but he only said, "Hungry? Nothing like boysenberry preserves and six slices of bread to dial back that inflammation."

She couldn't suppress a laugh and winced.

"Sorry," he said, concerned.

"No, it's good. Laughter is good. I just won't throw my head back and cackle," she said. "Let's eat. That second nap really gave me an appetite. What time is it?" Was he fooled by her bravado? He didn't seem to be. Yet. She'd get him eventually. She got everyone.

"Around seven thirty," he said, passing her a plate.

The meal was an elementary school feast, she saw with delight. Huge dinner plates stacked with almond-butter-and-jelly sandwiches, cut diagonally. *Diagonally! Be still my heart!* Two different flavors of chips. Pickles stacked in a tower on their own plate. Sparkling water in . . . what were those? Old-fashioned sundae glasses? *Divine.*

"Paul had lemons?" Melinda asked in surprise after her first sip of bubbly water.

"He had a bottle of lemon juice concentrate," said Grant with half a sandwich in his mouth.

"Nice job, Chef Grant!" she said with real appreciation. She inspected a sandwich. "What kind of jelly, did you say?"

"Strawberry and boysenberry," Grant answered as he opened his second sandwich to layer both barbecue and salt-and-vinegar chips inside. The crunch satisfied her even vicariously. "So I used some of each." A third of a pickle disappeared between his teeth. Then the next third. Then it was gone.

Melinda watched the show with her first sandwich still untouched in hand. "Wow."

"I'm tall," he managed through crumbling chips and sticky jam, and she laughed, but delicately this time.

Melinda took a bite. "Ohhhh." She closed her eyes. "It's like fourth grade all over again. This is the best." She stopped talking. The meal was humble and perfect. Soft slices of bread, sticky and sweet almond butter and jelly, crackling, salty chips, and crisp, tangy pickles. The bubbly water balanced the palate. She made it through two sandwiches and most of her chips before her stomach said uncle.

"That was incredible," Melinda said with what was surely a dopey expression. Her hand toyed with chip remnants. "Is there more water?" she asked. "And lemon? It was so fancy."

He chuckled. "On my way," he said. When he returned from the kitchen, he squatted next to the coffee table to refill her glass. "A capful is just right," he said as he tipped lemon concentrate into her glass and followed it with sparkling water. "I added more to mine by mistake and I think the acid ate its way through a couple teeth."

She laughed. "Good to know." She rubbed her neck and his eyes narrowed.

"Would you get me the ice pack?" she asked. "And maybe I need some fish oil or something with this meal. I might not be acting in the best interest of my head."

Grant stared at her and she laughed. "That probably made

no sense. Fish oil helps inflammation, and with that bump plus all the bread, I bet there's no small amount of that going on. But it was worth it," she hastened to add.

"Yeah," he said, "Yeah, I was just thinking what an idiot I was."

"What?"

"My dad is going to kick my ass," he said. He disappeared into the kitchen again. She heard cupboards opening and pill bottles rattling.

"What?" Melinda repeated to the empty room.

Grant returned with a bottle of fish oil capsules. "I should have thought of this right away. My dad's a big off-the-grid health nut and raised me on this stuff. I take it every day, but I know not everyone's as weird as we are, so I forget to suggest it to other people. I bet this'll really help your head. Despite the landslide of carbs we just ate," he said with a smile.

He shook four capsules into her palm and passed her the refilled sundae glass of water. She downed the pills and smiled her thanks.

"We're going to repeat those every few hours, okay?" he asked her, and she nodded. "We want to get ahead of the pain, and as much fun as that dinner was, that wasn't the way to do it." She nodded again.

"Are we allowed to converse, Doctor?" she asked.

"If you're a good patient, yes," he answered with false sternness. "Do you have everything you need?" She watched him scan her body and imagined his assessment: Ice pack on her head, heating pad on her shoulders, blanket across her lap as she stretched lengthwise on the couch, two pairs of socks on her feet.

"Do you approve?"

"It's not the ICU but it'll do," he said without humor.

"Everything beeps in the ICU," she said. "Not exactly conducive to rest."

"True, and in the ICU I'd have to wear scrubs, and I'm betting they don't come in my size."

That's better, she thought. She liked him better happy. Not somber. He sat on the floor near her feet with his back against the couch, both of them facing the fire. "So how do you know this Paul character?" she asked. "You play hooky together?"

Grant snorted. "*Hockey*," he said. "We play ice hockey. There's a league that meets on the lake every Saturday. Paul plays when he's here on the weekends. He's some financial guy at a bank down below, but he loves his cabin and comes up here as much as he can, which isn't often. The type who's married to his job, you know?"

Melinda nodded. It was nice to hear about Paul as a relatively normal person instead of keeping him in the Psycho Bad Guy room in her mind. Paul was Grant's friend. Grant was turning out to be a Good Guy. Paul needed to be a Good Guy, too, otherwise Grant might be a Bad Guy by association, and that wouldn't do. Bad Guys wouldn't carry you through the snow after you'd ignored their warnings and gotten a smackdown from a vengeful tree.

"Three questions," she said. "All equally important, and I don't want to get sidetracked, so I'm asking them all at the same time. One, what does Melisa do? Two, how long have you and Paul known each other such that you have never met her? And three, if you play hockey every week, do you still have all your teeth? Hang on, one more, does Paul still have his teeth?"

Grant's laugh reverberated through his chest, curling Melinda's toes.

"Despite how much I want to talk dental damage, I'll tell you about Melisa first, since she's an important player here."

99

Melinda shifted on the couch and he waited.

"Melisa's some kind of water therapist." Grant searched for the word. "Washer. Washu. Watsu. That's it. She's a Watsu therapist—like a massage therapist who works in the water or something. I don't know much about it, or her. Like I told you before, she and Paul met because she was kidnapped by some guys that were after her brother. They wanted to get to him through her. She and Paul happened to live in the same building. He got wind of what was happening and got to be the hero."

"How do a water worker and a fancy bank guy live in the same apartment building?" she asked.

"Good question," he said. "Maybe she got in when it was rent-controlled. I think he has the whole top floor," Grant mused. "A few years ago he bought the building."

"And you've never met her," she said.

"And I've never met her," he repeated. "Paul doesn't talk too much about her, but that's how he is—private. Plus, I see him mostly up here and she's down below."

"Do we look alike?" Melinda asked, suddenly curious about the face that so resembled hers that she'd ended up a captive on a snowy mountainside.

Grant grabbed his phone from the end table. He swiped the screen and pushed icons and a woman's face appeared.

"Here," he said, passing her the device. "You tell me."

Melinda took the phone and there she was. Dark, shoulder-length hair, though Melinda's was more unruly. Long nose, though Melinda's curved more at the tip, with delicately flared nostrils. Wide mouth, wide eyes. *Melisa's features are more Caucasian*, Melinda decided. *Probably since she isn't half-Bengali.*

"I can see it," she said with a smile, handing the phone back to him.

"Are you serious?" Grant's head jerked back.

"What?"

"She's nothing like you!" he said.

"Grant . . . You stole me from the airport because you thought I was her!" Had she entered the Twilight Zone?

"That was before!" He brushed aside her logic. "Besides, it was night. The lighting was bad. You were in the wrong place at the wrong time."

Melinda's mouth dropped open. Grant turned fully to face her, and she gaped at him.

"Her face is a shadow of yours." His eyes pierced hers. "Yours has life. Character. Richness. Warmth." He stopped, then started again. "It's all there. All the things you do and think are there on your face, waiting to be shared with everyone around you. Her face is a closed book." He shrugged and the tension cleared. "Which could be attractive, if you're into that look."

Melinda's mouth stayed open.

"I've known Paul for a year and a half or so, to answer that question. He seems really careful with letting people into his circle, so it didn't really occur to me that I'd never met his lady. I realized later that it was all strategy.

"About the teeth: We wear face masks. I'm not trying to lose my teeth before I'm ninety. And Paul's not trying to get less pretty," he said. "Not all the guys wear them, but we do."

She was staring at him.

"Any other questions come to mind?"

She shook her head.

"Okay, then. It's time for bed."

Her mouth closed with a snap. What had just happened?

"What? That's not fair! I'm not tired." But as she took a breath to argue more, the breath turned into a yawn, and the aches in her body swelled and grumbled. "You made me tired." She massaged her temples. "All those compliments were

101

exhausting and I need to recover."

A quick guffaw was his only answer.

At least Melinda was willing to see reason that she should rest. Grant thought less and less that she had a concussion, but he didn't want her staying up late and exerting herself.

He paused as he refilled her water. Actually, that was exactly what he wanted her doing, but not after a head injury.

He carried the water back to the coffee table and knelt in front of her.

"Okay, Gorgeous, let's hit the bathroom before I impose martial law and quarantine you to the couch."

Grant's shoulder muffled her laugh as he gathered her into his arms.

"I can walk, remember?" she protested, but he heard her pleasure at being carried, or at least imagined he did.

"This is a full-service kidnapping outfit," he said, puffing up his chest. "Now come with me into the kitchen. I need you to carry a flowerpot full of water."

She melted against him with laughter, but he suspected it had more to do with her fatigue than his wit. They made a quick stop in the kitchen for a pitcher of water.

"Got it okay?" He watched her grip the handle. "I can come back for it."

"Let me do something," she said as she balanced the pitcher with both hands. "You're carrying it by proxy, don't worry."

Grant walked through Paul's bedroom and into the bathroom, taking the pitcher from her and depositing it on the countertop before gently lowering her to the toilet's closed lid.

He stood in front of her, part rescuer, part oaf, all uncertain.

"Um. Do you need me to help you . . .?" Grant hated the flush that crept up his neck but he needed to know how unstable she felt.

"Leave me my pitcher and get out." She swatted him with what he hoped was mock irritation.

Grant went. He listened to the sounds of her brushing her teeth, rinsing the toothbrush, and pouring the water from the pitcher into the toilet to flush it. Not bad for a blogger. He might teach her this mountain thing yet.

He knocked. "You call for a lift?"

She laughed from behind the door. "How do I know you're the right driver? Tell me your name."

Uh oh. This could go badly. Was she being funny or was he on thin ice? He mentally crossed his fingers and went for broke.

"Grant Samson, and I don't always kidnap people, but when I do, I make sure to follow it up with a blizzard and a head wound."

Melinda opened the door mid-laugh and Grant swallowed his sigh of relief.

"You're right on time," she said with a smile. Then the smile dropped. "You're not going to let me walk are you."

"Glad that's not a real question," he answered, and lifted her into his arms. "How do you feel about more fish oil?"

"Ecstatic."

Grant tried to keep his laugh subtle since his mouth was at her ear.

"Actually, I think that first dose made a difference," she said, fingertips to her scalp where the branch had struck. "When I stood earlier, I didn't feel like an elephant was using my skull as a Thighmaster."

"You stood up earlier?" Grant was instantly incensed. "I

thought we had a deal!" They were in the kitchen now and he snagged the bottle of pills with one hand.

"For a Kaar driver, you're kind of bossy," she teased.

"Okay, okay, sorry. I just don't want you taking a dive on my watch. Will you promise to tell me in the middle of the night if you have to go to the bathroom?" He navigated the doorway between the kitchen and den, watched her nod, and didn't believe her for a moment. He lowered her to the couch. "I'm going to sleep on the floor next to you. If you move, I'll hear it. This is a threat."

Melinda sighed and rolled her eyes. "All right, Boss Man."

Grant liked Boss Man less than he liked Mountain Man, but he knew he was right. What if she stood up too fast, lost her balance, and keeled over? Then where would they be? No ambulance was getting up these roads, and he couldn't handle seeing her blood. The guys on the ice hockey team, sure, no problem. It was barbaric fun when someone bled on the ice— not a lot, of course, just a split lip or gashed eyebrow. Something that raised the stakes a bit. Seeing Melinda's blood would be a different story.

"Good," he grunted. *Animal*, snapped his mind.

Yeah, well, I'm the animal keeping her alive, he snapped back.

Grant shook four more pills from the bottle and handed them to her along with the glass of water. It was time to melt more snow. He'd do it after she dropped off.

"Get comfortable, Mel. Get as warm as you can without overheating. I'm going to stoke up the fire and melt some snow, then I'll come bed down. Don't worry about me," he said. He held up a hand to stop her concerns. "You need the warmth of the fire, and you get the couch. I'm not leaving you alone while you're out here, and the floor is fine for me. I've got pillows and I'll steal the blankets from the bed. We're both sleeping in jackets. Get comfortable," he repeated. "Get some sleep."

He saw with relief that she wasn't going to push it, wasn't going to resist or cajole. Instead she shimmied her body until she lay horizontal on the couch, head propped on a pillow, blankets snugged nearly to the hat she wore.

"Night, Mountain Man," she said, faint smile on her lips.

"Good night, Melinda," he said solemnly and watched her breath slow and deepen in the firelit room.

Her ears were crying.

Melinda touched trembling fingers to both earlobes and found them wet and sticky. She floated frozen fingers before her eyes and saw the tips red with blood.

Her head throbbed. Someone had hit her. Who had hit her?

She scanned the white ocean in front of her. No one was there. Was he behind her, would he hit her again?

He would. His malevolence closed around her like an evil mist.

She had to get out of there.

Her feet wouldn't move, why wouldn't they move? She looked at her feet.

That was why.

Hip-high snow locked her in place. She clawed at the snow to free herself only for it to pile higher against her.

Melinda twisted her torso left and right, frantic to prevent whoever he was from hitting her again. She gasped at the cold, at the exertion, at the fear that choked her lungs.

And then, after her body was drained to exhaustion, he struck her, and the crack echoed inside her mind and throughout the trees. Down she sprawled as her blood slashed the snow. Snow choked her mouth, ice cascaded inside her jacket and she lay in a heap of agony, waiting for him to finish her.

Melinda moaned in her sleep. Her eyelids flicked back and forth, her head jerked from side to side on her pillow. Grant sat in his makeshift bed on the floor, jaw set, eyes locked on her face. It was 2:00 a.m. She'd been tossing and turning off and on since 10:00 p.m. and he'd not slept a wink.

He'd woken her up around midnight for more fish oil. He'd worried about the Advil on an empty stomach and now regretted not giving her any. Earlier, when she'd been peaceful, he'd built up the fire, melted snow, and done a cursory check of their supplies. Then he'd returned to her restlessness.

Now every whimper ended in a sob and every moan in a muffled shriek. Damn the snow in the damn trees. Damn him, too. Grant turned to the fireplace in desperation. No time like the present to heat things up, though he'd tended the fire not thirty minutes before.

Anything to keep his mind off what her mind was on.

As if in agreement, Melinda let out a soft wail. Grant gritted his teeth. Unless she woke up, he wasn't disturbing her again. She needed the rest too much. Instead, he crawled the short distance to his post by the stove, twisted the handle down to release the door, and swung it open.

Hot air singed his face and his stubble fairly crackled with the dryness. He rubbed his jaw where she'd stroked it earlier when she'd kissed him.

Might be time for a shave.

As if another kiss was happening.

There's no need to brutalize her face as well as her head, he snapped at his conscience.

He shook his head. Not a good sign that he was arguing with himself again.

The fire. Make the damn fire.

Grant's shoulders settled as his body moved through the motions of building up the blaze. Heat gloved his hands as he wedged more wood into the stove.

Even with the creak of the door as he closed it, Grant heard Melinda's sigh. He whipped his head around, heart in his throat. But her eyes were closed and she looked peaceful.

"Grant," she murmured. "So nice to meet you, Grant." She smiled and nestled her head on the pillow.

Grant's hands stilled, one on the stove's handle, the other twisted behind him.

Melinda sighed in her sleep.

"Okay, then." He checked that the stove was secure then crawled back to his place on the floor below her.

"Okay, then," he repeated. He laid his head on the pillow and tugged the blankets over himself.

Grant lay awake long after she drifted into more contented sleep, listening for signs that she was in pain. He heard none, and it was close to 4:00 a.m. before sleep claimed him.

CHAPTER FIVE

The fire that warms us can also consume us;
it is not the fault of the fire.
Swami Vivekananda

The snow had stopped when Melinda woke the next morning. She knew it as soon as she opened her eyes. She knew where she was this morning, knew she was on the couch. She also knew her head felt better. Not perfect, but better. And she knew she had to pee.

Melinda shifted cautiously. There was a mountain man below her waiting to pounce if she so much as sniffled, but she longed for a little autonomy, especially with regard to a full bladder. That was what she got for hydrating.

Slowly, gingerly, she raised herself to sitting, careful not to drop blankets onto the sleeping man at her feet, and careful not to move too quickly.

He seems pretty out. Melinda peeked at him with raised eyebrows. Did he always sleep like this?

She scooched toward her feet on the couch, away from Grant's head. Success! She reached the armrest, crested it like a speed bump, and slithered awkwardly free of her couch castle and captor.

"*Oof,*" she whispered, standing stiffly and rubbing her shoulders and neck.

Her bladder squeezed its impatience and Melinda hustled through the kitchen and into the bathroom in her socks.

Several minutes later she returned to evaluate the landscape of the kitchen. From the reflective menagerie of water-filled stockpots, saucepans, vases, and jars, it was clear that Grant had melted snow last night while she slept. She raised an eyebrow. The mountain man was serving his purpose.

Melinda's stomach growled—it was time to cook. Still loath to bow to the insipid blandness of cereal, she ducked into the pantry again. What was left? She eyed boxes and bags of nonperishable items.

Oatmeal! Sprouted and steel-cut, to boot. *Of course. Nothing but the best for the Mastermind.* What could she add that would give it some energetic staying power as well as some flavor? She dug further.

Jackpot! Melinda pulled nuts, nut butter, and dried fruit from the pantry. *Paul, I almost don't hate you.* And then she remembered that without Paul's perversions she wouldn't be cut off from friends and family and sleeping on a sofa, and she scowled.

But what about Grant? Her mind whispered, and after that she didn't know what to think.

"Better to cook than to think." Melinda burst out laughing— she'd just found her new motto. Melinda measured water into a saucepan, sprinkled in salt, and topped the pan with its lid. While she waited for the water to boil, she turned to the butcher block with her collection of culinary accessories. She slivered, chopped, and julienned Marcona almonds, dried apricots, cherries, and pears, then stirred the oats into the water.

"Let's gussy this up, shall we?" Melinda murmured as she remembered Grant's spectacular sandwich spread from the night before. She went on the hunt for serving dishes. Because of course Paul had them, right? Yes, of course, he had them. *Cabin: Four stars. Hospitality: Zero.*

Melinda's scalp tingled where Grant had stroked her hair as his mouth plundered hers.

Fine. Not quite zero.

She shook herself and collected a half-dozen small, shallow dishes and filled them with toppings. She checked the oats and gave them a stir.

What next? Melinda readied bowls and spoons and found more oatmeal complements. Almond milk, honey, coconut oil, and cashew butter, too. Melinda placed the jars at the center of the table and laid out the bowls.

Now what? Now she waited for the oats to cook and had a little snoop. *Sorry-not-sorry, Paul.*

Melinda wandered into the bedroom and her eyes fell immediately on the gun. The gun. What was she doing with that thing? She remembered the first hours of their arrival at the cabin—the hopelessness, the fear, the flimsy illusion of the revolver's protection. Two days later she knew she was as likely to shoot off her own foot as she was to protect herself. Plus, if Grant were going to harm her, he would have done so already.

He wasn't like that. He didn't want to hurt her. Somewhere in the region of Melinda's heart a spark flared and she drew a quick breath. It was time to get the gun out of circulation. She tiptoed through the kitchen and turned left to open the coat closet. She located the shoebox and placed the revolver inside.

That was done. She spied the wood stove. That was it! She could build up the fire. Grant wasn't the only one who could be resourceful, right? Right.

She spared a glance for Grant, who slept heavily with an arm flung across his face. *Don't stare. He's just a man.* How long had it been since she'd had a boyfriend? Six months? *Try a year.* The corners of Melinda's mouth turned down.

The fire, darn it. Right. The fire. She hadn't built a fire in years. Maybe it was like riding a bicycle and the perfect steps would come to her, one by one, and a roaring blaze would leap to life and delight them both. *Yeah, and maybe we'll be rescued by a serenading SWAT team.* Melinda sat cross-legged by the hearth and willed the stack of wood to float into the stove and catch itself on fire.

Maybe if she treated it like a kitchen experiment. Hopefully one that didn't explode in her face. Melinda sat up straighter and took a deep breath. *First step: observe.* What was inside the wood stove? She peered through its small window. Whitened coals and odd bits of blackened wood, but minimal ash. Maybe that's what the tray underneath was about? Should she empty the ash? No, that was his call, she decided. So what, then? Melinda was used to the cold. She'd grown up north of Seattle and moved to Denver, after all. But her family had had a gas fireplace, which meant no mauls, no axes, no coals, no questions about ash disposal.

Melinda vaguely recalled camping with the Girl Scouts and building a tower of things that burned. *Second step: find things that burn.* She reviewed her surroundings: a shiny brass oblong rack stacked high with split wood, a subdued-looking brass fireplace tool set, a low-slung rack with a leather gusset stacked high with newspaper, and a second similar rack full of split kindling.

Sure, just like riding a bike. How did she open the darn thing? Melinda ignored the tremble in her hand and reached for the slender black stove handle. The catch released at her downward twist and she enjoyed a brief thrill of success. *Look at that, I didn't explode. The crowd goes wild.* She tugged the door open wide and warm air sucked the moisture from her eyeballs.

Melinda perused the ingredients at her disposal. *Third step: newspaper.* Newspaper—was that right? Should it be flat? Tented? Folded into a crane? Melinda closed her eyes and tried to remember. What had her troop done? She was thirty-two now, so it must have been twenty-three years ago, when she was nine. Who could remember building a fire twenty-three years ago? Melinda squashed three sheets of paper into something resembling snowballs and dared the coals to contradict her. She added the newspaper to the coals and watched them smoke lightly and then incinerate themselves into nothing.

"No, no! Stop!" she hissed. She grabbed a handful of kindling and shoved it on the expiring newspaper with a desperate prayer.

The kindling rested with what appeared to be cool comfort atop the mocking coals. She had better hurry up with step four.

"Easier said than done," she muttered and grabbed two rough-split logs. She manhandled them into the stove and groaned as she knocked aside the underperforming twigs.

"*Kuttar bachcha,*" she whispered at the place where a fire should be. *Son of a bitch.*

"You tell 'im," rumbled a voice behind her, and Melinda jerked around to see Grant propped on one elbow as he watched her from the floor.

"This thing won't work," she sputtered, simultaneously frustrated and embarrassed.

"You're off to a great start, though," Grant said. Smooth as a panther, he sat upright, stretched, and rolled his shoulders. He dropped his head to elongate his neck and twist his torso left and right.

Melinda forgot about the fire.

"Want a hand?" he asked.

"I need way more than a hand," she muttered as she watched his display, and then she blushed. "I need an intervention," she added hastily. Was everything she said innuendo? "Can you do this and I'll take care of the oatmeal?" She stumbled to her feet. She couldn't get out of there fast enough.

"Getting paid in food for lighting someone's fire works for me."

Melinda hid her smile and Grant threw back his blankets to stand.

Suddenly serious, he asked, "How's the head? I'm glad to see you moving around, even though I wish you'd let me take care of things this morning."

"I'm a little stiff but the pain is much less," she said, brushing her skull with tentative fingertips. "It's a little tender for sure. But I can turn my head all right. I even bent over in the pantry earlier!" Melinda's face flamed at the picture she'd painted. Grant's words appeared to stall in his mouth.

"Uh, and did you feel pressure?" he managed.

Melinda imagined his face got a little redder at that comment.

"In your head. Did your head hurt when you were, uh, in the pantry?"

"Not really. Definitely not as bad as yesterday," she said, hoping the oatmeal would boil over and give her an excuse to leave.

"Well, progress, then," he said. "Have you had any fish oil yet?"

"Ick, no. Not before breakfast," she said. "It should be done by now. Do you think Paul has a serving tray?"

"He must. This place is deluxe," Grant said wryly.

Melinda laughed and escaped to the kitchen.

Grant shoved his hands through his hair and stretched both arms overhead to work the stiffness from his involuntary slumber party. He wished Melinda hadn't beaten him to wakefulness today, but perhaps last night had been worse for him than for her. She seemed to be moving around well. Her attempt at a fire was heartening as well as endearing. He walked to the stove, whose door she'd left ajar in her haste, and evaluated the scene. It was about time to start from scratch, anyway.

Grant carefully extracted the ash tray, dumped the contents into the metal ash bucket, then recreated the fire. He fingered his stubbly jaw and realized it was time to ask Melinda's permission to intrude on the bathroom.

He found her in the kitchen, tinkering with something on the range.

"Hi," he said, relieved when she didn't jump.

"Hi," she replied and half-turned to face him, a question in her tone.

"Mind if I use the bathroom to weed-whack my face?"

"Not at all," she said. "Need warm water? I have extra from my tea." She extended a white mug to him, "Big Spender" scrawled across it in curvy gold script. Paul must love that one.

"Thanks," he said. Grant took the mug carefully from her hand and made his way through the freezing bedroom into the bathroom. He hunted through Paul's bathroom drawers until he found shaving lotion and a razor and got to work. A few minutes later he wiped his shorn face dry on a towel and rinsed the soapy remnants down the drain.

He joined Melinda as she loaded a large wooden tray with

114

their breakfast.

"Let me carry that," he said.

"No, you have to move that beastly coffee table so we can eat." She swished past him with the laden tray.

As if he would allow her to carry a four-course meal in her damaged condition.

"I can do both," he replied, intercepting the tray and gesturing that she precede him into the den. Grant watched the sway of Melinda's hips until she stepped between the couch and the coffee table. Grant laid the tray on the table, crouched to grab the table's turned legs, and gently positioned it between the sheepskin rug and the couch. "Here okay?" he asked.

"Perfect." She dropped more quickly than he would have liked her to sit, her back against the couch. Two stoneware bowls full of steaming oats wafted their wares amid smaller dishes full of chopped nuts, dried fruit, and strips of pale somethings that were frankly questionable. Beside them waited a small stoneware jug, a jar of honey, and a jar of cashew butter. His dad would be so proud. Hell, a bed and breakfast would be proud. All it lacked was a sprig of lilac.

"This looks professional," he said. He crossed his legs to sit opposite her on the floor. "But did we need the sliced albino ears?"

Melinda giggled and drizzled honey on her oats.

"Those are dried pears, I'll have you know," she said with pseudo-indignation, or so he hoped. "*Some* snowbound guests consider them a delicacy." She accessorized her dish with nuts, fruit, and whitish liquid from the pitcher. "Almond milk *du* box," she said to his questioning look.

"Of course," he said. Grant added fruit and nuts to his own bowl and dug in.

"Another masterpiece," he swallowed and said after a while.

115

"Who taught you how to cook under fire?"

She burst out laughing and Grant's chest warmed when she didn't flinch. "That's a good way to put it. I think . . . I think it was my mom, actually. My dad's Indian, West Bengali, and I got my love of sweetness and spice from him. Plus coconut milk, soaking things, sprouting things, all the concoctions. But my mom taught me to stare down a kitchen, make friends with it, and become one with it." She laughed and took a bite of her oatmeal. "That's abstract, I guess, but that's the essence of it. She took any twist you threw at her, fearlessly."

Melinda swirled her spoon around her bowl to capture the last bite, then continued, eyes on the air between them. "She and my dad used to have fun in the kitchen together. His collection of family recipes plus her inventiveness meant they'd be in there arguing, laughing, combining, you name it. My brother and I learned to stay the heck away when they were in the kitchen together. But there was also this sweet magic about it, so sometimes we'd end up tiptoeing to the doorway and watching."

Grant watched her face come alive as she spoke of her family. But what had she said? *Used to.*

"Do they not cook together anymore?"

He cursed himself for a fool as her face shuttered and closed.

"My mom left when I was fifteen and my brother was twelve. She never divorced my dad, never tried to, but she also never came back. They're still married."

Her broken expression twisted his gut.

"After my brother and I were born, my mom got pregnant again. Their third. Planned. She lost the baby at seven months along, when I was seven and my brother was four." Melinda's spoon froze in the air. "After the initial shock, she seemed okay. Like, for years she seemed okay. But it did something to her that she couldn't recover from. And how could a seven-year-old fix

116

heartbreak like that?"

The question was rhetorical, and Grant knew it.

"When I was about thirteen, she kind of . . . snapped." Melinda's face had gone blank. "She started criticizing us all the time. Telling us all the problems we had and stuff we did wrong. She was a psychologist and had always been so amazing at letting me have my own experience and not telling me how to feel, all that psychology crap. That completely changed. She was like an attack dog about every decision I made. I was so confused, and I was so pissed."

She laughed without mirth and the sound tore at his chest.

"'Resentful' is the grown-up word to use. I felt *resentful*. It was all her shit! All of her pain, her loss, her confusion at . . . at . . ."—she hunted for words—"at being alive when her poor baby had died. Our sister," she finished. "Our poor baby sister."

Melinda set her bowl on the coffee table and sighed. "My dad didn't know what to do, and of course he was getting her attacks, too. He was 'too stubborn,' 'too locked in tradition,' 'too hard on us,' 'too easy on us,' too everything. She was relentless. Eventually she moved out. Blamed him for some made-up thing." She toyed with her necklace. "He's close with his family, but he's hardly locked in tradition. We celebrated the major Indian holidays, but in no way was he into any archaic inhibiting behavior from anyone's tradition. Nothing she said made sense."

Her eyes flashed with hurt as well as anger.

"You were fifteen when she left?"

"Yeah."

"That's a hard time for a girl to lose her mother."

"Yeah," she agreed and her eyes flashed again. "Part of me wanted her to go, but then afterward I was so bloody lost. I totally shut down. I had to invent a socially palatable personality because I turned into a zombie for a while."

She paused and he wondered how deep the pain of that abandonment ran.

"Bet you didn't expect that when you asked about oatmeal," she said with an empty laugh. She stacked her bowl and spoon on the wooden tray and cast around for other things to tidy.

"Did you ever see her again?" he asked, undaunted.

"All the time. That's what was so awkward about it. She moved, but she stayed in the same suburb in Bellingham and we had to pretend everything was normal. Our parents treated it like joint custody in a divorce. We spent half the time with her, half the time with him. We knew she was unhappy, but we couldn't do anything about it. How could we? We didn't understand it. We still don't." She stopped. "Well, I still don't. Maybe she and Max have reconnected. That's my brother, Max. We haven't spoken in a while." She stared at the fire.

Then she laughed, a sound so void of joy he gritted his teeth. "All this before 10:00 a.m.!"

"Don't be embarrassed," he said. He felt for her but he wanted to know more. Needed to know more. "Why don't you and Max talk anymore?"

"I don't know." She sighed, and dragged her eyes back to his. "It's like we experienced this traumatic thing together, the dissolution of our family, the dissolution of love, and we couldn't recover from it. He broke inside, too. And he turned away from me." She shook her head and stared at the floor. "Now I'm just being dramatic. Lots of families grow apart. It's not like we're special. Or were special."

Grant didn't buy it. "Your mom disappeared into her pain and your dad couldn't cope. They both abandoned their kids. So you and your brother abandoned each other, and all hope of connecting with anyone ever again."

Melinda's face swiveled back to him, her eyebrows raised.

"Uh, sorry, I don't know where that came from," he said with an apologetic laugh, then immediately came clean. "Actually, I do. It's because I did a heap of therapy after my mom, uh, died in a car crash. So I know some shrink speak. But I shouldn't have said that to you. I sure as hell don't know if it's true."

Grant watched her turning over his words in her mind. Why had he said "anyone"? Why not just "your family"? Because he wanted her to reawaken and reconnect. He wanted her to recognize that she shut out everyone who could ever possibly hurt her. *And I want her to connect—with me.*

"Your mom was killed?" Melinda took back the reins.

"Yeah. Car accident," he said. "Ten years ago. Damn nightmare." He took a deep breath, surprised that talking about something he'd put so much time into healing could still sting.

"Can I ask what happened?" she asked tentatively. "You don't have to talk about it if you don't want to."

"It's okay," he said. "I don't get upset about it anymore. The event is upsetting, the loss is awful. But it's over. It happened. We dealt with it the best we could." Grant paused. Long version or short version? Definitely short.

"She was driving home from down below and a drunk driver sideswiped her into the guardrail on the way down the grade toward Dillon. Her car flipped and ended up upside down in rush hour traffic. She didn't have a chance." He looked away from her. To give her space to process what he had said or to collect himself after sharing his own family tragedy, he wasn't sure.

"Oh, my God," Melinda breathed, concern written on her face. "How old were you? How old was she? What did your dad do? Do you have brothers and sisters?" She almost laughed at her urgency. "Sorry. Any one of those questions is fine to answer."

119

"I was twenty-eight," he said. "She was fifty-three." That part hurt. Why did that part hurt? Because that was too young. The older he got the more he realized how young that was. And she had suffered. There was no need to mention that, though. This conversation was intense enough. "I have a younger brother. His wife just had a baby a month ago, their second. I was at the airport after visiting them, so Paul harassed me into joining this circus."

"That's why you were so adamant about me not driving away from here the other night," she said, her voice small.

"That, and it was freezing, and you were half in shock, and I was already struggling with a horribly guilty conscience." He caught her eyes. "Still am."

She looked away. Fair enough. He didn't know how to deal with it either.

Grant rubbed his shoulder and rolled his neck. "What was the other question? What did my dad do?" He chuckled. "My dad's got life figured out. He mourned, wholeheartedly. He fully felt his pain. He read a bunch of self-help books on grief and made me read them too. We basically had a damned book club about them. He found a therapist for himself, found one for me, and threatened to pay the guy even if I didn't go, which he knew I wouldn't let him do, so I went. What can I say? Blackmail works with me." He scanned her face. Was this too much for her?

"So now that that's all out in the open," he said with a half-smile, "would you like to take a tour of the back deck?"

Her eyes widened. "There's a back deck?"

"Yes, indeed. It's Ipe or something equally as bulletproof and expensive. It's through that wall." Grant gestured toward the ten-thousand-dollar slider and curtain.

"Ee-what?"

"Ee-pay," he enunciated the short word. "*Ipe.* Nothing's too good for our Paul."

"Let me clean up." She piled plates and bowls onto the tray.

"Let me help," he said.

"You do the fire," she said as she stood. "I'm not getting near that thing again."

"Sounds good. But the next topic of conversation is how you grew up in the Pacific Northwest and never learned how to build a fire."

She threw an almond at him.

Melinda melted snow on the stove for dishwashing and thought about what Grant had said. What she had said. Nothing like captive sexual tension to bring out your deepest truths. She hadn't seen that conversation coming, though. Any of it.

She squeezed dishwashing fluid into the pan and swirled it to a bubbly lather, then tackled bowls, saucepan, spoons, and serving dishes. Was he right? Had she responded to her parents' crumbled relationship by closing herself off to them? To her brother? To everyone and every relationship? Probably.

Bollocks.

That was an unfortunate revelation. Painful, even. Especially when it came to her brother. Melinda bowed her head over the sink and pressed her palm to her forehead, grimacing against the regret that barreled down on her like a train.

Was it time to be an adult about it all? She cursed her mother for the thought. What did being an adult about it even mean? First it meant surviving this experience. And after that . . . it probably meant calling Max and coming clean about her inadvertent repetition of their parents' emotional shutdown.

Double bollocks.

Couldn't she just do the dishes and stay alive, and worry about growing up later? Melinda's mother stared at her in her mind's eye, lips poised to comment on her lack of emotional dexterity. *Ugh.*

Melinda dried and shelved the dishes. Now what? A date on the deck, it would seem. She walked through the cabin, collecting warmer items—gloves, hat, boots, jacket—and moved to the living room to assemble herself. Fire tended, Grant sat on the edge of the chair across from her and laced his boots.

"Ready?"

"As I'll ever be." She zipped up her jacket. Her puffed sleeves swished against her torso as she walked across the room behind him.

Grant pulled back a luxe-looking curtain to reveal a sliding glass door. He released the lock and shimmied the door open.

"Whoa!" Icy air shocked the breath from her lungs.

"Yeah, what you said." Grant grinned. He followed her outside, then slid the door mostly closed after them. "I'd rather lose heat than have the door freeze shut on us," he explained.

Melinda looked around. Whatever the deck's material, it was inconsequential, as the whole thing was buried in snow. She trudged to the railing and looked over the snow-covered meadow they'd traversed the day before. Drifting snow erased the boundary between sky and earth.

"Looks harmless, doesn't it?" Grant looked sideways at her from her elbow.

"Ha," she said, straight-faced.

"So why can't you build a fire?"

"Oh swell, you remembered."

"Of course I did." He grinned at her, then added, "Does this feel like a cross-examination?"

She laughed. "No, it's fine. Better get it all out in the open. Yeah, I grew up north of Seattle, just south of Canada. I did go to Girl Scouts, and they taught us how to build a fire, but we never went camping so the skill faded." Shoot, was she really thirty-two? That meant her last boyfriend was two years ago. *Dammit.* No wonder she was Mountain Man-crazy.

"So you guys had a gas fireplace?"

"We did. We loved it. Used it all the time. Sometimes we lost power, so that was inconvenient, but never for very long. We were on city water, so we didn't have to melt snow to make hot chocolate."

Grant laughed. "You guys were pampered. So your dad . . . He's first generation?"

"No, he's second. I'm third. He was born in Seattle but his parents were from New York, and their parents were from West Bengal. He retained a lot of customs and culture, but it's impossible to keep it all. Plus I went to American public school, so . . ." She shrugged.

"So you love peanut butter and jelly," he finished for her.

"Exactly," she laughed. "But also *dal* and curry and all his favorite dishes. My dad used to act like he wasn't allowed in the kitchen—like women were the only ones allowed, even though my mom wasn't like that at all—so it always felt like a sneaky indulgence when he and I cooked together." She remembered what it had been like to revere her father and sighed. After a moment she continued.

"You know, I kind of respect them for staying together despite not living together. I think she loves him. He loves her. I don't think he knows who he is without her. He just doesn't have the skills to help her pain, and she's stuck in it." Melinda stared past the meadow at the silent giants, the trees weighed down with days of snowfall. "And the problem is that she's just . . . wonderful."

"Wonderful?" This was clearly not the adjective Grant was expecting. It wasn't what she expected to say either, but it was the truth.

"She is," Melinda admitted. "She's so full of life. Or she was, once. Pure, straightforward life. Sharp as a knife. Loving and honest. It was wonderful to know her. It must have been wonderful to be married to her. He proposed on their second date. Can you believe that? He would always say that he 'just knew,' whenever it came up. He just knew she was the one for him."

Melinda allowed herself to marinate in the fantasy she'd been raised on. Then the bitterness flooded back and she set her jaw.

"But really, he was the complacent type and 'just knew' she'd tolerate it. She had enough spitfire for both of them, he didn't need to have a spine. And now she's like a washer that's stuck off-balance and he can't fix her. Now she's perpetually . . . coping." She tossed in a word from her over-analyzed youth. "Or at least she was, the last time I spoke with her. Maybe if we'd never known who she was before, then it wouldn't have hurt so bad when she turned on us." She tasted her own anger and wondered if Grant could taste it, too.

"But you're right," she said quietly, more to the trees than to him. "I'm doing what they did: to myself, to them, and to Max. Do you know, when we first got here, I wanted to use your phone, but I had no one to call." The pained laugh caught in her throat. "I'm just as lost as she was. As she *is*. All of my relationships are hollow, kept at a distance, and that's how I want them. I don't even want a cat because it's too much commitment." This time the laugh escaped and the sound was as raw as she felt.

"I've never let a boyfriend get close to me." Her voice was louder now. Louder and unhinged, but she kept going. "I never leave them; they always leave me. Because I never let myself get vulnerable, not even once. I'm out of the relationship before it even starts."

Melinda stared at the bleached forest until reason whispered in her ear. *Figure it out, Sen. No one needs your melodrama. Give the people what they want.*

She spun to face Grant who raised both hands to catch or contain her, she couldn't tell which.

"Dammit, Mountain Man, you did it to me again! When is it your turn for twenty questions?"

"Whenever you like," he said, hazel eyes glittering in the cold light. "Don't expect the same revelations, though. You'll have me beat on that."

Grant wasn't kidding. He was impressed with Melinda's candor. Still, he braced himself for her inquisition.

"Where are you from?"

"Here. Colorado. Born at home, actually." He laughed. "Hippie parents."

"Are you dating anyone?" she asked, point-blank.

Grant started, but then this is what attracted him to her so deeply. Her directness, her acceptance of—no, her *pursuit* of the truth, bitter as it may be.

"Uh, no, not really."

"Such a male answer," she scoffed. "How many women are you sleeping with, then?"

"No, no. None. No one," he hurried to explain. "I said that because it's never serious with me. With them." Grant sighed. *Smooth as always, Samson.* She had gotten real with him. The least he could do was try to do the same with her.

"I date here and there, but mostly it's a quick, uh, interaction that sometimes leads to a relationship that's just as quick. They like me because I'm big and"—he rubbed the back of his neck— "uh, mountain-mannish as you say, but they don't think of me as a long-term option. I don't know why."

Grant squirmed in his boots at the lie. But what could he say? He'd never allowed himself to get close to any of the women that paraded through his life, and who would want to invest their time in someone whose main goal was to resist their invasion? No wonder they cheated or sabotaged things or flat-out disappeared. *Issue number one could be that I view them as an invasion.* It was too much to convey on an Ipe deck, he reasoned, regardless of how open she had been.

"Is it about your mom?" Melinda asked as she brushed snowflakes from her cheeks.

"My mom?"

"Yeah, you know, leaving you, in a sense." She looked sideways at the railing. "Maybe that's the wrong thing to say."

"It's okay," Grant said. "You can ask whatever you want. It was a long time ago, and I already psychoanalyzed you, so it's only fair." He cleared his throat. "I think you're right. I haven't worked on my feelings around my mom since it happened, and they've probably changed from what I dealt with at the time." He stared at the flurries descending on the meadow.

"I think you're right," he repeated. "Death renders you powerless. We think that with enough safety measures, wearing our seatbelts, saying 'please' and 'thank you,' et cetera, that we can postpone death to a time when it's convenient for us, but that's not how it works." He leaned toward her. "I pick women who will leave me so I don't have to face the fact that they're not right. Because if the right one came along and she left, I would die. I can't go through the pain of losing someone."

Grant searched Melinda's eyes. How would she deal with that analytical yellow brick road? *Send me packing to meet the King of the Lollipop Guild, probably.*

She tilted her head to the side.

"So how does it feel to hear yourself say that?"

Grant laughed out loud, the sound nearly garish in the quiet.

"This is like being with Bernard all over again," he chuckled. "My therapist. Dad thought I'd do better with a guy, for some reason. Probably thought I'd try to hook up with a woma—" Grant stopped. *Perhaps not the best audience,* his mind postulated. *Thanks a lot,* Grant shot back. *Isn't your job to stop me before I say something stupid?*

In that moment the wind picked up speed. Fat flakes swirled in from the north to frost Melinda's eyelashes and nose. It looked like they'd reached the end of their sojourn.

☙

Probably thought I'd try to hook up with a woman, Grant had almost said.

"Got it," Melinda bit out as she fought against the pang of jealousy in her chest. "Well, I'm freezing. Mind if we go inside? Not that it's not magical out here—it is," she added shortly. "It's beautiful."

"Yes," Grant said. "Beautiful."

Melinda swallowed, envy replaced by another sensation as the timbre of his voice softened her joints and melted her defenses.

Grant bit at the fingertips of one glove and shook out his hand. Slowly, he reached to take a lock of her hair between his fingers.

127

Melinda couldn't have moved if the trees had erupted in songbirds. Or elves. Or singing elves.

Eyes on hers, Grant traced his index finger down the curve of her cheek. Then his thumb ventured across the trembling surface of her lips. Her weak gust of breath escaped into his palm.

"Dammit." He wrapped both hands around her upper arms. "Tell me to leave you alone, to stop touching you."

Melinda stared, dazed at the fire in his eyes.

Well, look at that. Oatmeal with a side of sob story and the mountain man was all torn up. But did she want him to leave her alone? Melinda's stomach flipped. No. He scared her, disoriented her, and saw inside her, but he drew her to him like the proverbial moth to the flame.

"No," she whispered.

Relief washed over his features and he shifted his weight from hers.

"No," she repeated hastily, "I'm not stopping you."

And then she moaned into his mouth as it crushed hers. His kiss was hard. Distraught, like there were words unsaid, more to be understood. Her arms hung at her sides as his body ruled hers.

"Stop me," he urged, his breath hard against her mouth.

"What?" Her eyes could barely open.

His hair tickled her face as he angled his forehead over hers. "This is wrong. I'm taking advantage of the situation. Of you."

She slid her arms around his neck and pressed her body into his embrace.

"Dammit," he growled and took her mouth again.

His kiss told her everything. She tasted his remorse at the way they'd met and the ways he felt he'd failed her. She tasted his loathing for himself and his desperation to be forgiven.

As suddenly as it had begun, it was over. Grant ripped his mouth from hers and she stumbled. He steadied her and she blinked at him, mouth ajar.

"What the hell was that?" she demanded. She could barely keep upright.

Grant laughed and her intoxication evaporated.

"I'm cold too, Gorgeous," he said. "Let's forgo the majesty of nature for some warm beverages on the couch."

Melinda was grateful for his arm as they made their way through the snow to the mercifully warm cabin.

Melinda appeared only a little dazed as she shucked off her boots and padded over to the fire to warm her hands.

Grant secured the slider beneath the roar of blood pumping through his ears. He sat hard in the alcove's straight-backed wooden chair and shoved numb fingers through his snow-frosted hair.

What the hell was that?

Grant had been dreaming of Melinda's lips for nearly forty-eight hours. Surely no one could convict him of kidnapping or assault if they saw her mouth.

He snorted. He was pretty sure that was what all kidnappers said. Time to beef up his legal defense.

But her lips had been so soft.

No, idiot. Knock it off.

Snow crystals had iced her lashes and she had looked like an ice princess. Frozen and fierce. Had there been a visible spark as their lips touched?

Idiot!

He couldn't think. He needed to think.

He should melt more snow.

He should chop more wood.

He should bury his head in the snow and cool the hell off. Or walk through that field of snow again. Maybe the snow had reached waist-deep and one of his more pressing problems would solve itself. Grant vaguely recalled promising something warm to drink. How was he going to talk his way out of that?

Appear confident. Easier said than done.

"We need water for dinner." Grant stood abruptly and clomped toward the kitchen. He saw Melinda's startled look, but he was too busy stiff-legging past her to care. He grabbed the first empty vessels he found in the kitchen, tucked his tail, and stalked out the front door.

His relieved breath was short-lived as he stared at the items in his hands. Two coffee mugs and a sauté pan. Idiot.

Grant scooped a useless amount of snow into the mugs and pan and wondered how he was going to avoid her until the cops arrived to arrest him. Why wasn't there a side entrance to Paul's infernal cabin? Maybe he could walk to town. *Great idea, Lewis and Clark.* Maybe he could leave the mugs inside the front door before he grabbed the maul and snuck out again. *Coward,* his mind jeered. *Survivalist,* he growled back.

In the end he got lucky. He tiptoed into the house, listened for movement, and found that Melinda was miraculously in the bathroom. Like a stumbling paramour, Grant deposited his offering, snagged the maul from the closet, and fled.

He nearly sprinted to the end of the walkway and found a lamentably small stack of pine rounds. There weren't nearly enough to quench the fire coursing through him. *Maybe I could dismantle the cord and restack it again.* He eyed the wall of stacked wood. Better yet, he could dismantle and reassemble the house.

Half an hour later he'd split the whole pile and got to work adding it to the cord. *Now what?* Splitting wood brought minor relief, just not enough to survive another night in close proximity to Melinda.

Grant pulled the tarp over the freshly split wood and eyed the other end where the dried wood lay. Probably, they could use more kindling.

Probably, you could grow some balls, his mind taunted. Grant gritted his teeth and headed down the walkway to the cabin. It wasn't tiptoeing, he assured himself. It was being cautious. He pushed through the front door, traded the maul for the hatchet from the closet, and shut the front door with care.

He would never tease Paul about his tool obsession again. He grabbed a few lengths of wood and turned to the splitting round. He crouched down. Time to get his mind straight.

Sure.

Maybe I pick women who'll leave me so I don't have to face the fact that they're not right, he'd said.

Where had that come from? He didn't know. Well, he might.

Grant slid the hatchet into a split in the quarter round and pounded the blade through.

He hadn't answered when she'd asked how it felt to admit that. Grant stared at the hatchet, fingers frozen in the act of finding the best vein. How did it feel? It felt scary as hell. It felt ludicrous. It felt contrary to what he'd been telling his friends, his father, his brother, even himself for the past ten years: that he couldn't figure out why he hadn't met someone already.

When the truth was that he was too scared of failure to do anything other than hook up with placeholders.

Grant's fingers twitched.

Well, that sucked. *Don't do that with this one,* he told himself. *Don't pull the same shit you always do.* He'd started to, he knew. He'd started in on the charm and humble bravado BS when they'd first met. Unfortunately—maybe fortunately?—his standard approach had been significantly derailed when he'd ended up the villain in this drama.

Grant assessed his meager pile of kindling. It wasn't happening. His mind wasn't letting up and he wasn't fool enough to go on a psychological journey while playing with weapons. He needed his fingers.

Grant snorted. Who was he kidding? He needed his fingers so he could touch her again.

Melinda checked the label on the box of falafel mix. Falafel! In the boonies? For as much as she loathed Paul, she was starting to appreciate him. Almost absently, she circled the lump on her head with her fingers, grateful that the roar of her headache had quieted to a hum.

What was the best meal to serve a man who had run through a blizzard to save her, and who was outside battling his desire for her? What was the right boxed, canned, or jarred meal to seduce said man into keeping her warm, without building her yet another fire?

Spanish Rice? *Yeah, that reels 'em in.*

Canned ravioli? *Absolutely, if he were ten.*

Pasta, she decided. Maybe canned white beans and jarred red sauce would pass for eggplant and beurre blanc. She laughed aloud. Time for more garlic powder and onion flakes.

Now that she knew where the wine fridge was, Melinda made her own selection. They'd start with pinot and move on to the Grenache-cab blend. She uncorked and poured herself a glass of the former—light but smoky. *The perfect complement to a mountain man.*

No, that was wrong. She tried again.

The perfect complement to a snowy evening.

Better. She had to play a little hard to get.

Melinda poured Grant a glass of pinot and walked to where he was stacking wood by the stove. He'd made himself scarce for most of the day, after the peck on the deck. Now he was reorganizing kindling, firewood, and newspaper for the second time. She could smell the avoidance like cloying cologne.

"We're starting with pinot tonight."

He glanced up and reached for the glass she offered. "Starting?"

"Yes," she said, archly. "This is a high-class cabin. We serve wine with ice crystals but we serve it in courses, darn it." She giggled at her own joke and was rewarded with his short laugh.

He wouldn't meet her eyes, though, not yet. She narrowed her eyes at the top of his head. He would. She'd make sure of it.

Back in the kitchen she rinsed and gently heated the beans in a saucepan, then added salt, dried sage, and olive oil before they joined the tomato sauce.

"Got any more of these wine-flavored popsicles?"

Melinda turned to find Grant leaning against the doorway between the kitchen and den. "My pleasure, sir. And would the gentleman enjoy an appetizer? Tonight we have a mayonnaise-topped Ritz cracker for hors d'oeuvres."

Something clenched in her belly at his low rumbling laugh and she held her breath for courage. She snagged the bottle from the counter and sauntered forward to tip the wine into his glass.

"Is there anything else I can get you at this time?" She held his gaze.

"I'm all right for now, thanks."

"Just let me know," she said, voice unaccountably husky. "I'm here if you want me." Melinda turned carefully so as to not ruin her exit and returned to the stove. *Take that*, she thought

133

as she stirred the sauce. *I dare you to go play with your wood now.*

Grant stood in the doorway for another moment or two, then crossed to the dining table and sat.

Gotcha.

He cleared his throat. "I'm not going to be able to finish all of this," he said, gesturing to his glass. "I don't really drink that much, and I want to stay conscious with the weather. The refill was just an excuse to watch you work your magic in the kitchen."

She raised a brow at him. "I believe that was a compliment, Mr. Samson."

"Don't tell anyone," he said, bringing his hand to his chest with counterfeit concern. "You'll ruin me in the kidnapper club."

Melinda choked on a laugh and Grant's eyes searched hers. She saw his mind working: was the joke too far? Would she take offense? No, she would not. She officially thought he was a decent human being, and she was officially very interested in being kissed again.

Which means I'm officially off my rocker.

"Actually," she said, tapping the wooden spoon delicately on the saucepan, "I'm outing you as a knight on a white horse in my upcoming post, 'Savory Survival Sauces and Decanting in Subzero Temperatures.'"

Grant slapped his forehead and groaned in defeat, and Melinda giggled. He was joking with her. She liked that he was trying to heal their—what was this? It sure wasn't a relationship. Was it a situation? Yes, that was it. He was trying to heal their situation, and she liked it. She also liked that he was calling it quits early on the booze. That was fine, she didn't need him inebriated for what she wanted from him. In fact, this was better.

Chills raced up her neck. She'd be gentle with him. But eventually, she'd get him.

Melinda hunted for the box of matches next to the range

134

and came up empty.

"Are we out of matches?" she asked, rummaging among the spice jars.

Grant stood from the table.

"Don't get up, you can just tell m—"

Grant slid behind her and Melinda froze. He planted one hand on the counter beside her, his chest a warm wall against her back, his thighs rock-hard against her backside. His left hand painted flames down her arm, and then he reached above her head to a slender cabinet. Its opened door revealed stack after stack of matchboxes.

His warm breath caressed her temple. Melinda's heart stumbled and nearly fell.

Grant took a box of matches from the cabinet and slid it beside her hand, his thumb light across the back of her trembling hand.

"Is that what you needed?" he asked, his voice a low purr.

Melinda didn't speak. Couldn't. She trembled as she nodded.

"Tell me if there's anything else you want." His words pulsed through her ribcage like lightning. She nodded again. Her breath came hot and short. If he hadn't been behind her, she'd have slid to the floor. He stood behind her a moment longer, a pillar of radiant sensuality. Then, at last he stepped back, leaving Melinda gasping at the almost physical rending.

"I should check the fire," he murmured and turned on his heel.

Melinda gripped the countertop as her heart galloped away with no one in the saddle. The back of her whole body hummed. First the kiss on the deck, then his epic shutdown, and now he'd put her in her place with the electric shock treatment. What the hell was going on?

But she knew what was going on. *He picked up the gauntlet*

I threw and tossed it in my face.

Melinda steadied her breath. She had no idea what to do now. Yes she did. It was time to cook. Having neither brain nor legs was no excuse. What was the food parallel for brainlessness? Flan? Tapioca pudding? Yes, tapioca: pleasant, insipid, entertaining. An edible lobotomy.

Melinda grimaced at the unappetizing phrase. She was out of practice. She knotted her hair at the nape of her neck. Brainless or not, she got back to work, heartened by the familiar task. Within half an hour, she walked into the den with pasta and sauce-filled bowls in hand.

"Should we eat in front of the fire?" she suggested. Grant closed the door to the stove and nodded.

"Gotta take every chance we have to get warm." He brushed wood splinters from his hands.

Melinda nodded. She was back in control. She could do this. She wouldn't allow him to waylay her again. As long as she did the touching, she could do this.

"Great," she said. "Could you grab my wine from the kitchen, please?"

With the fire popping and wine beside them, they sat on the floor and ate.

"Again, this is incredible," Grant said, his legs stretched out before him. "Not just because you poured water from a vase for the noodles," he added, and she laughed. "This is just straight-up good. What's your secret?"

"First of all, you have to consider the conditions." Melinda twirled noodles onto her fork. "We're cold, hungry, traumatized, scared for our lives. That makes anything taste good. To be honest, I could have saved myself the effort and just done the Ritz crackers and mayo thing and you would have thought it was amazing."

Grant laughed and prodded her knee with the handle of his fork. "Nope. This is straight-up good. How'd you do it?"

"Well," she began again, "I see food as a spectrum of tastes." Her heart skipped as he put down his bowl to listen to her.

"You mean like salty, sweet, sour, and all that?" he asked.

"Yes, exactly. Like that and more. Aged, fresh, colorful, colorless, thick, thin, crisp, soft. It's like a continuum of opposites." Melinda realized she'd never articulated this before. "I start with one element and identify its features." She held up a noodle. "The pasta is smooth, kind of starchy, kind of savory. The beans are small, round, pleasing to chew. Salty." She plucked a bean between her thumb and forefinger and held it to his mouth. Her eyes held his in challenge and at last he took the bean between his teeth.

She ran a mental victory lap but continued as if nothing had changed. "The tomatoes are tangy, seasoned, liquidy, and so on." She sipped her wine. "So when I cook, I balance out a certain element with its conceptual opposite." She chuckled. "According to me, that is.

"Tonight I started with the pasta and kept adding elements based on these perceived features, and eventually I had a meal. Within reason, it wouldn't matter if it were a ribeye or a can of ravioli. Once those elements are balanced, the meal tastes good." She smiled. "Well, that plus wine." She raised her glass at him. "Okay, now it's your turn. What's the continuum of opposites in plowing snow?"

Grant stretched his arms wide and laced his fingers behind his head.

"The secret in plowing snow is that you always include wine."

Melinda laughed and put down her own bowl, tucked her feet under her body and turned toward him.

"Who do you have to be to enjoy plowing snow?" she asked.

137

He thought for a moment. "You have to be someone who likes driving, likes thinking critically, and who likes getting up freakishly early. Fortunately for me, I like all of those things." He dropped his hands and let one rest near her knee, and her heartbeat crept faster. "There's some caveman part of me that enjoys mastering nature all winter long."

He waited until she'd taken a sip of wine before adding, "Plus, I like wielding a huge appendage."

"You beast!" Grant watched Melinda choke with laughter. "You did that on purpose."

"I can't help it. My appendage commands attention."

She laughed again but didn't touch him, didn't want to make him retreat into good behavior now that he'd dallied in inappropriate humor.

"Actually," he continued, "while the 'boys and their toys' thing is pretty true, it'd be foolish of me to think I'm ever really mastering nature. I'm more like a surfer riding the waves who hopefully has the good sense to head back to shore when it gets too rough."

Melinda watched as he sank into his thoughts for a moment.

"I started when I was twenty-seven," he said, eyes on the fire before he turned back to her. "I'd done odd jobs here and there before that. Worked at a couple breweries down below. Then my dad had knee surgery and needed help getting around for a while, so I moved up here to be with him. I took a job for a plowing outfit and after a few years the guy wanted out and sold it to me. I've got six rigs and twelve drivers. Even have an office manager to yell at me about receipts." He smiled.

"Impressive, Mountain Man."

"You know what I really like?" he asked. "I like the noise. It's strange, I'll admit. I love the huge noise of the engine, the sound of the plow breaking the crust of the ice, the slush hitting the side of the road. It's this visceral high. I never get to sleep in, but I get that high and I feel alive."

After a moment his gaze returned from the place it had been and he grinned.

"What do you do in the summer?" she asked.

"Since I moved in with my dad, I get to save a lot more rent than a typical business owner does. We keep the fleet at his place. He has acreage, and it's a central location for my routes. And all that means I save money and fritter it away on making hard cider in the summer."

Melinda's eyebrows rose. Cider was having a heyday of late. *Wait a minute.*

"Was that a play on words?" she demanded.

He nodded.

"Did you just make an apple fritter/apple cider joke?"

He nodded again, his smile smug.

"That was terrible!" she moaned.

"What can I say? I'm a fruity kind of guy." She smacked him on the stomach with the back of her hand.

"Ow!" he feigned, and grabbed her fingers. Their eyes sparked and caught but again she didn't push. When he stroked her knuckles then released her hand, she took it back without touching him again.

"So. Cider," she said, certain she was blushing.

"Yeah, cider," he said. "My dad let me plant three hundred trees up there twelve years ago and they've been in full production for about eight. We grafted bare root varietals so we had a head start. We've got Spitzenburgs, Golden Russets, Arkansas Blacks, Gilpins, and your more common Braeburns and Granny Smiths.

"I use almost the same crew on the trees as I do in the trucks," he continued. "We harvest from August to October, but of course the snow starts around the same time, so I lose some of my pickers and have to hire short-term."

Melinda's mouth had fallen open at the number of trees he'd planted and now she cocked her head at his attention to growing the perfect crop.

"When does the booze part come in?"

He laughed. "Well, we have apple-pressing parties that are more like Thanksgiving feasts. The extra apples become pies. After we get as much juice as we can, we age it in wine barrels. Then it ferments with the help of some natural yeasts, plus some stuff for flavor, for eight or so months. Then we rack it and pour it off the lees. The stuff that settles at the bottom of the barrel, I mean."

"This is an art form!" she exclaimed.

"It started out as a hobby," he said, "but it's grown into quite the production."

"Do you sell it anywhere?" Surely after twelve years and three hundred trees, he'd be floating in bottles if he didn't distribute them.

"We sell at the markets up here," he said, chin lifted in slight pride. "The ski crowd really goes for it. Local, organic, gluten-free, craft product, all the good stuff." He grinned. "Plus, we charge a lot so they feel like they're getting quality."

Melinda shifted and felt something stab her in the behind. What was she sitting on? Her fork? No, it was those zip ties. Had they fallen out of her pocket when he'd undressed her after the tree branch incident? *Poky little things.* What should she do with them?

Grant's eyes traced Melinda's face as she toyed with something in

140

her pocket. Firelight caressed her skin and set her hair to burnt-umber flame. She was so beautiful his teeth ached.

Then bile rose in his throat. How could he have done this to her? Disbelieved her? She fairly broadcasted truth—pure, unapologetic, clear-eyed truth. She'd been through so much with her family and was trying to work through it. And he'd called her a liar and carted her off in a death carriage to God-knows-what. He was a criminal.

"How can you sit here with me?" he burst out. She jerked to face him, startled. "How can you sit here listening to my bullshit stories about apples after what I did?"

She looked confused. "The fritter thing . . .?"

"No, dammit, the car!" Grant stabbed his fingers through his hair. "The ride up here! I was a bastard. I stole you. You're stolen now. Trapped." The truth roiled in his gut.

Melinda tilted her head at him, evaluating. He hoped she judged him and found him unworthy.

"You're making all of this your fault," she said. "Why are you doing that? Do you control the weather? You thought you were being a good friend."

Grant gritted his teeth. "What happened in that car was my fault. I'd like to sink the damn thing in the lake. With me in it."

Melinda studied her shoes and he kicked himself for tainting their evening by seeking absolution. Then she seared him with her gaze and he stilled.

"Would it help to understand how I felt?"

Grant shook his head, confused. "What are you talking about?"

"I can explain until I'm blue in the face what it's like to feel helpless," she said. "But most men don't really understand that. They haven't been shown and told that they're powerless from the beginning of their lives, the way that women have."

Melinda paused. "Have you ever been made powerless, Grant?" Her voice was low, her eyes hooded.

Wordlessly he shook his head. He wasn't completely oblivious to women's issues, but as a man, a large man, he'd never given his personal safety a moment's thought. Perhaps another reason why he enjoyed plowing snow—it brought him closer to the edge of vulnerability. He'd never considered that women lived there every day.

"Would you like to be?"

He didn't know what she meant but fortunately she didn't seem to need an answer.

"Have you never felt the least bit powerless, Mountain Man?" She rose to her knees then, hands on her thighs as she stared down at him.

"I . . ."

"Well then," she breathed. "I should give you an education. Hold still." She crawled behind him. As if he could have moved. On her knees beside him, delectable curves pressed to his side, she was both innocent vixen and calculating seductress. Grant gave himself a mental ice bath. No, she was neither of those things. She was trying to explain something to him. Something vulnerable. Something important. Right? God help him. Maybe he should check the fire.

"Can you reach your hands back here, both of them?" Melinda asked as she fidgeted with something behind his back.

Grant might have been out of his element but he wasn't about to cry off. Whatever she wanted to teach him, he knew he had it coming. Gamely, he clasped his hands together at the small of his back and awaited her cure for the ignorance that ailed him.

At her fingers' urging, a sharp line drew itself around both of his wrists. The line grew tight, then taut, then cutting.

"Ow!" What was she doing? He wriggled where he sat but couldn't free his hands.

Melinda sat back against the cushions.

"There," she said. His lungs stalled at her beatific smile. "There's your taste."

She looked part exhilarated, part giddy. Grant struggled against the band around his wrists but all he got were lacerated wrists.

"What is that? What did you just do?" he asked.

"Paul has zip ties." Her eyes sparkled.

Grant groaned. If he'd had a free hand he would have slapped his forehead with it.

"Of course he does."

"*This* is helpless, Grant," Melinda said. "This is powerless. Not completely, of course. You could escape if you really wanted to. Something that wasn't available to me," she added. Grant closed his eyes against another wave of disgust at himself.

"That's a good idea," she said, though he'd uttered not a word. She searched around them and Grant's pulse kicked up a notch. "There!" His bicep burned where her breast brushed it.

"What—" he managed before she wiggled what must have been her hat over his head and in front of his eyes. She shifted and the tantalizing pressure of her legs on his evaporated, leaving them cold and bereft.

"Now," came her voice from farther away. "Imagine you're in a car."

Grant stiffened.

"Imagine it swerves, but you're in the back seat and you can't do anything. Maybe you offer advice to the driver and he doesn't like it, so he blocks you out. Imagine the windows are blackened. Imagine the driver hates you. Wants to hurt you. Wants you dead."

"But I didn't hate you." A feeble interjection. "I don't hate you."

"Yes, I know that now. But in the moment, let's imagine you aren't sure of that. You're only sure that you can do absolutely nothing to save yourself."

The slight whoosh of her exhale to his right was Grant's only warning before something exploded.

"What the hell!"

"Imagine the car spins out of control." Her voice was ice.

Something sharp scored Grant's arm from his elbow to his shoulder in a slow, teasing line. A knife? No, there was no pain. Before he could determine what weapon she'd wielded, Grant heard the unmistakable sound of the wood stove door opening. Why would she do that? The room was warm enough. The fan churned out hot air by the second.

"Melinda?" he asked. "You need help?" The scrape of wood on wood quickened his pulse. "You want me to do that?"

Melinda moved almost soundlessly, but the flames on the stick she must hold crackled menacingly.

"Can you feel this, Grant?" Her voice was a terrifying song. "Would you like to know where it's going?"

Grant opened his mouth to protest.

"I wish I'd known where we were going two days ago," she said. "I wish I'd known anything about who you were and what you wanted with me." Shame burned through him like the fire she brandished.

The crackling receded and the stove door squeaked as she closed it.

"Melinda—"

"Remember," she said smoothly. "I can't hear you. I've put a divider between us and I'm listening to all my favorite songs, so loud that you might go deaf."

144

Grant winced.

Her footsteps traced the couch behind him. Vivid color flashed before him as she yanked the hat from his head. He craned his neck to find her.

"But I think . . ." she continued from over his shoulder. "I think there's more you need to understand. Wait here," she said. "I have to get something."

"What? No you don't. Get back here!" Grant called as she disappeared into the kitchen. He heard her rummaging in Paul's bedroom and for a split second he thought of the revolver, but he refused to believe it. Someone who named their snowman Stanley wasn't the type to punish a guy by making him dinner and then shooting him. *Yeah, well, you trapped her in the car for three hours.* Grant struggled to his knees.

He levered himself upward, his bound hands a wedge against the armrest behind him. Melinda returned then and he froze.

She wasn't carrying the gun. She was carrying a small foil packet. She'd changed from her Michelin Man ensemble into a man's black t-shirt and nothing else. He gulped, more helpless now than he'd been without his sight.

"Is that Paul's shirt?" Was that high-pitched warble his voice? Had she zip-tied his hands or his balls?

"Yes," she whispered. Grant watched her pulse race at her throat. "It's all I could find."

"He's not getting it back," he growled.

She laughed lightly and moved closer.

"I'm cold again, Samson," she breathed.

"Holy hell."

She could have knocked him over with a feather. And then she did, or at least the next best thing. Fingertips against his chest, she pushed ever so slightly, eyes on his as he dropped hard onto the couch. She stood above him, bare feet, bare legs,

145

bare . . . What the hell was she doing?

Grant's eyes found the erotic angles of her feet and ankles—how were her ankles sexy?—and moved up the swell of her calves to the beginnings of her thighs. Melinda's warm brown skin glowed amber in the firelight. She was shapely, like a cello, and strong. His eyes glided up her legs to the place where her thighs joined beneath the t-shirt.

No, women hated that, right? He should be respectful. And keep going. He followed the stretch of the shirt over the breadth of her hip bones, up the smooth lines of her abdomen, over the soft swell of her breasts—her bra was gone, where the hell was her bra?—to her clavicles. His eyes found her jaw and then her mouth.

"What do you want?" he rasped.

"To be warm," she said, honeyed voice turned molasses. She tossed the condom to the other end of the couch, and he watched it, a silent firework in honor of his powerlessness. "It'll keep," she said.

She draped first one leg and then the other across his lap until she straddled his bent knees, planting her palms on his chest for support.

Panties. There's a layer of panties, he thought fervently. *Thank God*. Why he needed that extra scrap between them, he wasn't sure. He only knew that if she'd touched him with her bare sex while he was incapacitated he would have wept.

"How does it feel to be powerless, Grant?"

Grant could think of not a single answer. No word, no phrase, no glib reply. His brain had stopped working. He might well be drooling.

"I'd never fully understood it, before that night." Her hands slinked past his shoulders to tease and grip the back of his neck. "Oh, I thought I had, but I'd never felt that way so thoroughly."

146

Her ass swiveled against his knees. He didn't much mind, but he didn't understand. Melinda squeezed his neck and slid down an inch. *Ah.* She was sliding down his legs to his groin. Without thinking, he leaned back into the cushions to give her access.

Slide.

"Like the situation was so utterly wrong it couldn't be real."

Slide.

"Like it wasn't the way it was supposed to be. You had the wrong person. I was supposed to be anywhere but there." She pinned him with her eyes. "I don't need you to feel that fear, but I want you to understand what I went through."

Her fingers wove into his hair and Grant stared at her, a lot aroused and a little afraid. He grunted as she used his hair as a pulley and sank herself fully into the V between his legs and torso, her face millimeters from his. His shoulders screamed from their awkward angle and he didn't care.

"Samson," she whispered against his mouth, her hair a black shroud around them.

Grant's mouth opened to speak but she shook her head. He angled his head to kiss her but she pulled back. He tried to gather her in by contorting his body but she leaned away.

"Please," he said. "Please, I can't . . . I need to . . . "

"Yes," Melinda whispered into his lips. "That's how I felt, too."

Guilt slammed him in the solar plexus and he dropped his head. But she dipped her cheek to his, those magnetic lips a feather to his cheek.

"Never do that to me again."

"Never," he promised ardently.

She arched her pelvis against him and he froze.

"Unless I ask you to." She caught his mouth with hers.

147

Desire incinerated his guilt, and with overflowing relief he kissed her back. Her kiss was down and silk. Slow and deliberate, like she wanted to ingest him whole, little by little.

She may as well. There'd be nothing left of him after this. Her fingers stroked the back of his neck, slid down his shoulders, across his chest. Her lips kept their slow assault.

Grant groaned like an animal, desperate to match her power with his own. He'd never felt so impotent in his whole life. Strain licked his arms like fire and his wrists stung with broken skin, but he didn't care. He needed to touch her, to hold her. He writhed like a beast in a cage.

"Dammit," he tore out. "Melinda, you have to untie me. I can't stay like this."

Her eyelids fluttered open.

Melinda had never done anything like this before. She'd never taken control like this or seduced someone so aggressively, or at all. And it was too late to stop now! The notion intoxicated her. She'd never felt this wild, this alive, this free. Gone were the disappointments of men, the frailty of relationships. Someone was here with her and he didn't think she was too mannish, too brusque, or too complex. He wanted her. Plain and simple, he wanted her.

Grant's willingness to concede the reins flooded her with power. *Not that he has a choice*, she admitted. She'd thought to lose herself right then and there as he'd made his unconcealed appraisal of her body. His eyes had stroked her like a caress and she'd been left trembling and wanting. Now he was helpless beneath her and begging her for mercy. Things could be worse.

Except . . .

"Um, I don't have scissors," she confessed, and he choked out a laugh.

"My knife," he bit out. "On my belt."

Grant shifted sideways and Melinda leaned around him to find it. It was worn and aged, a simple five-inch knife with a bone-inlay handle. She tugged out the blade, then curled around him to reach his hands. Grant leaned forward to accommodate her and she tapped him with the flat of the handle.

"Don't move," she commanded, and he went like stone.

Dull side to his skin, Melinda slid the knife between his wrists and snagged the zip tie with the serrated edge. The knife tugged on the plastic and she heard his sharp inhale. She sawed and the loop snapped. Melinda winced at his raw skin.

Grant didn't flinch at what had to be pain as she unwound the plastic from his damaged flesh. She tucked the blade into its handle, then sat beside him on the couch, suddenly uncertain. Grant groaned as he flexed his hands and rolled his shoulders.

Then his eyes locked on hers and she froze.

"My turn," he whispered and lunged for her.

The bear was back. Or had she thought him a bull? His massive arms trapped her against the couch, her head pillowed on the armrest. His body, still clad in boots, jeans, and flannel, dominated hers, the thin cotton t-shirt riding over her belly and black panties.

Grant's mouth devoured her. Melinda expected his kiss to be aggressive, since she'd spent the last twenty minutes taunting him, but instead, he inhaled her, engulfed her, overwhelmed, and tormented her. She moaned into his kiss, free of the burden of control.

His hands traveled the length of her form at will. One hand lodged in her hair and guided her kiss where he wanted it. The other traversed the landscape of her legs, crested the jut of her hips, glided into the well of her waist, cupped and squeezed her breasts under her shirt.

Melinda moaned again. Her hands moved to the planes of his face to explore him as freely as he explored her. The hand in her hair coasted down her back to grip her ass so firmly that she whimpered, on the border of pain, until she was saved by his other hand sweetly twisting and torturing her nipple. Melinda arched her back and opened her mouth to his tongue.

She'd always been too large, too sturdy, too broad-shouldered. Now she was dainty, compressed into nothingness by this bear of a man. Her hands snaked down his back to his waist, intent on lifting his shirt to feel his skin.

"No," he said brusquely. "My turn now." He captured both of her hands with his own and tugged them above her head. He yanked the hem of the shirt until it, too, was over her head and her breasts and stomach were bare.

Grant stared at her and an actual growl reverberated through his chest. *Bear.* Mouth hot on her neck, he released her hands and forced her head to the side. Melinda moaned and dug her fingers into his hair as he kissed, licked, and nipped at her skin. His mouth traveled down to her collarbones, past her necklace to her breasts to catch a nipple between his teeth. She cried out as he attended her breasts in tandem, suckling the right and massaging the left, gripping and squeezing her ass with his other hand. Sensation engulfed her and she was helpless against the onslaught. She tightened and tilted her pelvis, aching for his touch there, but he deliberately ignored her and pressed her into the couch with the flat of his hand.

"Grant . . ." She struggled to twist her sex against his hand.

"Wait," he said harshly.

She watched, dazed, as he slid from the couch to kneel on

150

the floor between her legs. Both of his hands slipped behind her back and down to cup her ass. With a squeeze he yanked her hips to the edge of the couch and fitted his body to the apex of her bare thighs. She gasped at the rough intimacy of it, of the fierce heat she felt through his jeans.

"I've been dreaming of this since I first saw you," he gritted out.

"Oh, you mean when you thought I was your friend's girlfriend?" she teased before she thought better of it.

"You're damn right." His hands flew to the buttons of his shirt. "It was hell. It's one of the reasons I put up that damn divider. I thought you were putting on a show for me, or for him, or for yourself, and I got so jealous I couldn't fucking think. You were so beautiful." He tore off his flannel and met her gaze. "You *are* so beautiful."

Melinda's stomach clenched at the rippled musculature of his torso. "I went crazy." He stared at her for a brief moment, as if assessing her interest. "Enough about Paul." He slid his fingers into the lace waistband of her panties. "It's still my turn."

Grant lifted Melinda's hips and slid her underwear over her thighs, past her knees and then her ankles. And then all she wore was a necklace. For a moment they stared at one another. Grant took in her nude form, sprawled on the couch, dark eyes on his. She was so beautiful it hurt, so perfect it was all he could do to force air into his lungs. She bit her lip and his grip on sanity snapped.

"Mine," he growled. Grant grabbed her arms and jerked her to a sitting position to crush her mouth to his. One hand molded the small of her back as he kissed her, the other hand sought pillows to wedge behind her. He pulled back to loosen his belt, and she followed his movements with heavy-lidded eyes.

"Get the condom." He shoved his jeans down his thighs and off one leg as she complied. Melinda tore at the packet but he took it from her, unable to wait. Her fingers circled his sex and he groaned as she rendered him more and more senseless.

"You're right, this *is* a glorious appendage," she whispered, and he laughed, drunk with desperation.

Finally, much too soon, she removed her hand and Grant rolled the condom down the length of himself. He watched, mesmerized, as she guided the head toward her opening but not inside, teasing herself instead. He clenched her thighs.

"Holy shit" was all he could manage.

She smiled slightly, breath faster now, eyes closed. Back and forth over her clit, over her lips, around her opening, she used him as a tool.

Grant tore his gaze away from the erotic dance of their bodies and turned his attention to her face. Her eyelids fluttered, her lips parted, her mouth softened into a lazy O. Her hair was a wild tangle coursing over her shoulders.

"Melinda," he groaned, and tension gripped his body like a fist. "I can't wait, please—" He pulled her hips flush to his own to stop her hand, his cock pulsing between them.

"I like you begging," she whispered.

"I like you making me beg," he said.

"Your wrists . . .?" she began.

"Fine. Your head?"

"Fine."

At last Melinda pressed him into her. "Slow, please," she whispered.

"My pleasure." He kissed her. Slowly he drove his hips

forward to bury himself to the hilt. His breath left him in a gasp. God help him, she was like satin. Hot, perfectly soft, impossibly tight. He stilled, lost in the sensation of being inside her at last.

Melinda's fingers clutched his shoulders and, with an exquisite moan, her eyes rolled back in her head. Grant was pretty sure his did, too. He gritted his teeth against the pleasure and withdrew, then pressed forward again. She was silk. She was velvet. She was perfection. He wasn't going to make it.

Grant gripped her hips and thrust forward again, harder this time, and they both came to life, in search of more sensation, more heaven. She wrapped her glorious legs around his back, dug her heels into his ass and her fingers into his hair as he surged forward in pained pleasure.

Building tempo, building heat, he worked her against the couch cushions as her gasps bounced in time with his movements.

Hell. His movements were moving her farther and farther away from him. *Stupid couch*, he growled silently, then pulled out of her. Gathering her body to his, he laid Melinda lengthwise on the couch and braced his arms beside her.

And then the couch collapsed.

"Oh!" Melinda couldn't help her burst of laugher. It was too much: the heat of the moment, the insanity of their makeshift bed falling to pieces. Hold on, was it a futon? Of course it was a futon. The couch had simply done its job and flattened into a bed.

And then all thought vanished, because as the couch had shocked them with its crash, so Grant shocked her with his body as he climbed atop her, placed himself at her entrance and

153

drove inside her. And with an aching gasp, she followed his lead. She arched and moaned, needing more, more fullness, more delicious pressure. She lifted her hips, captured his length with her sex, tilted her pelvis to swallow him whole.

Harder and harder he plunged into her. He was hurrying now, losing himself as she too became lost. Head bowed, Grant's hand moved to her ass and again grabbed her with a ferocity that stopped just short of pain. She shrieked and dug her nails into his back, legs strung like a bow around his back to urge him deeper. He complied and rolled his hips, so that Melinda felt full with him to her throat.

Her pelvis tilted to his and she met his pounding with the sensitive nub at her core. She was coiling, building. His body crashed over hers and she was the shore, pummeled, driven, carved, bathed. Deep moans took shape and he trapped them with his mouth.

And then it became too much.

Her hands couldn't find where to be and she flung them wide only for him to catch and pin them above her head with a growl. The immobility freed her body to arch with pleasure, to loose her scream, and it echoed as if from someone else's lungs. Her orgasm lapped at her legs and swallowed her whole. She was dimly aware of Grant's groans as his body clenched and released over hers.

Time stopped. All was one. Nothing was cold, nothing was hot, no one was captive, no one captor. There was no guilt, no uncertainty, no remorse or remembering. They lay still together, existing only as deep, ragged breaths that blossomed and collapsed in a mist around them.

Grant let his head drop from his shoulders against her neck and he nuzzled her. Eyes closed, Melinda nuzzled back, the movement almost unconscious.

154

Slowly the room reappeared, and with it the cold. Sensation returned in the form of a throw pillow half-under her head, a blanket wedged beneath her back.

Was this okay? Was she okay? Would they be okay?

They weren't even a *they*.

Were they a *they*?

Melinda didn't know. She didn't know anything.

Well, she knew she had to say something. The silence couldn't stand. Figure it out, Sen.

"Five stars," she whispered.

"What?"

"I've been preparing my review since the airport," she choked back laughter.

Grant's chortle shook the couch-turned-futon as he flopped beside her.

"Well hell, that can't be good." With effort, he propped himself on his right arm, this time to kiss the corner of her mouth and fling one massive leg over hers.

"It got a little dark in parts . . ." His guffaw interrupted her monologue but she persisted. "But after the whole head injury/rescuing thing, and then this sex stuff, you really turned it around. So. Five stars."

Grant slid an arm around her and flipped her body atop his.

"No fair!" Melinda pushed feebly away from him. "I'm still reassembling all my cells after they exploded. I can't be expected to support myself."

Grant's lips found her ear, his breath found her neck. Warm hands swept up her back, his feet curled around hers, enfolding her in gentleness.

"You don't have to do anything," he murmured. "Just be with me."

So Melinda shifted her limp body over his solid one. She

dimly felt him reach under the futon and fling blankets over her cooling body. She heard his rumble of contentment, felt his kiss at her temple, and allowed sleep to lure her into its dark possession.

Grant studied the vaulted ceiling. If he didn't get this condom off soon it would be permanently adhered to him, and that part of his anatomy was decidedly opposed to that. But Melinda was asleep. On him. Poured, melted, crumpled on top of him as she breathed in and out and smelled like heaven.

And what's heaven exactly? his mind challenged. *Spices,* he shot back. *Warmth. Her incredible skin.* Grant turned his face into her hair and inhaled. Cardamom?

He craned his neck to check on the fire. *Dammit.* It would need improving soon.

In a few minutes he would shift her body from his, sneak from beneath the blanket, and deal with the condom as best he could. In a few minutes he would walk on his knees to the stove, tug open the door, and, as quietly as possible, introduce four more logs into the waning blaze. He'd watch them catch and then crawl back to the couch-bed and the amazing woman it held.

But not yet.

Grant's fingers waded through her hair as it streamed across his chest. For now he lay there enjoying the wonder of her body as it softly, sweetly weighed down his own.

What on earth had happened? Who the hell was she? Had she really just tied him up and had her way with him? And what about the couch?

"Shit. The couch," he breathed aloud. It was looking like he owed Paul a new couch.

Grant hadn't met anyone quite like Melinda before. Someone secluded enough to be alluring but warm enough to meet him with joy when he broke through her walls.

Is that what they call kidnapping these days?

It might have been the best thing that ever happened to me, he answered himself.

Until she had him arrested.

His mind was a stick-in-the-mud, but it did have a point. What did tonight's encounter mean for his future as an accidental kidnapper? Did it count as sexual assault? Shit. The law was a tricky place. Terrible people freely committed terrible acts every day and innocent people were locked away for decades at a time. Not that he was innocent, but he wasn't a complete psychopath. He hoped she knew that.

He hoped it was true.

Grant tilted his head more acutely to look at Melinda's sleeping face. Did she know that? Was she simply under duress? Would their lovemaking this evening be considered a crime?

Too much thinking. Time to fix the damn fire.

Grant shifted his hips away from hers, eased her body onto their makeshift bed, and slid his legs off the couch. Righted, he made his journey to the stove to fight the storm for two hours more, and worried all the while. What did she want from him? Would she regret this seduction in the morning? Resent him? Hate him?

Could his mind not shut up? Grant crawled back to their couch and then stopped, uncertain. Did she want him in bed with her? Should he take the floor?

He'd bank on sentimentality, he decided, and went to the other side of the couch to keep her closer to the fire. He slid beneath the blankets and lay next to her, figuring that if she woke and he was gone, it might be marginally worse than if he were there, in all his kidnapping glory.

Here's hoping.

He closed his eyes.

CHAPTER SIX

Never seek or avoid; take what comes.
Swami Vivekananda

Melinda was warm. Sleepy, languid, boneless, and warm. Luxuriously, she stretched both arms free of the stack of blankets that shielded her and her eyes flew open.

"*Whoo*," she breathed aloud.

Oh. That's right. She lay on a futon in an igloo of blankets that insulated her against the frigid temperatures around her. And the giant man with whom she had recently been indecently intimate lay beside her.

"'Whoo?'" He grinned in the cold light.

Melinda giggled and wrapped a silvery-gray throw more tightly around her shoulders. "Yes, *whoo*. This room is so much warmer than the bedroom! But it's still winter and there's still only the fireplace, and I'm still naked, so *whoo*."

She cuddled into the shelter of his limbs. "Thanks for helping me get warm last night."

"Gorgeous, it was my pleasure," Grant said. He wound an arm across her waist and trailed his fingers down her back.

Melinda closed her eyes, relishing his touch.

"What time is it?" she asked, afloat in her moment.

"Can't be more than 6:30," he said, a scant inch from her face.

"Early." She felt his lips at her ear. "My clothes!" She'd have to risk frostbite in order to dress. Grant chuckled and pulled back.

"Don't give them a second thought." Grant relinquished his blankets, and Melinda allowed her eyes to feast on his naked form as he stood and stretched. *Such a bull.* With those ridiculous back and chest muscles he was definitely a bull. But those arms and that scruffy hair, those were all bear. She was back to square one.

"Thanks. Don't freeze," she said, her gaze mid-thigh.

"Thanks for your concern," he said wryly and she jerked her eyes to his. Busted. "I'll get you something to wear," he said, unperturbed by her assessment of him.

She thanked him with a small smile and snuggled further into the blanket. Her back was comfortable; it was time to turn and heat her front. The fire had died but the coals gave off enough heat to warm her exposed face and fingertips, and she closed her eyes.

This is what he's been enjoying by sticking me in the bedroom!

The night before she'd been on the couch, she admitted, but that was with a head injury. No one on bed rest could fully appreciate their surroundings.

Grant returned with her jeans, another of Paul's shirts, one of Paul's sweaters, a pair of her socks, her bra, and her own jacket and hat.

"I couldn't find any panties," he said, eyebrows raised in a poor show of innocence. "So I figured you could just go without."

"Pervert." She laughed.

"Hey, who tied up whom last night?" He dropped the clothes on the futon and raised upturned palms.

"Hmm?" she asked with her eyes on his flexed biceps.

"Eyes up here, Gorgeous."

Crap, he was on to her.

"I did what I had to in order to avoid sleeping in the icebox again," Melinda said primly. "It's not my fault if you enjoyed it." She grabbed the clothes and dressed, resentful of the cold fabric kissing her skin instead of Grant. After a minute she turned to find his eyes on her. She laughed.

"What is this, a reverse peep show?" She pulled Paul's shirt over her head, completing the performance.

"I take what I can get," he answered, straight-faced.

"Well then. Now it's my turn to watch." She turned to face him where he stood wafting testosterone in the mountain air. "And go slow."

Grant's short burst of laughter went straight to her sex.

"Pretty sure my stuff is bunched up over by you." He jutted his chin in her direction, hands on his hips. His fingers strummed the satiny skin of his hip, and she was immediately lost in his anatomy again. Stubble lined his jaw already, she noted. It suited him.

Grant cleared his throat.

What had he said? Right—clothes. Clothes? His clothes! Melinda scanned the floor beneath the futon. He was right, they were there. She passed him the boxers, pants, and socks, but kept the shirt. She might as well have some compensation for being trapped in a snowstorm with no underwear.

Grant donned what she'd given him, slowly, as per her instructions, and then turned to her in surprise when he failed to find his shirt.

"You're fine as is, Man Candy," she said, grinning.

He made as if to grab the shirt in her hands and she thrust it toward the fire. "One more step and it's cabin food."

161

He froze. "That's better," she said. "Now, how's about you stoke our fire," she said. His eyes flashed. "I'll scrounge up something to eat. Post-coital comestibles."

What was a good after-sex companion? Cinnamon rolls would do nicely, she decided, and lamented that they couldn't use the oven. What else was indulgent and celebratory? *Nothing else has a gooey center for a prize.*

Melinda paused in her reverie to realize he was staring at her. Eyes on hers, he circled the couch to crouch in front of the stove.

"I'll do the fire," he said. "But I'm reporting you for harassment."

Melinda burst out laughing. "Just for that, I'm using your shirt as an apron." She scooted across the futon away from him. She thought about making good on her threat but instead tossed the shirt to the couch and fled to the kitchen, his chuckle floating after her.

But seriously, what was there to eat? Besides that beast in there. Melinda turned halfway for another peek of a shirtless Grant building up their fire. This is where the going got tough and the tough wished for a coffeemaker and pastries.

At least there was tea. Melinda set about boiling water and selecting bags from the tea canister. She returned to the pantry and waited for it to speak to her. This was getting trickier by the day. Should she use the mung beans? No, she'd spring those on him for lunch. Oats, dried fruit, chia seeds, nuts . . . *Lost Cabin Muesli?* Perfect. Okay, not perfect, but it would do. She stacked the jars on the counter.

Melinda poured half a cup of the super-small chia seeds into two stoneware bowls. She added boxed almond milk to each, gave them a quick stir, and set them aside to thicken up. Time for tea. The water was boiling, so she dropped in a few fragrant tea bags, added the lid, and wrapped a towel around the pan to keep it hot.

Back to the muesli. The oats, she set aside. The cashews and walnuts, she diced into small chunks, and gave the same treatment to the dried apricots and apples. Cinnamon? *Yes.* Nutmeg? *Of course.* Cardamom? *Why not?*

That was the theme of this insane adventure, wasn't it? "Why not?" Why not, indeed. *Why not forget to charge your phone? Why not get into a car with a stranger? Why not cook for and sleep with said stranger?*

Melinda's hands froze and her stomach tightened. Here came the guilt storm. The panic attack at having done something wild, out of control and out of character. The panic at who knew what the consequences of this would be. They would be crippling.

She knew nothing about this man and had all but launched herself into the sack with him. Was he anything like what she looked for in a man? Who knew? Would he disappoint her like every other man had? Probably. What on earth had she been thinking? And what about her safety? Had anyone even wondered if she was missing?

Melinda set the spices on the counter, unable to concentrate. *Max?* No, she disappeared from her brother for months at a time. *Remy?* No, her editor wouldn't hound her until Friday of this week and it could only be . . . Wednesday. Melinda blinked. *Mom and Dad?* Why should they? She'd shut them out for years. Pain knifed her chest and she stiffened against it. *No, that's not true*, she haggled. It wasn't a complete shut-out. She emailed them annually.

But she told them nothing. Asked them nothing. Believed in nothing. Maintained nothingness. Melinda's hands trembled against the counter. What the hell had she been doing with her life? Who did this to their family and friends? Who did this to themselves? Deep breaths. No one had a panic attack in a chalet.

She had to get it together.

What had actually happened? What had she done that was so wrong? If she examined it closely enough, broke it down into a simple sentence, maybe she could deal with it.

It. What was *it*? She was the princess and there was a pea in her mattress. What was it? Embarrassment? Pain? Shame? Melinda squeezed her eyes shut.

Disappointment. That was it. Grant hadn't had the balls to seduce her, so she'd done it herself. She had to do everything herself. Why would a roll in the hay be any different? There was the nutshell. She'd found it. She inhaled. Exhaled strongly. Repeated it a few times for good measure.

And there was nothing she could do about it now, so she might as well cancel the pity party.

Melinda yanked a mug from the dish drainer, filled it with hot tea and got back to her stupid muesli. She added half and quarter teaspoons of the seasonings to the chia mixture, then added the dried fruit and nuts. The chia would turn breakfast into more of a porridge than a muesli, but who the hell cared? She poured a generous splash of almond milk into the bowls, then added the uncooked oats for texture.

"Do I smell spice?" asked Grant from the doorway.

What now? Could she speak with him after her breakdown in the kitchen?

She tightened her stomach. *Socially palatable. Jaunty, spunky, witty, cold. Keep him over there and you over here.* She'd done this before, she could do it again.

"You love that spot, don't you?" she asked as she turned. "Yes, you do smell spice, and I'm freezing. Want to eat in the living room?" He collected the bowls from her, his expression slightly puzzled.

"Thanks." She centered herself in the familiar role of

164

hardened jokester. "Just for that I'll pour you a cup of tea."

Grant's gut twisted as he sat. Melinda had hunched her shoulders—in pain?—and then had straightened her spine and gotten back to work. Things had gone too far for him to keep quiet anymore. *She's a prisoner because I brought her here.* He burned to unburden himself and achieve, if not absolution, at least acceptance.

They settled in front of the fire with tea mugs and bowls of cold cereal. It was another rich, flavorful meal, and he wondered distantly how she did it every time. He wished he could experience her cooking outside of this entrapment. He wished he could experience who she really was.

Grant's chewing competed with his thoughts for volume in his mind.

"Why the heck didn't I warm this up?" she asked, just as he said, "I know you don't want—"

They both smiled and he bowed his head toward her.

"We'd be warmer if I had." She smiled lightly, thought completed, expression caged. "Your turn."

Grant sighed. "I know you don't want to hear it, Melinda, but I'm sorry about how this happened. I don't know how I could've thought you were someone else, and I don't know how I could have—" He rubbed his hand across his face and forced out the words. "How I could have thought you were just being dramatic." He glanced at her, sick with aching for forgiveness and knowing he deserved none. "While you were begging for help." The shame of the truth clung to his mouth, reluctant to reveal itself.

"You've been so resilient with the stress." He cut the air with his hand to encompass the blizzard, the lack of amenities, the lack of freedom. "You're even cooking for me. And last night . . . last night, you . . ." Grant raised his head to look at her. She watched him with an unreadable expression, not eating.

"I don't know if you lost your mind last night, or felt like you had to do that to protect yourself, or what. I don't know what that was for you." He took a breath. If she was listening he was damn well going to make himself spit it out. "Last night meant something to me, and it's okay if it didn't mean anything to you. I understand if it was just a . . . reaction to all this pressure. But I want you to know that I think you are pretty damn amazing. And I want to thank you for sharing more of yourself with me," he finished lamely. Had he really just thanked her for sex? He wanted to bellow with frustration.

There was no way to apologize for what an ass he was, to ask if she had had sex willingly, and to thank her for trusting him with her body, if that had been what she had done. There was no way to logically do any of this. Grant searched her face. What was she thinking? Were his fears correct? Was she following his plot instead of her own and responding to his attraction? Was she feeling manipulated into liking him, and even worse, into sleeping with him? Was she even looking at him anymore?

Grant looked at her sideways.

No, she wasn't. Her face had gone blank. Limp hands held her half-eaten bowl of cereal.

Suddenly Melinda jerked to life, looked past him, and stood abruptly.

Then she left him, not pausing as she placed her bowl on the kitchen island and walked into the bedroom, closing the door behind her.

Melinda sat cross-legged on the millionaire mastermind's bed and tried not to hyperventilate. Grant's friend's bed, the man who loved his girlfriend so much he healed her pain with a yearly adventure to celebrate her strength.

Melinda's ragged breaths fogged and dissipated in the freezing bedroom. She snorted. No, she wouldn't hyperventilate, she'd die of hypothermia. But the cold contained her, hardened the edges of her body so she couldn't explode into a thousand pieces.

Get it together. She was being ridiculous. Why had she fled the scene like a lunatic? Her lip curled. *Because he's sentimental and weird.* It must have been even longer for him since he hooked up with someone.

Steam bloomed from her short laugh.

Shut up! Melinda screamed at her inner harpy, her relentless distraction from real life, from real pain and real emotions. The truth was that Grant had bared his soul to her and she'd panicked and run. A man wanted her and she had almost literally run away. Did she not want to find a partner, to settle down and . . . have a baby or something? She laughed bitterly at the reference to instincts she barely understood.

Melinda hugged her knees against the frozen ache in her chest. What was wrong with her? Why didn't she connect with that life? Was she as broken as her mother? Why didn't she want to accept the affection of a man that she knew she had feelings for? Confused feelings, but feelings nonetheless.

Because connection scares you to death, the voice inside answered. She squeezed her eyes shut with her face against her knees. *Any connection at all.* Real connection meant no more false fronts, no more hiding behind her computer screen and proclaiming audacity but practicing fear. Melinda cracked open an eye and grimaced at the room. The room did not grimace back.

"This sucks," she spat. It sucked to be a chicken cowering behind a wall.

So what was she going to do about it? Did she climb the wall? Did chickens even climb walls?

She didn't laugh this time, tired as she was of her mind making light of her culpability. It was all well and good to scale this boundary and jump into a relationship—or *situation*—with this man.

Because it was only a matter of time before she poisoned it. Not with infidelity or cruelty, but with her overpowering instinct to hide from anything real. Like every single relationship with those she already loved. Like with her family.

Melinda tightened her arms around her knees to hold the recriminations at bay.

They would not be held.

Truth crushed her in an avalanche of twisting discomfort: if she couldn't face those hurts and heal those insults to her pride, she would resort to the same pattern with Grant. She would toy with him, pretend to love him, name him as a problem, treat him as a contagion. Shut him out, shut him down.

No, no, no, no.

Did psychological spiraling happen in all life-and-death situations, or just hers? It had happened in the car; it had happened after the tree branch. It had happened after she'd slept with Grant. Did that say something about him? Or her? Or tree branches? Melinda growled.

The answers weren't going to come to her in cold storage. Melinda unwound her legs and dangled them over the edge of the bed. She stared at the walls for one final moment, then dropped to the floor and walked to the door.

Grant sat abandoned, empty dish in his lap, his eyes on the fire. What the hell had just happened? He snorted. What had happened was that he'd used his pseudo-psychology on her again and she hadn't appreciated it. She was in Paul's bedroom right now throwing her clothes into her suitcase, lacing up her boots, and preparing to hike out.

Dammit.

She'd been right, he was avoiding the pain of significant loss. For all his reading and ruminating, he was still doing the dance of denial and protecting himself from happiness like he had protected himself from pain. He suddenly longed to right that wrong, to learn the lessons he'd missed while he mourned his mother.

Grant stood. No. He wouldn't let her leave. He would fight like the white-horsed knight she'd accused him of being. Determination readied his legs and flexed through his arms. He caught sight of the bowl gripped fiercely in his hand and laughed. Fine sword for doing battle.

No matter. He marched into the kitchen, laid his bowl next to hers, and stared down her door.

And then he stopped. What exactly was he going to say? *I think I have feelings for you; could you help me get over my mommy issues?* Yeah, the ladies loved that.

Why was he even there? He had nothing redeeming to say, nothing useful to her in her process of discovery. Or in her process of condemnation, wherever she was. Hadn't he held her captive enough? Were his feelings really her problem? No, they were not. *Dammit.* Why didn't he have a sword to fidget with?

Maybe he should be casually cleaning the kitchen when she emerged.

He was doing a disturbing amount of staring at her door. Stalking, rather.

Could we call it monitoring? he wondered.

Try haunting, his mind answered.

In the midst of his semantic crisis, Melinda's door flew open.

Melinda shrieked. One hand flew to her chest. The gargoyle was back and this time it was hunched outside her door. "You scared the hell out of me!"

"Sorry," Grant said sheepishly. His weight shifted side to side, his hands flexed closed and open, then worried the front of his shirt.

"Uh," he began.

"It's all right," Melinda said. "It's *all* all right. It's my fault. I'm sorry I left." She closed her eyes. Opened them again. Wished they were closed. Stared at his chest. "Okay, sprinted."

She raised her eyes to his. Was he sick of her games yet?

"Um." She drew a breath and exhaled. "Want to come in and talk?" She hadn't stepped foot out of the bedroom. Couldn't. She'd found clarity in that ascetic space and didn't want to become tangled in the web of warmth he'd spun in the den or the clutch of joy she'd created in the kitchen.

His eyebrows lifted. "Sure?"

She nodded. "Sure."

Melinda stepped back and Grant stepped forward. She faced the room and wondered where they should sit. She settled for cross-legged on the bed. Grant chose the straight-backed chair that had served as her lock the first evening. It felt like a year ago.

"I . . ." *I what? Say something. Say anything!* "I think you're right," she forced out. "There is something between us." She lifted her gaze from her hands to his face. "It's not just you. It's me too. I . . . feel it too." Deep breath. "And not just that, it's the other stuff you said—my mom disappearing into her pain and my dad not coping and them abandoning us." Another deep breath, shakier this time. This was hard. "Me checking out from my brother. And from all hope of human connection."

"I was way outta line—"

"No, you were way right, and it was hard to hear. You sat out there in the den and put a name to the face of this thing, a name to whatever that's happening between us, and I felt . . . cold creep in and try to freeze me over. I had to get out of there." Melinda tucked her knees against her chest, balled her fists into her eyes.

"It's what happens when I'm faced with my own BS," she said. A laugh rattled free of her throat. "It's a self-defense thing, I guess. My mom would be so proud." Melinda peeked at Grant's face again but didn't see boredom, so she pressed on.

"I didn't want to have abandoned my brother." She felt the threat of tears. "But I did. I did what I felt was done to me. It was immature and really sad. Heartbreaking. It was the best I knew how to do. And I was afraid that I would do that to you. There's something happening with you, with me—with us, and if I'm not careful I'm going to fake my way through it."

Did he understand? Was he asleep? No, he was still here, still listening.

"I'm afraid to leave this room," she said, her voice weaker than she would have liked, but it was too late to stop now. "I'm afraid to leave this cabin. What if what we are only exists here? I don't want to lose it. I don't want this to turn out to be nothing."

There. She'd said it. She'd said a lot, but was it too much? Too crazy?

Grant's heartbeat pulsed in his ears.

This was not what he had expected.

There she sat, a ball of tension on Paul's bed, uncertainty painted across her face. Her fingers twirled and untwirled her hair.

He blew out a deep breath. Time to come clean, just as she had.

"After knowing you a really short amount of time, I can't imagine you faking your way through anything, Melinda," Grant said finally. He cringed. Way to sound like every other sex-crazed male. "What I mean is, you put your heart into everything you do. And it means a lot to me that I could mean something to you."

Melinda's eyes flickered but stayed trained on the floor.

"I'm freaked out too," he admitted. More than anything, he wanted her to feel less alone. "I don't want to be, but I am. I've been telling myself women are crazy and vindictive, they don't want to be with me, they all cheat—every lie in the book to steer away from sticking around." He sucked in a breath. "The truth is that I'm choosing women who are too young, too wild, too wrong, because choosing the right woman means death. If I chose the right woman and it ended, I would die. I would be broken, the same way I was broken when my mom died. I'm still recovering from that . . . robbery. It feels like theft. She should have had more time left, and in under the span of an hour, the rest of her years were taken from her. And me. And my dad, and brother. She never got to meet my brother's wife. Never got to meet her grandbabies. So many nevers." His jaw hurt.

Did she hear him? Did she believe him? He had to get closer to her, to touch her. To see if she understood.

Grant sat beside her on the bed, aware of the force field of tension surrounding her. He didn't get too close.

"I'm not trying to force you," he said, "or get serious too fast. I wanted to honor your revelations and tell you some of my own. See, meeting you has brought some things to light for me. And not just that I should never do a favor like this again."

His joke won a half-smile.

She was so beautiful, even in the cold winter light, even swaddled in layers of clothing. What was that look on her face? Contemplation, he guessed. Hopefully the good kind.

Grant watched and worried as she mulled over what he'd said. Would it be enough? Would she make a break for the car? He'd never made a declaration of affection like this before. It was terrifying.

Melinda turned slightly and reached a hand to fidget with his shirt.

"So what are you saying?" she asked.

Grant's stomach clenched. "What do you mean?"

Her dark hair veiled half of her face as she drew designs on his shoulder blade with her fingertip.

"I mean . . . what kind of woman are you calling me?"

Melinda slid from the bed to her knees on the floor and faced him where he sat. She wiggled forward and wedged herself between his thighs, working her fingers down the buttons of his shirt one by one.

Grant's breath hitched as they met the resistance of his belt and idly traced the shape of the buckle. *Christ.*

"Mel?" he squeaked.

"'Too young?' 'Wild?' 'Crazy?'" She opened his belt.

"Melinda," he rasped again. This wasn't where he had been going. A simple "I like you too" would have sufficed, but no words followed. He checked his hands and found them gripping the comforter of Paul's bed—Paul's bed! What the hell was she thinking? Not that he could bear it if she stopped now.

Melinda's fingers went for the zipper of his jeans. Grant's pelvis lifted of its own accord and she worked his pants over his hips and tugged them from his ankles. She reached into his boxers to free him, then stopped and gazed up at him, her eyes dark.

"Is this why you wanted me commando?" she breathed. "It makes this so hot." The tip of her tongue teased the corner of her mouth and Grant's breath failed.

And then she took him into her mouth.

Oh my God.

Grant groaned and his body lurched. The boldness, the directness of the sensation sent him reeling, even as he grasped at lucidity and held on for dear life. Her mouth worked up and then down, stretched wide around his cock, getting to know him slowly. Her tongue swirled and suckled as his mind stalled, free-falling in pleasure, his teeth locked together. Her hand snaked beneath his shirt to strum the muscles of his abdomen; the other cupped him from below as she lifted her eyes to his and impaled her mouth on his cock.

He'd never witnessed a more erotic scene in his life.

Her lashes slipped closed again and she pushed further onto him until he touched the back of her throat. She gagged, and he felt guilty at the immediate surge in pleasure. She slid her mouth up and off his length and then back down as far as she could, her moan of pleasure muffled by his girth. Was he a little deeper inside this time? He fought the urge to press himself fully into her throat. Up and down she stoked the fire inside of him, choking when she went too far, until he thought he'd explode.

"Mel," Grant croaked. "Melinda. Please, Melinda, please," he begged. In response, she sank onto him as far as she could go, drew her cheeks close together and slowly withdrew. Her lips had blossomed from caressing his cock, her eyes brightened with mischief and desire.

"Tell me this isn't going in the blog," he said weakly and she broke into laugher.

That was the break he needed to regain control, and he took it. He grabbed her arms and pulled her bodily onto the bed.

"What are you doing?" she asked, breathless against his lips.

"Turnabout's fair play," he replied and rose above her on his elbows to brand her swollen mouth with his. Who was this woman? What had she been thinking, changing the subject that way? Grant didn't know, and he didn't much care. He'd figure it out later. Now it was time to even the score.

Grant broke the kiss to see his own body, half-dressed in sturdy flannel and half-naked, and very . . . engaged. More importantly, Melinda was wearing too many clothes. Her sweater, he dragged overhead, leaving her disheveled and panting against the pillows. Her shirt, he shoved below her chin; her bra, he unclasped and threw who-knew-where in his haste to free her breasts for his tongue. Grant groaned as he took one perfect, dusky tip into his mouth and suckled.

His hand fumbled at the button on her jeans and released it, found the zipper and lowered it. Both hands shimmied her jeans over her bare ass and down her legs. Grant dropped to the floor, coaxed her hips to the edge of the bed for his turn to kneel and worship.

He slid both hands up her thighs to caress her skin as he licked a line up her leg. Melinda moaned and Grant pressed her knees wide, as wide as they could go against the bed.

"Ohh," she breathed, and Grant grinned.

"You're so gorgeous, Gorgeous."

Grant's hands went to work on her ass as his mouth worked up her thighs. He kneaded, gripped, and squeezed as he licked, breathed, and caressed with his lips. Melinda's moans and whimpers spurred him on. By the time his mouth reached the junction of her thighs, his hands were completely under her ass and partway up her back to feed her into his mouth.

"Melinda," he called to her quietly.

"Mmm?"

"I want to watch you," he said.

"Mmm," she repeated, head thrown sideways, bottom lip between her teeth.

Grant crawled next to her, swept his hands beneath her to cradle her, and hoisted her up the bed until her head met a pillow. He snagged two throw pillows, spread her legs high and wide, propped a pillow beneath each knee and returned to his task.

He had traded his comfortable position for a better view and it was beyond worth it. Grant lowered his mouth to her body and rejoiced as a whimper escaped her. He let his mouth move slowly, lovingly over her flesh. He laved, caressed, and stroked the folded shape of her with his lips and tongue. But he was not trying to bring her over the top. Not yet. He wanted her body as awakened as his had been. As it still was.

Melinda garbled something as his attention focused on a particular zone of her body, near but not quite at the bud at the center of her body.

"What's that?"

"Grant," she gasped. "Grant, I can't take it, please stop and come up here."

Thank God, because he was coiled near to exploding. He pushed up from the bed and surveyed her bared, disheveled body like a conqueror, growing harder still.

"Where'd you get the condom?" he grated, voice hard.

"That nightstand." Grant reached for the drawer, tore open the package and fitted himself with the sheath. He searched her face. Was she still hungry for him?

"Please," she said, panic in her eyes.

Please don't stop, he heard her say without words, and he growled in response.

"Please," she repeated, and pulled his hips to hers. Grant lowered himself onto her and she opened her thighs, her knees at his sides. His sex found hers and he nudged at her opening. How could something so soft be so tight?

She was already moaning as the tip of his cock entered her. Her eyelids closed as he pulsed slowly forward, further into her, further, until they were joined completely. He itched to move fast and hard, to plunder her body and repay her the agonizing bliss she'd bestowed upon him, but she was already in another place and writhing in an effort to intensify her pleasure.

Eyes glued to her face, he pulled back then pushed slowly into her. Her shriek flared between them and he gritted his teeth to drive forward again. Slow but hard. That's how he wanted it. That's what he wanted to show her. Because he was powerful. He was strong enough—for her. Whatever fears she had for their future could be doused in the intensity of his passion for her. Melinda flung back her head, eyes tightly closed, lush mouth wide and gasping.

Grant grabbed her breasts, kneading, demanding, as he thrust into her, and she arched off the bed in sensual offering. He dropped to his forearms, unable to hold back any longer, at last allowing himself to build momentum. He thrust quickly now, slamming into her, watching her face for signs of pain. She kept pace with him, legs taut, head thrown back, throat bared, her breathing short and choppy. Her desperation was his undoing, the pitch of his passion capsizing him as he lost all reason.

"Melinda," he groaned as he tipped over the edge.

"*Yes*," she said, not to him, not to anyone. "*Yes, oh God.*" Her words dissolved into shrieks as his world crumbled around him.

Melinda concentrated on breathing in and out and prayed her heart could maintain a gallop. What had just happened? What had she done—had she completely lost her mind? *God, I hope so*, she thought fervently. She'd relish being free of its insistent chatter.

After a time, her heartbeat slowed. The room returned, too. Unsurprisingly, it was freezing. Cold air iced her cheeks and frosted the tip of her nose. Grant's body pinned hers to the bed and she was grateful for the warmth, albeit lung-crushing. She turned to look him in the face. What was she going to do about him? She'd pulled her standard trick: steered away from something significant and toward distraction. But was that all it had been? Or was it true desire, sparked from his openness with her?

Melinda didn't know, and it left her uneasy. What had she said earlier? Better to cook than to think.

"You hungry?" she asked, and felt the bed shake with his laughter. "Good, you're alive," she said, then added indignantly, "Come on, it's almost lunch time! Be grateful I'm so focused on food—"

She turned her face away from his kisses. "Stop!" She

laughed, pushing him away. "You're lucky I'm focused on food, otherwise we'd have died three days ago!"

He loomed above her, forearms planted beside her head, smile broad. What was that expression on his face? He leaned down, closer, closer, until his lips brushed her ear.

"It's barely 10:00 a.m.," he whispered.

Oh, he was laughing at her.

"What?" she cried. "No way! It has to be time for lunch! I'm starving!"

"Yeah, I'm getting that that's a theme for you." He yanked the blankets over her and returned to nuzzling her neck. "Is this your preferred way of staying fit?" Grant kissed her ear and licked a line down her throat.

Melinda laughed. If only he knew how backward that was.

"Think of me what you will." She shifted to give his mouth access to her collar bone. "You'll thank me if you ever get a meal from me that involves a refrigerator."

"I think you're a goddess, Gorgeous," he said as he reached her mouth, and she smiled into his lips. "And I will do everything in my power to get another meal from you."

Melinda's toes curled beneath the blankets.

"Sure, it's easy to say that now," she teased. "All you have to do is chop wood and carry me around and keep us alive."

Grant encircled her with his arms and tucked her into his side. *Bear*, Melinda decided languidly.

"What brought on this workout?" He stroked her cheek with his fingers. "Not that I mind in the slightest."

She tried for coy. "I guess masculine vulnerability turns me on." Flippant, but also kind of true. Would the answer placate him?

His stomach growling broke the spell. No, not his stomach. Hers, more likely.

"What's that noise?" She cocked her head to decipher the deep rumble.

Grant froze.

"Shit!" he exploded, flinging back the blankets. "*Shit.* That's my plow. They're here. Paul. The cops. The cavalry. *They're here.*"

Grant launched off the bed like a pommel horse champion. He grabbed her clothes and shoved them at her before jerking on his own. Melinda lay stunned for a moment, then forced her fingers to manage her bra, shirt, and sweater. She dashed to the bathroom to dance on the remaining cold pair of clean underwear. She shrugged on her jeans and jacket and yanked her fingers through her sex-tangled hair.

Grant was dressed and giving the room a hard look. For conjugal evidence, she guessed. *What's the food parallel for—Not now!* she screamed in her mind. *Not now! Not now! Not now!* Did she always have to interject something to keep from feeling anything, even fear? Did she always have to escape the present moment? Could she never just *be* without judging and evaluating and picking everything apart? *Shut the hell up! Shut up shut up shut up!*

Car doors slammed and Melinda froze.

And then, blissfully, the cold descended and as if punishing her rebellion, her mind went petulantly, utterly blank. The noise of the raiding party floated in from a mile away.

Grant's footsteps became muffled and distant.

Why was that?

Oh, he was leaving the room.

That seemed smart.

Melinda trailed mutely after him as he abandoned the scene of the crime. Voices sounded from the driveway and Grant stationed himself at the front door. Melinda floated behind him, mind retreated, body numb.

Grant reached for the door handle, then twisted back to glare at her.

"Can I call you?" he burst out.

Melinda blinked. ". . . What?" Of all the questions she expected, this was not one.

"Can I call you? Sometime. After this." His nostrils were flared. There was urgency. Why? She heard it but didn't understand it. They weren't at a bar and they were well past his asking for her number. They were stranded in a frozen love nest and about to be exposed.

Grant stared at her.

"Uh, okay?" It was all she could manage from her ice palace far away.

Footsteps reached the door.

There was no time left.

Grant yanked open the front door and Melinda disappeared into his shadow.

A black boot crossed the threshold. Melinda's eyes traced the boots up heavy dark pants to a black trench coat and soft-looking scarf. Her breath quickened. Why was this almost as frightening as being back in that stupid car? Maybe she'd get lucky and faint.

"Samson." The measured voice cut the air like a blade.

The Mastermind. Paul.

"DiMario," Grant answered, cool as a cucumber. Neither moved forward to shake hands or embrace, she noted. Accidental kidnapping was serious business. Was that almost a joke? Melinda chided herself for hiding behind humor as well as Grant's body. That was the bitter spark she needed.

In a stop-motion rush, Melinda's mind came back online. Her heart took off racing and her hands trembled. She blinked and looked around her.

Paul DiMario was tall. As tall as Grant, but leaner. Lithe. Fierce. With a gentlemanly brutality, if there was such a thing. Even with the stress of driving through the snow to meet some unknown fate, he was dressed in new-looking slacks and a knit sweater. Plus kidnapper gloves and a dark coat. The guy had it together, she had to give him that. More striking than his wardrobe were his pale blond hair, aquiline nose, and ice-blue eyes.

"Where is she? Is she all right?" Paul was asking.

"She's here," Grant said. Melinda took a breath and stepped from behind her human shield.

Paul's eyes flashed.

"Melinda," he said in greeting. She thought maybe he paused then, to let her speak if she chose. She did not choose, and he continued. "Melinda, I wish I could say it was nice to meet you, but that would make a mockery of what you have been through, and I do not wish to do that." He stopped. Melinda waited. *Let's hear it, then.*

"I deeply regret what has happened to you. For what I did to you. It is completely and utterly my fault, and if you wish to pursue legal recourse you will have my wholehearted cooperation." He stopped again, and when she didn't reply, he went on.

"I'm sure Sams—that is, Grant has explained it to you, but I'd like to share in my own words why I have put on this production year after year, for my beloved's benefit. Would you mind?"

Melinda nodded.

"A few years ago, my girlfriend's brother made certain catastrophic financial decisions. I didn't know who she was other than that she was a tenant in my building. She didn't know that her brother's creditors were getting anxious about his ability to repay them. Instead of dealing with him directly," Paul said, lip curling, "they resorted to absconding with her person and holding her for ransom for over a week."

Melinda shivered. Over a week. A lifetime. Melisa must have been terrified.

"Melisa was essential to her own rescue but I, as well, played a role in it. And as such, when she was freed, she continued to be plagued by fears that she was not strong enough to save herself should the need arise in the future. Quite cleverly, she came up with the idea of someone mock-kidnapping her and of her escaping on her own power."

Melinda nodded. Most of this was familiar. It was fitting to hear him recount the tale, however, as this appeared to be the end of her own kidnapping scenario.

"Since we had subsequently begun a friendship, I volunteered to play the role of abductor. She outwitted me brilliantly," Paul said with pride, and Melinda almost smiled. This was the Mastermind, after all.

"Since then," Paul continued, "it's been an anniversary we've kept to celebrate her escape as well as our union. I can assure you, however, that this is the last time I'll ever rely on a friend to commit the act for me." Remorse was writ large across his face. Was it real? "We might need to find another way to celebrate."

Melinda didn't know why that made her feel better, but it did. *Oh I don't know, because the margin for error on this was always ridiculous, and no one should go through this again?*

"Melisa is with me. She'd like to be the one to take you home," Paul went on. "We imagine you want to get far away from this hellish place as quickly as possible. Grant and I will tidy up affairs here, and Melisa will take you home and stay until your friends and family arrive. She's a very soothing presence," he said with a quick smile, "and has an unfortunate familiarity

183

with what you've endured. Although I hope I can assume that your stay in my cabin has been marginally more tolerable with Grant as your chaperone."

"What the hell?" Grant burst out, hands balled to fists at his sides. "She's not some tenant with a leaky sink! She got kidnapped, man! Get your managerial head out of—"

"Grant was a total gentleman," Melinda said before things could get worse, and felt Grant's jolt of surprise. "After the first misunderstanding, he's been a savior to me. As for your offer of legal action," she went on, "thank you. I will think about it. I believe I'll have a lot to think about in the next few weeks."

Lighter, quicker footsteps crunched down the snow-covered walkway. A woman several inches shorter than Melinda slipped into the house past Paul. He stepped sideways to accommodate her. *Melisa.*

Melinda's gaze flicked between the two of them, then settled on Melisa. Melisa's hair had slightly more brown than her own, and her lips were slightly less full. Her skin was slightly lighter and she was slightly thinner.

She took in their expressions. Paul's face had changed from polite diplomacy to something tighter, something strained. He was afraid. Why was he afraid?

Melisa's face . . . Melisa's face was more difficult for Melinda to see because of the anguish in her eyes. *She's intimately aware of my experience. She knows the fear. She thinks I've been in hell for the last four days.* And by all rights, Melinda should have been, except that somehow things had gone surprisingly right, after they'd gone horribly wrong.

Had they? Could she say that for sure? Melinda stole a glance at Grant and found him watching her. Where were things now? Surprisingly right or horribly wrong? Melinda returned his look until the atoms between them crackled.

Who knew? Who knew what any of this would be like outside of the cabin?

Then Paul drew Melisa close with one arm and Melinda jerked her gaze to them once more. Melisa's eyes had filled with tears.

"If there's anything you need, Melinda, we . . ." He seemed not to know how to finish his sentence. "We're here for you," he finished, flatly. His face remained calm, if tense, but now he was pressing Melisa into himself as if to envelop her completely.

He's afraid for her. He's afraid of what she's feeling now.

"Melinda," Melisa said with a soft, delicately feminine voice. "Melinda . . ." The tears took over and her face crumpled. "I'm so, so—" Her lower lip trembled, hand flying to conceal her mouth.

Melinda took a cautious step forward, and then another. She reached out a hand, until she caught Melisa's.

"I think I understand what you two were doing," Melinda said. "I see that you think you contributed to someone being tortured, as you were." Melisa's eyes shone with tears and she nodded.

"Please know that I was very well taken care of." Again she felt Grant's movement at her side, this time a stiffening. "Grant melted snow so we could drink water and cook. He kept the fire going constantly. He gave me the bed so I would sleep better." *Don't blush don't blush don't blush.* "He even gave me your revolver so I could shoot him if I wanted." Melisa sniffled a short laugh. "And he carried me, unconscious, through that meadow after I went for a walk and got knocked out by a tree limb."

Melisa's face froze in an expression of concern.

"He saved me," Melinda said. "He was there for me. I was protected. I was not alone." Melinda didn't know where her words were coming from, she just knew that she wanted to reassure Melisa that she herself hadn't gone through the same hell. She guessed that that thought had been haunting Melisa for the entire time the blizzard had kept them all trapped.

"I'm so sorry," Melisa managed. "I've been sick thinking of you up here. Scared . . . hopeless—" She turned her face into Paul's chest. His arms immediately enfolded her, and Melinda saw his face was tight with pain as he bent his head to whisper in her ear. She imagined the words he'd use to comfort her, imagined the way he'd warm his voice to soothe her guilt and memories.

"Melisa." Melinda spoke quietly. "It's clear that the last few days have been more traumatic for you than they've been for me. I don't want that for you; please consider that when you're thinking about this later." Melisa pulled her head away from Paul's chest and Melinda saw her deep, forced breaths, her efforts to be calm.

Melinda wished she could take Grant's hand and steady herself, too. She wished he could wrap his big bear arms around her and cocoon her in safety the way Paul cocooned Melisa.

She watched them together and saw that Paul might be a millionaire but that he adored the woman in his arms, and really was trying to make the best of the situation where she'd found herself.

I bet if I were a millionaire everything would be a game to me, so I'd want to create my own game. Melinda didn't know which way was up. *Remember, Grant is good, so Paul is good. Grant is good, Paul is good.* Grant was good. Was he good? Was he right?

And was there a way for her and Grant to live a happily-ever-after? Perhaps, if . . .

If what? The words were a bitter gust through her mind.

It was impossible. Pathetic. She was trying to turn a hookup into a fairytale, and life didn't work that way. Life offered windows of fun but eventually everyone disappeared or disappointed. It was a matter of time.

Melinda shivered. Cold wafting from the open door? No, it was a wake-up call from a distant land called reality. The reality was that with their rescue, their window was closing. Time to figure it out.

Suddenly the room was too small, the chilled air too thick. Her legs were stuck to the floor. Her clothes wrapped her too snugly. She tugged at the collar of her sweater. She couldn't breathe, couldn't think of anything but escape.

They were staring at her. She kept her voice as cold as her heart.

"Right, then. What's the timeline on getting out of here?"

Grant watched the train wreck in front of him as if in slow motion. How the hell was it up to these three people to hash out his future, and he, ringside and useless? What if, after this damned abrupt interruption, Melinda never wanted to see him again? What if DiMario said something that threw Grant's credibility into question? Grant's mind raced to find anything over the past year and a half of friendship that would send him sprawling under the bus. Dammit.

But Paul seemed to be behaving himself, if a bit pompously, and Melinda was holding her own. Melisa was in no state to drive anyone at the moment, but Grant knew she was made of strong stuff. She'd pull it together.

Melinda's comments had warmed him but not eased his uncertainty.

Foolishly, he'd imagined a leisurely morning together, a further softening of the questions between them, developing a plan that they reconvene after the cabin. Another amazing dinner tonight.

This is not a vacation, his mind reminded him. This was an experience she wanted to put behind her. *He* was an experience she wanted to put behind her.

"Who drove what?" He aimed to match Melinda's cool.

"I met Bryan in Dillon to pick up your rig with the plow," Paul answered, and Grant's eyebrows rose. "It's more difficult to manage than I've given you credit for."

Grant nodded slightly in acknowledgment. Not too little too late, but about damn time.

"I drove the Land Cruiser," Melisa said, her eyes clear now. "And I stopped by the grocery store to send you home with food." She looked from Melinda to Grant. "Both of you. Grant, we've been in touch with your dad and let him know where you were." Her gaze jumped sideways. "Uh, the gist of where you were. You can share other details, if you like."

"Thank you," Grant said as he met her eyes. "That was thoughtful. And"—he extended his hand—"it's nice to meet you. I've been hearing about you for a while."

Melisa turned to Melinda.

"Has Paul told you that I'd be happy to drive you home, Melinda?"

Melinda nodded.

"Excellent. Please allow me to do that for you. You can kick me out immediately, if you like. The past few days, as you said, have been pretty brutal for me. I'd see it as an act of kindness if you let me rest tonight with the certainty that you've been escorted home safely."

Grant was relieved to see Melinda nod again. He longed to be the one to tuck her in at home, but if it couldn't be him, then Melisa. She struck him as the nurturing type.

188

"All right, then," said Paul. "Where are your things? I'll carry them to the car. Ah. Perhaps you need a short while to collect them? Please go ahead. Grant and I can discuss our next steps."

"Can I help you make sure you've got everything?" Melisa asked, and Grant stiffened.

Melinda's things were in the bedroom, and the bedroom had sex written all over it. The blankets were mostly off the bed, Grant's belt was on the floor, and—*Oh, God, the condom.*

"Thank you, but I can take care of it," said Melinda.

"Can I help?" Grant asked.

She turned to him. "I can take care of it," she repeated. He tried to hold her eyes, to penetrate her mask. Her face remained impassive, clinical, even. *Dammit.*

Every second of this falsehood put a mile between them. All Grant needed was a moment with her. A brush of her hand against his, a softening of her face as he caught her eye. Something that said he hadn't imagined the past four days, or at least, the past twenty-four hours.

Instead, she headed toward the bedroom, and away from him. *From all of us,* he told himself. *Just to get her stuff.* He imagined her folding her clothes into her bag, tucking her toothbrush into a side pocket, stripping the bed.

He itched to help her, but he knew it would be suspicious if he did. But why? Surely any two decent people trapped by a blizzard would have connected somewhat, and that connection could be safely witnessed by other people. Right?

Connection, yes, but not intimacy. If he went near her now, he'd pull her close and never let her go. He'd breathe in her scent, kiss her cheek, stroke her hair, tell her everything would be all right. That they would make it through this confusion.

And that wouldn't do at all.

There were too many doubts. Could he call her? Could they

see one another outside of this place? Did she never want to see him again? The thought gave him pause. She said he could call her, right? *Yes, but she's skittish as a deer. For all you know, she's imagining a knife to her throat.*

As he thought about it, he figured that was exactly how she felt. She was on autopilot right now. She was doing what needed to be done, and that was all. His gut twisted. But wondering about her with acid churning in his stomach wasn't doing him any good, so he marched into the kitchen and grabbed clean dishes from the drainer.

Melinda emerged from the bedroom just then, and they stared at one another. An ocean of unspoken words rolled between them. Could she feel his yearning?

She looked exactly as she had the night they'd met—duffel bag slung from her shoulder, black puffy coat zipped to her chin, scarf looped around her neck. Maybe there was more fatigue around her eyes. More strain at the mouth, a different set to her shoulders. *Dammit, dammit, dammit.* All he wanted was to hold her.

"Melinda . . . please," he said quietly and reached out a hand.

Melinda's eyes cut to him but she said nothing.

"Please, won't you talk to me?"

At that moment Paul and Melisa walked into the kitchen and the mood shattered.

"Did you find everything?" asked Paul.

"I got it all," she said, her eyes still on Grant. It was a message, and his heart swelled with gratitude for her even as it burst with pain.

"All right, then. Let's get you out of here," said Melisa.

And Melinda turned on her heel and left.

The air was crisp, and the vastness of the snow blinding, but Melinda could almost see the sun in the bleached sky. There it was, an ultra-white pinprick beyond the haze of clouds tracking her steps to the waiting SUV. She hadn't been out front in two days.

"I'll move Grant's groceries into his truck," said Melisa. She lifted a brown paper bag from the back of the Land Cruiser and took it to the enormous silver Dodge with its equally massive yellow plow. *There's the appendage.* Melinda didn't laugh. She didn't smile, not even internally. How could she? There was no joy left.

Then Melisa was back and standing outside the open driver's door.

"Ready?" she asked. "You can put your bag in the back seat if you'd like."

This time, Melinda did laugh, but it was cynical and short. A laugh of despairing familiarity—was it only a handful of days ago that she was having the same conversation with an enormous, handsome stranger? It was a laugh of being near tears. Fat chance. She was heartless and empty.

Melinda extracted her phone from her bag and dropped the duffel in the back seat.

"Do you have a charger?"

"Sure," Melisa replied, scooting into the driver's seat. She handed the charger to Melinda and started the car. As Melinda plugged it in, a small icon appeared on the phone to indicate that it would need a long charge. *You and me both.*

"How are the roads?" asked Melinda.

191

"Not bad," Melisa said as they pulled out. Melinda watched the cabin disappear in her door's side mirror. "Everything's been plowed, which is a blessing. The snow stopped last night and we got on the road first thing this morning. It took a while to coordinate with Grant's guy, though."

Trees blurred past Melinda's window. After days of stillness and solitude, speed was a foreign language.

"There was no hurry."

She felt Melisa mulling over her statement and hoped the other woman would leave it be. The whole drive could be in silence, for all she felt like chit-chatting. And for a while, it was. Melisa left Melinda to reacclimatize to the surreal experience of being in a moving vehicle, of seeing houses, storefronts, other cars, and other people. Before long, though, Melisa broached safe topics like the weather and Melinda's job. Melinda queried in kind, and soon they were passing the community of Genesee, less than a half an hour from the Park & Ride where her car was parked.

"So," Melisa said, her voice a little softer than before, and Melinda's neck prickled. "Did you and Grant get along okay, after he explained what was going on and who he was?"

And like a movie, a stream of images flashed in front of her eyes. Grant swinging the maul over his head as he split wood. Grant's eyes closed in pleasure as he ate her food. Grant's eyes locked on hers as he moved inside her, just that morning. Her pulse quickened and her heart wrenched. This was madness.

"Yes," she managed.

"He's a really decent guy, from what Paul's told me," Melisa continued lightly. "Did you guys get to know each other at all?"

That was one way to put it. But how much to tell her? How much to admit? To Melisa? To herself? Would the people they had briefly become have any place in the real world? And was

192

their affair even worth exposing to the light of day?

Melinda didn't know. The amount she didn't know was suddenly significantly more than she could bear, and her tenuous grip on sanity slipped away. Everything slipped away. She stared at the dashboard, at her hands limp on her jeans, at the freeway beyond the windshield. Her lungs tightened, a self-made corset that cinched her waist and robbed her of breath.

How much did the other woman suspect? Clearly something, given her careful phrasing. Would she empathize, or would she judge Melinda as being easy, for letting her kidnapper have his way with her?

Melinda felt easy. What's worse, she felt empty. Where was Grant now? Was he, at this very moment, drinking a beer and laughing at how the dumb chick had given it up, not once, but twice?

Melinda's face fell into her waiting hands. Back hunched, eyes squeezed shut, the tears pushed their way out of her. She wept. She sobbed with heaving shoulders and whimpers from deep in her throat. She cried until her sense of self was gone.

And then, suddenly, awkwardly, with one last shaky inhale, it was over.

Well, that didn't take very long. Her sarcasm was still intact, if not her pride. What was that, a three-minute breakdown?

Melisa was still waiting for an answer.

Melinda wiped her eyes. "Um," she began. "Would you believe me at this point if I said no?" She was grateful for the compassion she heard in Melisa's low chuckle.

"Absolutely." The other woman's face went impassive. "Totally plausible." Then a smile tugged the corner of her mouth and she sighed.

"Okay, yeah. I thought, or I imagined, that I had seen something between you two up there," Melisa said. She turned for a moment to catch Melinda's eye. "Are you okay?"

"Yes, I guess. Well, no. I mean . . . No? Yes? I don't know. I don't know anything." The tears took Melinda again. What the hell was happening to her? She jammed her knuckles into her eyes and rubbed hard to stem the grief. Grief about what? A weekend hookup? Ugh. She laid her palms on her legs and squeezed firmly, determined to not hide behind her hands again.

Melisa strummed a rhythm on the steering wheel. "Do you want to talk about it?"

"No. Yes. I don't even know," Melinda laughed at her flip-flop answers. Wasn't there anyone else in whom she could confide? No, actually, there wasn't. "You know what, why not? Not that I know what the hell to tell you. Where do I start? The beginning's the obvious choice. Okay."

She hesitated to relive the clawing dread of the back of the Mercedes.

"The beginning was terrible. He was so bloody cold. He thought I was you, and role-playing, and he got pissed. But after that drive, he was . . ." She stole Melisa's word. "Decent. He just kept showing up for me and was so strong. He really cared that I felt safe, and empowered, even as we were stuck in that place. He gave me my own space, let me have the kitchen, kept me warm . . ."

Her pause was more incriminating than the phrasing itself.

"Bloody hell." She wrestled with the wording, the rules, the truth. "I just don't know if it's real!" she burst out. "I don't know if anything outside of that place is real. How could it be? How could we be anything to each other out here?"

She pinned Melisa with a glare. "How could he and I be real in the stupid so-called real world? How could it work? It couldn't. Nothing works long-term out here. Everything is upstaged by the next best thing. Everyone leaves, eventually." Her gaze slipped from Melisa's profile to the road, and she saw they were almost to the Park & Ride. *Great. Way to keep it together.*

Perhaps cued by something in Melinda's voice, Melisa kept silent as she engaged the turn signal and steered the car toward the exit. She followed the ramp off the freeway and turned onto 44th, then Ward Road, then into the lot.

Melinda stared silently at the rows of snow-covered cars. She hadn't seen this many vehicles since she'd dropped her car here Friday morning. Was it really only Wednesday? Friday was a lifetime ago. Why were there so many cars? Where were all these people? Why weren't they at home and making the most of their running water and electricity? After her brush with scarcity, the audacity of abundance was discomfiting.

Melinda couldn't tell which marshmallowed car was hers. *What's the food parallel for death by marshmallows? Something to do with Willy Wonka.*

"Just tell me where I should go," Melisa said as she idled the car near the entrance.

As if Melinda could remember.

"Um. Maybe down that fourth row?" she suggested, and Melisa started the car forward. They reached the end of the row. Melisa suggested they double back and Melinda nodded. Six passes later, Melinda was ready to give up. Melisa was as well, it appeared.

"Melinda, I think we have to call it," she said. "Even if we found your car, it would take us an hour to dig you out." She paused. "I'd be happy to take you to the police station . . . ?"

Melinda heard the question but wasn't interested. She wasn't ready to face that decision yet. "If you have time to double back to my place in Golden, that would be great," she said. "Thank you."

"Of course." Melisa steered the car toward the exit. "I

imagine they'll have been lenient with the parking restrictions here, but in case you find a ticket on your windshield, or in the mail, Paul and I will take care of it." She pulled the Land Cruiser back into the slush of Ward Road and then merged onto I-70. Only then did she resume her delicate interrogation.

"So . . . ?"

Melinda burst out laughing.

"I think I know where this is going," Melinda said with a sidelong glance at the other woman.

Melisa laughed as well. "So he's a heartbreaker, is he?" she asked.

"God I hope not," Melinda answered, and that same organ quickened in her chest. *My heart? Love? No way.* It wasn't possible in that short amount of time. She thought of her parents. Nothing good came of pressure-cooked romance.

"But . . ." Melinda picked up where her reverie had left off. "We . . . connected. He was so constant. So dependable. So caring. And if I'm honest, so sexy."

It was Melisa's turn to burst out laughing. "I can't disagree with you there," she said. "The man is a mountain! And that touch of silver in his hair? I mean, wow. Killer."

Her tone softened from conspiratorial gossip to supportive girlfriend. "I can totally see it. Paul and I got together way too soon after I had been abducted, but I was helpless to stop it. He made me feel safe. That was the opposite of how I felt every other minute of the day. And he made me feel seen when I'd always felt invisible. I think it's those rare times when your skin gets peeled off that you really see the truth of who someone is and how they affect you."

Every nerve in Melinda's body tingled with recognition at the truth of Melisa's words. *He saw me. He made me feel safe. Even after scaring me to death.*

"It might even be *because* he scared me to death that I felt so safe with him later," she mused. "I could juxtapose the decent man with the brute and could tell which one was real and which one was operating out of desperation."

Melinda stared at piles of dirty snow kicked to the side of the road. Stupid snowplows. She'd never be able to look at winter driving the same again. *Shit. He's ruined this whole state for me. Time to move to Florida.*

They had reached Sixth Avenue, partway into Golden. Melisa exited the main road, following Melinda's directions to her condo.

"Take my spot. Number seven, over there. Oh." She blinked. Melinda's spot hadn't been occupied for six days and was bracketed by two cars, so the plow hadn't cleared it.

"No problem," said Melisa as she steered the car into the lake of snow. "What's the point of an SUV if you can't deal with a little white stuff?"

The Land Cruiser's tires chewed dully through the snow as Melisa nudged the vehicle forward. Then Melinda gathered her things while Melisa grabbed the groceries and they met on the mostly shoveled sidewalk.

"Would you like me to take those?" Melinda asked.

"Not at all," Melisa answered. "Unless you'd like me to drop you here and not come with you. But I'd prefer to see you safely into your place, make sure your electricity is working. I'd hate for you to be out of the frying pan and into the fire. An ice-cold fire, that is."

Melinda smiled. "That's fine with me. Thanks for the concern. I'm this way." They picked their way over the icy walkway to her front door. Keys, she realized. She would need her keys. She unzipped an accordion compartment in her bag to locate her small set of keys: one house key, one car key, one gym locker key.

197

No office to speak of, no storage unit anywhere, storing stuff she cared about. No boyfriend's house key weighing down her bag.

Stop wallowing. She jiggled the key in the lock, cranked the handle, and pushed open the door into a freezer. She'd known to expect it, since it was she who'd turned down the heat before she left, but still, the cold air was less than welcoming.

"*Whoo!*"

"Yikes," said Melisa. "That's some homecoming. Where's the thermostat?"

"Right behind you to your right."

"Want me to blast it?"

"God, yes." Melinda continued tentatively into her foreign home. "Come on in. It's no luxury cabin, but it's got electricity."

The living room was richly, if sparsely decorated. Two soft brown leather couches faced the pale amber partial wall of windows and Melinda's television. A *khorjin* rug dominated by reds, browns, yellows, and aquas linked the perpendicular couches, and a square coffee table provided a landing pad in the space between them. The unfamiliar sight of her belongings overwhelmed her. She scanned each item like an amnesiac. Could she absorb their history within herself? Who had she been when she'd used these things? She was so different now.

She set her bags down and continued the reintroduction to her home. A trio of books about cooking, a set of orange, pink, and red pillar candles, and a deep green hoya house plant in a hammered brass pot adorned the low table. "Thank goodness I watered you before I left," she murmured.

Melinda had long ago exchanged the condo's modern pendant lighting for pierced brass pendants, and as she flipped their switch, she met their dappled illumination like a familiar acquaintance. Beyond the carpeted living room was her round-tabled dining nook, and adjoining it, her kitchen.

Her kitchen. Looking at her kitchen again was like seeing a loved one after years of painful estrangement. Had she betrayed it? Moved beyond it? Forgotten it? Why was she getting emotional again?

Kuttar bachcha. Her kitchen reminded her of Grant.

While the living room and the dining nook shared the western-facing wall, the kitchen spanned the length of both of them. Unlike the boho-modern chic of Paul's cabin, Melinda's kitchen had the feel of a professional culinary zone. Cream cabinets softened the sharp steel of the fixtures and appliances, and she'd brought the space to life with rich jade green, robin's egg blue, and aqua—the colors of her strainer, stand mixer, utensil jar, stacking bowls, and drawer pulls. She stared in horror at the refrigerator, stocked with all manner of ingredients. Her gaze dropped to the butcher block-topped island, and she steadied herself on it. She'd bought this place because of the kitchen, and now food reminded her of Grant.

This was robbery.

"Would you like me to put away the groceries for you?" Melisa asked, and Melinda jumped. Would she? Would she like someone else to open her cabinets and pull out crisper drawers, the way she had done in the mountains?

"No, thank you. It's something I have to do myself." She cringed at how odd that sounded. But she had to reclaim her kitchen. There was nothing else to do. She couldn't call Melisa back tomorrow because she was frightened of the cold-cuts drawer.

"Okay."

Melinda watched in surprise as the other woman walked into the kitchen like it wasn't covered in landmines and deposited the groceries on the counter. "Tea?" Melisa offered.

Melinda sighed—whether from relief or exasperation, she wasn't sure. Apparently Melisa intended to stay a while.

❧

Grant was back in his rig. The engine chuffed along with its comforting hum and the wheels gripped the road. The snowfall had officially stopped, but blowing snow kept his wipers busy. Heat piped steadily through the truck's vents to wick moisture from his chapped face.

The road was in good shape, plowed mostly clean. Only tracks of compressed snow remained. The road. That was it. His mind was on the road. It had to be. There's no way he could function if it were on her. *Her.* After she had stalked out of the cabin without so much as a peace sign, Paul had wasted zero time getting to the heart of the matter.

"What the fuck?" Paul said in time with Grant's *"Dammit."*

"What the hell happened up here?" Paul demanded.

"I sure as shit don't know, man." Grant rubbed first one and then both hands roughly over his face.

"Please tell me you guys didn't hook up while you were up here. Are you trying to get life in prison?"

"I'm not telling you anything, DiMario," Grant snapped, but he knew he was doing exactly that: telling him everything. His poker face had always been a joke. He slumped into the chair's forgiving embrace.

"Christ, man. I thought I was a dumbass. You made me look like a good Samaritan! Or worse, a pimp." Paul's eyes seared him alive.

"You got us into this mess, DiMario. Don't go shifting the blame to me."

"Okay, okay." Paul's hands went up. "At least we're sharing culpability now. Can't say I'm not grateful. It was lonely in the gallows."

"Things got wild," Grant said, eyes closed, head tossed back against the chair. "I may owe you a new couch."

Paul's eyes widened. "Are you fucking kidding me? Out here? In front of the fire? Could you get any more trite?" He rubbed his temples. "If she tells Melisa, she won't have to call the cops—Mel will do it for her."

"What are you talking about?" Grant asked, head still thrown back and ignoring the ceiling.

"You had sex with someone with whom there was a very clear inequity of power. For all you know, she thought sleeping with you would prevent her being murdered."

They had been Grant's thoughts as well, but hearing them from a trusted source was not heartening.

He had to talk with her.

No, he had to leave her alone. And find legal representation.

But she said I could call her. He was a madman grasping at nothing. She had also said, "Please stop, please, I'm not who you think I am."

Grant groaned.

"Let's get out of here," Paul said. "What do we have to take care of first? Also, it's freezing in here. You didn't have to worry about the expense of the propane, this was an emergency."

Grant's head snapped up. "The expense of what the hell did you just say?"

"The propane. The heat. You used the generator, didn't you?"

Grant counted to ten. "No. Remember, Paul, you don't have a damned generator," he said in a low voice, near conversational. "I've been telling you for a year to get one. When in the frozen-over hell did you get a generator?"

Paul had the grace to look abashed for a millisecond, Grant saw with satisfaction. Paul could apologize until the cows came

201

home, but he lacked the sincerity that made humility ring true.

"Oh hell, man." Paul squeezed his eyes shut. "I'm sorry. Shit. We just had it installed a couple months ago for situations like this. It's under the back deck. The transfer switch is in the coat closet."

Grant's eyes locked on Paul's. *Keep it together, Samson. Remember you're already going to prison for kidnapping. Don't add murder charges.*

"I woke up every two hours to keep the fire going," he said through clenched teeth. "I collected snow in your damned beer steins so we could drink water and make food, and flush the damned toilet. Melinda slept in her clothes and your stupid fancy jacket! We were freezing in here! No, you didn't tell me about *the fucking generator!*" Yelling was helpful; it took his mind off the pain that awaited him.

"I'm sensing some frustration," Paul said delicately, and Grant leapt to his feet. Paul didn't flinch. He knew Grant better than that, unfortunately. But it would have been nice to scare the overgrown elf for a second.

"I'm getting my stuff and then I'm out of here," Grant growled. "Hire a housekeeper to take care of the rest. Turn on your damned generator and watch a damned movie."

"Fair enough, fair enough," Paul said, all amiability and easy condescension. "Happy to. In fact, why don't you go home, get showered, and I'll take care of things here."

"Perfect," Grant bit out, and stalked behind the futon to collect his bag. He checked that his phone and the infernal phone charger were inside, then walked to the bathroom to grab his toothbrush. The bowls from breakfast awaited him in the kitchen. *Who cares? Let Paul melt snow to wash up for a change.*

He scanned the bedroom for evidence of recent relations. Melinda had smoothed the comforter across the bed enough that it didn't look recently tumbled. Grant hoped he didn't either. There was nothing more embarrassing than carrying on as if you had the moral high ground and later realizing your ass was out the whole time.

He slowed and stopped. Maybe she'd forgotten something here, something he'd have an excuse to bring her. He checked beneath the bed, on and in the bedside tables, and under the chairs. Nothing. *Dammit.* If he contacted her, it would have to be because of the truth.

And what was that?

He stared at the bed and saw her sitting there, bravely laying her heart bare to him. He remembered the way she'd turned on a dime, desire somehow ignited, and taken him on the adventure of a lifetime. He saw her naked and laughing, naked and moaning. He saw her unselfconscious passion for food. The woman was insatiable. She was also amazing. He pinched the bridge of his nose.

Footsteps sounded. Paul.

"You come back here to cry?" Paul asked.

"Go to hell," Grant said, eyes still on the bed.

"That heartbroken?" Paul prodded.

"We have to get out of this room." Grant was grateful to Paul for not asking why. Paul wasn't truly a pompous ass. He just played one really, really well.

Grant returned to the den armed with his pack and toothbrush, but the urgency to escape had passed. Maybe he could hang out for a few minutes more. He chose the same lounge chair as before and sat.

Out of his sight, Paul might have raised an eyebrow, but Grant didn't care. Paul moved fluidly across the den to sit and stare candidly at Grant.

"You have my attention."

Grant couldn't help a rueful smile. That was Paul being warm and fuzzy. "I think I met someone," he sighed.

Paul nodded. "So I surmised. What happened?"

"At first it was awful. Actually, no, at first, it was . . . chemical. When I picked her up at the airport, it was on. And I was freaking out because I thought she was Melisa and that I was into your girl. I felt like dog shit." Grant tugged at his shirt collar.

When he told Paul about how he had raised the partition, his friend inhaled sharply, but to Paul's credit, he said nothing. Grant told him about how he'd received all the texts at once and realized his colossal mistake. His stomach was acid. How could he have been so stupid and so brutal?

"It took me some doing to get her into the house."

"And you gave her my revolver. You do know it's kept empty, don't you? Did you load it first?"

"No, of course I didn't *load it*," Grant snapped. "I wanted her to feel like she had some control over her situation; I wasn't asking her to end her life or mine." He went on, describing the difficult first night and the breakfast she had made the next day. He warmed slightly at the thought, and he realized what he felt was pride. *This is a new one.* He never got invested enough to feel prideful of a woman.

"We went for a walk and she got nailed by a dead branch." He winced at the memory as well as his choice of words. "My fault. I took her out in a damn snowstorm. I got her back here and kept her by the fire on the couch. She slept on and off, but when she'd wake up we'd . . . talk," he finished lamely. "We both slept out here. Me on the floor, her on the couch. Then the next day we talked more, and—"

"What is this, a soap opera?" Paul interrupted. "How did you get from kidnapping to sex-a-thon?"

"That's what I'm trying to tell you," Grant shot back. "I've never talked to a woman so much in my damn life. There's something different about her, but I can't figure it out."

"Perhaps it's that you couldn't wait until you got home to sleep with her, and you had to do so in my home away from home." Paul shook his head. "I'm going to have to sell this place," he said, more to himself than to Grant.

Grant waved him off.

What was it? What couldn't he shake? Maybe that she didn't need anything from him. She wasn't vying for anything. She wasn't looking for a matador or a hero, and that made him want to be exactly those things. He wanted to save her, to earn her trust, to wake up the parts of her that had gone to sleep, to rekindle life where it had gone dormant.

So then why did he feel rooted to this chair?

He closed his eyes.

"This is most entertaining," Paul intoned. "I certainly hope you're enjoying your meditation." Grant raised his head to see Paul staring at him over the pyramid of his joined fingertips.

"Go to hell," Grant said without heat. Then, almost as an aside, "How do I know if she's the right one?"

"Do you feel like you want to puke?"

"Uh, yeah," Grant said, surprised. "Yeah. I thought it was the breakfast at first, and then the adrenaline of you guys showing up, but the nausea hasn't gone away. Why is that? And why do you ask?"

"It's because she's the one," Paul said without affect. "What you're feeling is fear at the potential loss of selfhood."

"Are you kidding me right now?"

"I picked up some things from Mel's—" Paul stopped to correct himself. "I suppose we'll need to adjust our nicknames, won't we? I picked up some things from Melisa's therapist. The vagal response can be triggered by stress and its symptoms

205

include nausea. Feel a little warm? Light-headed?"

Grant stared at him. "If you think I'm going to call you Dr. DiMario, you've got another thing coming."

Paul laughed, and there was a smile at his eyes. "You've had a lot of stress for the past four days, but it sounds like the physical discomfort and fear of mortality are taking second place to your anxiety over the introduction of this woman into your psyche. I agree, she seemed quite engaging."

Grant narrowed his eyes.

"Relax, friend." Paul's platitude was kind. "I'm trying to be supportive. Do you really think I could compromise my Melisa by hinting at an encounter with your lovely Melinda?"

No, Grant didn't. He just didn't like Paul thinking more clearly than he was or pointing out what should have been obvious.

"But like you said, what if she just cozied up to me out of self-preservation?"

"Does that appear to be true?" Paul asked.

Did it?

Grant stared at the fire, imagining Melinda laughing in the snow, the softness of her face as she talked about her family, the way she watched him as she listened to his stories. No. It couldn't be true. She wouldn't have slept with him—twice—in some masochistic attempt to save her own life, would she? His heart hoped for that answer, while his mind was quick to point out that his heart was an idiot.

"I haven't been serious with anyone in ten years," he said. "There's something about her that scares the hell out of me. There's also something about her that I need now, like food. There's the chance I'll end up in jail. I haven't got a clue of what to do."

CHAPTER SEVEN

You have to grow from the inside out.
None can teach you, none can make you spiritual.
There is no other teacher but your own soul.
Swami Vivekananda

Melinda tapped her fingernails on the bistro tabletop. She lifted the half-empty water glass to her lips and drank again, even though she'd be running to the restroom two minutes after Melisa arrived.

Or I could just leave. There were only two other diners in the restaurant. A woman wearing too much paisley and a man staring at his phone from beneath his scratchy-looking orange beanie. They wouldn't care. She toyed with the thought for exactly three seconds before abandoning it. She'd been the one to call Melisa the day before and ask to meet for lunch; there was no reason to chicken out now. *Except every reason in the book.*

Why had she wanted this meeting in the first place? Because she was going mad. But also, if anyone could understand post-kidnapping malaise, it was Melisa. Her mind switched gears. *Post-kidnapping malaise . . . "Post-Kidnapping Hollandaise?"* It was catchy, but wholly inaccurate. The thought of rich sauces made her stomach revolt.

It had been a week since their rescue. A week since she'd been dumped into normal life. A week since their last snowstorm, and the streets were gray with dirt-crusted slush. It had also been a week since she'd seen Grant.

And if she were being honest, that was where the real mental instability lay. Did she want him? Or want him incarcerated? He scared the hell out of her. But why? The worst thing he'd done was erect a physical wall between them, which was so Freudian she almost laughed. After that, he'd begged her forgiveness, kept her alive and wooed her senseless. Her glass empty, Melinda got to work tearing her paper napkin to shreds.

Who the hell pushes away a ruggedly handsome, business-savvy lumberjack with eye crinkles?

He's an egomaniac, she shot back, flexing for a mental tennis match.

Why, exactly? He gave you the best sex of your life and told you he had feelings for you. He's clearly a monster.

All of that can be faked, she backhanded.

Says the pot to the kettle. Ooh, an ace.

He uses women. He said so himself! He's a broken man, just like the rest, she lobbed.

He got vulnerable with you. Vulnerable is not the same as weak. He threatens you because he doesn't need you to manage him, plus he gets you, and you don't know how to deal with that.

If he's so great, then why isn't he beating down my door? She dove across the court for that one.

Loaded silence. She imagined her ego walking past its fans, tennis racket raised to acknowledge the cheers.

Why don't you just talk with him?

Melinda ran after her victorious opponent. *Because it is*

always better to be alone. It is never helpful to keep anyone close. Ever. Wasn't that obvious?

Melisa had written her phone number on Melinda's grocery list notepad that first night.

"I know you'll want to go deep for a couple days," she said. "Hibernate. Call your parents, tell your friends, all that. But if you emerge on the other side and feel a little confused, or want to talk with someone who knows a bit of what you've been through, give me a call. My schedule is flexible. Lunch dates work great for me. You're choosing the restaurant, though." She'd gestured at the expansive kitchen. "You clearly know a thing or two about cooking and I'm not putting my foot in my mouth by suggesting hot dogs at the gas station."

Melinda had smiled wanly, accepted the other woman's hug, and escorted her out the door. She'd ordered Indian food that night. She didn't want to call her family but she could at least eat *masoor dal* with rice, chutney, and papadam.

It wasn't as if Grant hadn't reached out. The first night she'd gotten home, in fact, when she'd been wrapped in her chenille throw and staring out the windows at the blackness of Lookout Mountain Park, a text had arrived from a number she hadn't recognized. She'd picked up her phone from the coffee table with a fluttering pulse, unsure if she wanted to see what was written.

Fortunately he hadn't written *You up?* Or *Feeling lonely?*—pegging him for a player—though maybe it would've been simpler if he had. Instead, the ball was in her court, and her court was running scared.

"Did you make it home safely? If you need anything from me, let me know. I'll do whatever I can to help you through this. Grant."

She'd willed the words to unfurl into a letter, a novel, or at least a paragraph. And then she'd done nothing. She'd sent no reply, made no phone call. She'd stared at the message as if it was a snake on her coffee table. If she held still enough, it would slither away on its own.

Grant had excavated parts of her that even she didn't know existed, and she felt exposed, raw, and totally lost.

Now, Melinda twisted her pendant as she scanned the menu without reading it. *What Would Chandi Do?* Were her own actions cruel enough to earn the wrath of the goddess?

Cold air rushed the restaurant as Melisa pushed through the glass door. She scanned the seating area, found Melinda, and smiled her way toward her. Melisa wasn't scared of love or life or anything, Melinda guessed. She had experienced real terror and had emerged stronger for it.

Melisa set down her jacket and bag and moved to Melinda's side to hug her.

"How you holding up?" She pulled back but kept her hands on Melinda's shoulders. "I'm glad you called me. That was really brave."

The choice of words couldn't have stung more if she'd called Melinda a waste of space, and Melinda took rapid deep breaths.

"Oh, I'm so sorry." Melisa embraced her once again. "I know, it's the absolute worst when you're vulnerable and someone's nice to you. You can make it if you can fake it, right? And here I go rubbing salt in the wound." Melisa held Melinda until she got herself together, then pulled back, checked Melinda's face, and circled the table to slide onto her seat.

"What are we doing first?" Melisa asked. "Food or feelings?"

Melinda's lips twitched. "They're basically the same to me. Let's do food first. Otherwise I'll keep thinking that we could be eating now if we'd just ordered sooner."

Both women scanned the list of items and Melinda used the time to calm down. She had requested this lunch date. Melisa was the one person who could understand her right now. Talking about this would be therapeutic.

Right. That was why her stomach was in knots.

"I recommend the falafel." Melinda forced buoyancy into her voice. "And the hummus here is really good. Lots of garlic, if you're into that. Unless you have clients this afternoon?" she added as she imagined a healing treatment from someone with garlic breath.

"My afternoon client canceled. Bring on the onions!" Melisa grinned as the waiter came over and took their order. "Wine? Beer?"

"I thought you'd never ask," Melinda replied.

"And now . . . the rough stuff." A smile softened Melisa's face. "How's it been? The police haven't shown up at our apartment yet so I'm guessing you're still thinking things over?"

Melinda appreciated Melisa's willingness to discuss the legal side of the dilemma, but nothing was leading her in that direction.

"I don't know how much to tell you," Melinda began, and then searched the other woman's face. Melisa touched the back of Melinda's hand.

"I'm here," she said. "I'm not going anywhere. I've admired Grant, or the projection of Grant that I've heard about, for a while now. Whatever happened between you two is safe with me."

Melinda gave her a watery smile, but no tears came.

"I told you a little bit already. Well, to set the record straight, I seduced him." Melisa's brows lifted. "But I should start further back than that, because it started right from the beginning, when he picked me up at the airport." She thought a moment. "There was something about him. I'd never experienced that with anyone before. It was . . . magnetic. We were flirty, we talked. The air sizzled, you know?"

Melisa nodded.

"And then we passed my car and he turned just awful. There's a partition in that Mercedes, do you know that?" Melisa shook her head. Her face had worn an expression of convivial acceptance and now it broadcast shock. Melisa would know what that partition meant, what terror Melinda would have suffered.

"Yeah." Heat crept up her throat as she relived that night. "The driver can block out the back seat passenger. He didn't believe that I wasn't you, and he was all keyed up because we had this connection, and he took out his frustration on me by shutting me out. Good to know about a person, really." She studied an adjoining table.

Don't forget, though: you spot it, you got it, her mother said in her mind. The expression was shorthand for saying that Melinda, too, dealt with her feelings by shutting out other people.

Give it a rest, Dr. Sen.

"Anyway, he felt terrible when we got to the cabin and it turned out I wasn't you. We had driven all the way up there and were stranded, and he had the wrong person. There was no way out. And then he gave me Paul's gun." Melisa's eyes widened again. "But I stopped carrying it pretty quickly because he made it completely unnecessary. He didn't touch me once. He tried so hard to make me comfortable. And it turned out that he was into me." Melinda half-smiled at her shredded napkin.

"Also as it turned out, he's pretty nice. Handsome. Wonderful," she added quietly. Melinda traced her index finger around the rim of her wineglass. Their unorthodox adventure hinted at the edges of her vision. Building the snowman. The branch, and Grant carrying her back to the cabin.

"I cooked basically every meal. He ate everything I made for him, which is key for me, of course," Melinda smiled. "But he was the one going outside all the time to get snow to melt for water. He was the one splitting wood so he could keep the fire going. He tried so hard to make it up to me." Melinda gripped her fork. "For me. With me. I've never had a man do that before. He just . . . really listened when I talked," she finished lamely.

But it was more than that. What was it? Melinda's mind churned. It was time to talk about it. She dragged her fingers through her hair.

"I got a very distinct taste of what it was to not feel lonely," Melinda said, throat tight. "And instead I felt close, and connected, and wanted." The pain in admitting that hit her like a blow and her stomach clenched. "I guess not feeling wanted is kind of a thing for me."

Their food arrived, and Melinda realized they hadn't touched their wine. That wouldn't do at all. She took a long sip and said a silent prayer for salvation.

"I would have fallen for him, too," Melisa said. She leaned across the table and fixed Melinda with gray eyes. "Hook, line, and sinker. So if there's any part of you feeling shame about what you did, hug it and tell it it's okay, but then let it go."

Melinda closed her eyes and took a deep breath.

When she opened them, Melisa was lifting her glass, sipping, and sighing her appreciation. "This is the way to do it," she said. "Wine and feelings for lunch." She took a longer sip, and Melinda joined her.

Both women began their meals, and Melinda was relieved to find her choice in restaurants hadn't failed her. Neither spoke for some minutes.

"Well, how was it, then?" Melisa asked at last.

Melinda choked on her dolma. "It?"

"Yeah, it," said Melisa. "*It.* I figure, we've known each other about a week now. That's long enough for you to be able to comfortably explore your sex life with me, right?"

Melinda laughed.

"Plus, you teased me," Melisa continued. "You told me you seduced him. I'm dying of curiosity over here."

Why not? Melinda had no one else with whom to discuss her liaison. "It was . . . divine." Melisa grinned. "It was exciting. I did things I'd never done before. I haven't had that many lovers," she said. "I've never experienced anything like the freedom I felt with him. Up there, in the mountains. Despite our lack of freedom," she added, unable to enjoy the irony.

She picked up and then put down her fork.

"But what if that's all it was? Magic up there? What if I fell for some guy because we had crazy sex and he's a total jerk? What if it was just a hookup for him?"

"Have you talked with him about it?" Melisa's face was open, but there was something else there, too. A small tension at the eyes.

She knows something.

"No. Well, he texted me once, but it was the first night back and I . . . I didn't respond. I was too overwhelmed, just by being in my house, you know?" *Did* Melisa know? Had she experienced the same psychosomatic shutdown that Melinda had? And did she know when it would end?

"I totally get it," Melisa said. "When I was freed from those men, and was done talking with the cops and being checked out by the doctors . . ."

Melinda winced. What manner of hell had happened to Melisa?

"When I got home, it was the last place I wanted to be. It was like I could hear the walls breathing, like they were watching me. Nowhere was safe, no matter how many times I checked the doors and windows."

She smiled at Melinda. "Are you okay with this? Is this too much?"

"No!" Melinda jumped to answer. "It's not too much. This is like someone articulating the way my mind works now. It's great to not feel crazy!" She checked herself. "Not that you sound crazy. At all. Um."

Melisa smiled. "Don't worry about it. Nothing about the last week has been sane for you, and my experience certainly wasn't sane, either."

Melinda jabbed at her food with her fork. "Could I . . ." Would this be too far? "Could I ask you about being with Paul? After you got released and were putting yourself back together. You said it was too soon. How did you deal with having feelings for someone as you were simultaneously going through a breakdown?" She laughed. "Or at least, that's what this feels like to me."

Melisa smiled at her. "It was bizarre, is how it was. I felt guilty for getting all tingly over someone when I should be watching Jodie Foster movies and learning kickboxing." Melinda laughed again and the other woman tilted her head at her.

"But this is about you and Grant, right? Why do you feel bad about being interested in him? He sounds like he really came through for you."

"He did, later . . ." Melinda said. "But what kind of woman sleeps with a guy who ignored her when she was screaming for her life? The same woman who would fall for that guy, too, I guess." She tightened her stomach, which was suddenly close to rejecting her meal.

Melisa watched as she wrestled with her shame. Again, there was no disgust on her face, only compassion.

"What's wrong with forgiveness, Melinda? What's wrong with allowing him to not be the jerk you feared?"

Melinda's hands slid up to her shoulders, her arms crisscrossing her chest like armor.

"Why did I let him do that to me? What the hell is wrong with me? When did I become so bloody stupid?"

Melisa moved around to Melinda's side. "What did you let him do to you? Care for you under extreme circumstances? There's nothing wrong with that, or with you. You are not stupid. All of these feelings are totally normal." She wrapped an arm around Melinda's rigid shoulders. "You have a heart, you have a brain. You're learning how to use both of them, just like the rest of us."

Melisa sighed. "I want to tell you something, though," she said. Melinda turned to face her from behind her personal barricade. "Grant gave me a letter to give to you. Maybe it will ease some of your doubts. Would you like me to show it to you?"

Curve ball. Would I? She dropped her hands to the table. Who was she kidding? Of course she would.

As much as she dreaded it, Melinda was dying for some kind of contact from him, and a letter was the perfect vehicle. His words, his realness, his essence, safely contained on paper where she could put them aside if they got too strong. Too strong? No, that wasn't it. Too present. That was it. Grant had come at her with complexity, strength, vulnerability, and not a little bit of masculinity, and she had been completely thrown by it. He had put himself in her shoes and tried to help her. He hadn't lost interest at the first sign of resistance. He had completely shaken up her world. No wonder she had ignored him.

Melinda grabbed the envelope from Melisa's hand a millisecond early, but then she froze.

There was her name written on the outside. A simple word. Written with what? Haste? Urgency? Emotion? Rejection? Pity? Her eyes burned holes into the angled, blockish letters.

This is ridiculous, her mind offered helpfully. *Open it!* She turned the envelope over to reveal the flap, released the small patch of stuck adhesive, and drew out Grant's letter.

Melinda, the first page began—first page? Yes, it appeared the first page was addressed to her and a second page was addressed to the police—and the noise of the restaurant faded. Melisa disappeared. Even the table with its uneven tile and her stiff-backed wrought-iron bistro chair melted away.

> *Melinda,*
>
> *I hope you're all right with me writing to you. I wanted to say a few things, and Melisa suggested writing them down.*
>
> *Writing you is harder than I thought it would be. Not because I'm not thinking of you, because I am. I'm thinking of you every minute. But I don't know what you're going through and I don't want to complicate your life.*
>
> *I want you to know that if you need me, I'm there. If you want to ask me anything, all you have to do is call me. Talk to Melisa, she knows how to reach me. But if that never happens, I want you to know that meeting you changed my life. I had been living in a kind of okay state for a long time. For years, I guess. I hadn't been willing to go the ultimate distance and pass through old pain into the next level.*
>
> *Our car ride together showed me that I have some issues to work on. I'm sorry for that, and I also have to have gratitude for you for that realization. I wish you hadn't suffered so much in order for me to recognize that jealousy was rearing its head, and so was fear.*
>
> *Our time at the cabin together showed me that*

I'm ready to take the next step in loving a woman where it isn't destined to fail right from the start. Not that it was their fault. It was always mine. I was the one who chose them again and again.

I don't want you to feel like you have to make me feel better or that you can't go to the police. You need to do what's best for you and for what's going to help you sleep at night. I'm ready every day to hear from them.

But not talking with you feels like drowning. Because it's not any woman I want to be with. It's you. I want to be with you, only you. I'm scared just writing that, but I also feel better getting it out.

Whatever you need from me, I'll be there.

Grant, your mountain man.

Grant swung the maul and exploded the log in front of him. Shards and splinters flew at his legs and three split pieces dropped to the ground. He didn't trust himself to drive the plow, and besides, the snowfall had stopped after their rescue. Bryan and his team could handle it. And what if those felled trees didn't get dealt with? The whole property would go to ruin.

Keep lying to yourself as you waste a perfectly good Friday afternoon, Samson.

Wow, was he full of shit. His dad thought so, too, and made no attempt to sugarcoat it. The Sunday after he returned, Grant had finally come clean about what had happened at Paul's cabin.

"Well, what the hell is wrong with you, Rant?" Buck Samson had wasted no time in dusting off Grant's childhood nickname.

218

Not a good sign.

"What?" Grant had snapped the ends off a handful of green beans and chucked them in a bowl like he wasn't actively pondering that same question. They were ostensibly spending time cooking together, father and son, seeker and confidant. But Grant had a suspicion he was in for a tribunal instead of a supportive shoulder.

"Go after the girl, that's what." Buck slid a sheet of chunked beets, yams, sweet and purple potatoes, and onions into the oven. Grant's dad had gone vegan after his mother died, and even though Grant hadn't, he enjoyed the creativity his dad mustered up. They'd roast the root vegetables, steam the beans, and eat the leftover squash soup from the night before. All in all, a comforting meal for a winter night.

Grant had pondered his father's words all night long and wondered if his dad wasn't right. Should he go after the girl? What did that even mean? *Go after her.* It sounded like a risky proposition; he'd already done that, in a manner of speaking, and it left him waiting for the sheriff to arrive.

What could he say to her that he hadn't said already? He'd texted her the first night they'd been home. He'd been nearly climbing the walls from being away from her after such close quarters. She hadn't replied.

Grant hadn't slept that Sunday night after his dad's insights. He decided it was time to check on Paul again. *Because all good friends call each other at 7:00 a.m. on a Monday, don't they?*

"You again. I'll get Melisa," Paul had said, disgusted.

"No!" Grant had yelled. *Shit.* "Don't get—Oh, hey Melisa." Grant's voice was a full octave higher than normal. He cleared his throat to find his bass. "Yes, well, I was wondering if you'd talked with Melinda. To see how she's doing. You know, to check on her?" Not because he missed her body like a phantom limb.

Not because he yearned to pour her a glass of wine and talk with her by the light of a fire somewhere.

Melisa's silence was the answer he'd dreaded. "It's okay, it's fine . . . Yeah, fine," he babbled. "She had a rough time and I just thought maybe she'd want to talk with you. But, hey, no news is good news, right?"

"Grant . . ." Melisa's reply was measured. "Do you think maybe *you'd* like to talk with *her*?"

Was it that obvious? *Nah, probably only from space.*

"I mean, yeah, sure, I guess. To see how she's doing. If she needs any help."

Melisa paused for a moment. "Grant, would you consider writing her a letter? Then if she does contact me I could share it with her, and she'd know how you feel. That you want to 'check on her,'" she finished delicately.

"Yeah, sure. Great idea," he said, desperate to get off the phone.

After they'd hung up and Grant had been alone once again, he'd spent a full twenty minutes pondering the start of a letter to Melinda. Then instead of writing one he'd stood from his desk and gone back to the woodpile.

A good idea, maybe, but who had the time? There was too much work; on property like this, there was always work. There was comfort in work. There was avoidance in work.

But after an hour of splitting wood, the pressure of his thoughts had become too much. Was what he had done up there actually coercion? He tossed pieces aside, added another log to the block, and swung. Or worse, assault?

Grant rested the maul's head on the ground and stared at the property's frozen stream, forcing himself to further ponder the unconscionable. *Had* Melinda initiated sex with him, not once but twice, because she thought him dangerous and wanted

220

to stay in his good graces? The thought made him physically ill. Every moment, every kiss, every intimate touch—what if she'd thought they would save her life?

Disgust at himself surged through his veins. Barely seeing the round in front of him, he'd heaved the handle skyward and swung it home. A little too aggressively, it seemed, as the stump beneath the log had also split. Grant's arms burned with effort as his face burned with shame.

Suddenly he was done working. Grant left the split pieces on the ground and left the wedge in the stump—a big no-no, but he couldn't stop himself. He had something to do and something to say.

Grant had pushed through the back door, not bothering to remove his boots. He tromped down the hall, scattering wood shards onto his father's rugs. Grant didn't care. He had to get to his desk. He rounded the doorway to his office and dropped into the chair.

Just a quick note. He selected a piece of paper. He took a pen from the drawer and stared at it. He could do this. A few words would be okay. Nothing too aggressive, just a check-in.

Then he began writing, and then he was unable to stop. Putting the words on paper felt like a trance, and when he was finished he read them as if for the first time. Clunky but heartfelt. He folded the letter away. Worse would be to re-read and tweak it to death.

Grant felt better, but there was something missing. He needed to clear his conscience in a different way. He reached for another piece of paper.

> *To Whom It May Concern at the Police Department,*
> *I'm writing to confess to the kidnapping of*

Melinda Sen by means of a fake Kaar at DIA on Sunday, December 2nd, 2018. I took her to a cabin in the mountains and held her there for four days.

Her account of the story should be considered gospel. I am ready and willing to turn myself in at any time. Contact me at the number and address below.

Grant Samson

He tucked both letters into an envelope and sealed it, then wrote her name on the envelope's face. He felt lighter immediately. Something real had gone into those letters, and Grant felt free again. He felt alive. He drove down below to drop the envelope at Paul's apartment, then he turned around and came home.

The second he had pulled into his driveway, the anxiety kicked in. What the hell had he done? Could he never leave well enough alone?

Now, nine days later, he was a basket case. His thoughts were on paper, maybe already in Melinda's possession. Grant positioned a log on the splitting stump, eyed a crack that looked like it would give, and let the maul fly.

Thwack! He'd included a confession. Two pieces split. He grabbed the larger one to split again. She hadn't called.

Whoosh, thwack! More pieces. She hadn't texted.

Whoosh, thwack! Piece after piece.

She hadn't. She just hadn't.

But.

Go after the girl. Again, Grant let the maul rest on the stumps. Again, he moved as if in a trance toward the house. Where was his phone? *She said I could call her.*

Melinda stared at her phone. Her phone, fully charged, stared back from its place on her coffee table. It was always fully charged now; she couldn't sleep unless it was. *Oh look, a coping mechanism.*

Speaking of which, it was time to call her parents. Which one, she didn't know. But it was time. Three nights ago, she'd dreamed of her mother and father. Last night, of her brother. They were calling to her; it was time to return the favor.

Melinda hadn't told anyone what had happened, but she'd been overrun with blog topics after the first week of post-liberation hibernation. She'd barely sat down for the last seven days—she'd been too busy crafting and drafting "Rock and a Hard Place Chili," "Snowed-In Spaghetti," and "Lost Cabin Muesli," among others.

"Trapped Tiramisu" was an immediate hit among her internet friends. It was the typical concoction of ladyfingers, espresso, and whipped cream, but she'd trapped treasures between the layers—crumbled pistachios, bitter chocolate flakes, white chocolate mini-chips. The aim had been to represent the surprise joys of being snowbound; the taste had been unusual but satisfying.

"Can't Cry Cauliflower" had been another fun one. She'd oiled cauliflower florets, spiced them to within an inch of their life, and roasted them until tender and a teeny bit crispy on the edges. Then she'd eaten them like spicy popcorn on the couch while watching *The Notebook* and trying to release pent-up feelings.

It hadn't worked. Not since the lunch with Melisa a week ago had she been able to so much as tear up. Now everything seemed distant and dull.

It didn't fool her, though. Her poise was a veneer. Her stability was a time bomb. She didn't know when the collapse was coming, but it was coming. She checked her phone again. It was 9:17 p.m., or 8:17 in Bellingham. Was that too late? She hoped not. What was her excuse for calling them? *Umm. Right.* Of course.

Christmas was coming, and while Melinda normally pretended to glory in the holiday with its pomp, circumstance, and indulgence, this year was different. This year she felt intimidated to the point of inaction. This year she was a head case and felt like she should spend time with her family.

Or maybe, you big chicken, you actually want to spend time with your family.

Melinda dropped her head into the couch cushion and asked the light fixture for help. Help was not forthcoming.

With a sigh, Melinda lifted her head and eyed her phone. Now or never. She dialed her mom. The phone rang twice, and then there was Katrina Sen.

"Malina?" Her Swedish-descended mother had always used her Hindi name, and Melinda secretly loved it.

"Mom?" Melinda said, throat immediately tight with tears. Oh sure, there they were.

"Baby," her mom said. "Baby, do you need me?" Melinda's skin flushed with an almost ancient sense of safety. *How do moms know?*

"I don't know." And then Melinda cried. She didn't know if she needed her mother to step in, though she loved the offer, and she certainly didn't know how much to tell her about the kidnapping. Then, after a few choked and uncertain minutes, unexpectedly, fluidly, almost entirely, it came out.

"Mom, something happened," she began. Then hurriedly

she followed with, "But I'm okay. I wasn't for a little while, and then I was, kind of, but now I'm confused. Really confused. Can you help me?" Tears flowed now, hot and urgent down her cheeks. "I don't know what to do."

"Of course, my love," her mother said, her voice an embrace around Melinda's shoulders.

And so Melinda talked. She talked and told and shared. She omitted the racy details but alluded to the intimacy. She felt safe doing so. Her mother wasn't opposed to consenting adults; she considered it a step in the process of learning about love, and had never shamed Melinda when she'd had boyfriends. Even in the midst of her overanalytical fervor, Katrina had the grace not to pick at the romantic part of Melinda's life. Melinda was suddenly very grateful for that.

"Oh Malina," her mother breathed. "That is one hell of a story. Are you sure you're okay? Have you talked to anyone about this?"

Melinda knew better than to try to BS her mother. "Not really," she said. "It's weird, but I've felt pretty good talking to Melisa, that guy Paul's girlfriend. She gets where my head is, so I can tell her any crazy thing that comes to mind." She fiddled with the tassels on the pillow. "I don't know what to do about this guy, Mom."

"Do you have to do something about him?"

Such a shrink answer.

"Is it okay that I'm interested in him?"

"Why wouldn't it be?"

"Seriously?" That was too therapisty, even for a therapist. "Isn't it masochistic or codependent or something, to pursue something with him?" A rogue thread loosed itself from the tassel and she failed to resist the urge to tug it.

"Those are big words, sweetie, with a lot of meaning behind

them." Her mother could pacify an atom bomb. "What are you worried about? That if you follow your heart you'll have no self-worth?"

"Well . . . yeah," Melinda said. "Wouldn't I have no self-worth if I chased the guy who kidnapped me and ignored me when I needed help?" She spun her hair into a knot. "What the hell is wrong with me that I let that kind of person get close to me? Am I that broken?"

"You don't have to be broken to feel a connection with someone, sweetheart. I know you met under terrifying circumstances. But the beginning is simply that—the beginning. It's how you deal with the beginning that matters. And from what you told me, Grant did the best he could to make your situation as comfortable as possible."

"But what about everyone else? What am I going to tell Max? And Grandma?"

"That you're dating someone that you met at the airport."

Melinda's laugh sounded like a sob. "But won't Dad want to beat him up or something?"

"When have you ever known your father to want to beat up anyone?"

"Never." Precisely why Melinda was so mad at him.

"Do you want your father to want to beat him up, Malina?"

"Of course I do!" Melinda burst out. "I want him to defend me! Even if this guy's Mr. Perfect. He'd never dream of standing up for me like that. He'd never protect me. He never has."

"It's okay to let people evolve, my love," her mother said. "It's okay to let Grant change from the mistakes of that first day. I know I've had to learn more than a little from your father about forgiveness."

"What?" Melinda was confused. What did her father have to teach? Or forgive?

"After your sister died and I got so depressed, I took my anguish out on the three of you, something I know you're painfully aware of. He weathered that just as you had to. I had to learn that sometimes acceptance and stillness look the same."

"Mom . . ." Melinda had no idea how to query into what alternate universe they'd wandered, and she was more than a little afraid to break the spell by asking for specifics.

"I'm here, sweetheart," her mother answered, and it was like she really was. Melinda felt her mother's presence fill her living room, all acceptance and openness.

"Where were you?" Melinda's voice was small, and she realized the question made no sense. She didn't care. "Where did you go?"

"Oh, sweetheart." Her mother sighed. Melinda was afraid her mother would keep her answer topical, but she needn't have worried. Topical wasn't Katrina Sen's style.

"I don't know. Well, yes I do, I was in grief. I was in horrible grief and I took it out on you, and your father, and your brother. You didn't deserve it. I know you did your best to survive my pain. And then when my grief ended, I had lost my chance with you, and you were gone."

Melinda placed her fingers on her chest where the words pierced her heart.

"You were gone physically," her mother said, "and when I reached out to you, I felt like you were gone from me emotionally as well. And you had every right to be."

Melinda put the phone down on the couch and stared at it. Maybe it wasn't an alternate universe. Maybe it was the Bermuda Triangle, where all reason was lost, never to emerge again.

"But you tell me," her mother continued as Melinda took up the phone. "How does that feel to hear? I trust your experience as much as I trust my own. More, in some cases. What was it like for you?"

Her mother was right. She had reached out to Melinda after Melinda had gone away to college, but Melinda had assumed—wrongly, it seemed—that her mother wanted to pick up criticizing her where she'd left off. How many times had her mother tried? Melinda didn't want to count.

"Mom . . . Mom, it was so lonely." The tears returned. "I needed you, and the only way I could have you just hurt." Melinda could hear her mother's sniffing now, too. "We saw you all the time, but it was like you weren't there. And when you did talk to us, you just wanted to beat us down. Everything we did was wrong. I couldn't keep up with trying to make you happy." Melinda's words came fast, almost as fast as her tears.

"I know, baby, I know."

She's not denying it, Melinda marveled. *There's no wall here. Where the hell is the wall?* For the last fifteen years Melinda had either experienced or avoided a figurative wall of denial built wide and strong in front of her mother. And now Dr. Sen was owning it all.

"You do?"

"Yes," her mother said simply. "I get it. I hear you and I'm so sorry. That is not what I wanted for you. It's not who I wanted to be as a mother for you. And then to watch you shut down in the same way I had done, well, it absolutely broke my heart. That wasn't what I wanted for you either." Her mother drew a shaky breath.

It was time to take a risk. "I'd really love to see you guys. It's been so long. Are you all booked for the holidays?"

"Do you want Daddy and me to come?" her mother asked. "Dad and I will come. Aarjav," she called, and Melinda started. Her mother was with her father? "Aarjav, honey, Malina needs us." Her mother must have covered the phone as the two talked because then Melinda could no longer make out the words.

"Malina?" Kat was back. "Your father's students have turned in their final exams and he is free to travel. He has to grade their midterm accounting tests but he can grade while we travel. I don't have patients until after the new year. Would you like us to come?"

Melinda couldn't speak. What had just happened? Her mother was seeing patients again? Her mother was on speaking terms with her father? Speaking-in-person terms? She had thought she'd call her mother, tell her an abbreviated version of the truth, maybe get some sideways maternal support that would carry her through the holidays. Suddenly Mom and Dad were going to turn her Christmas into a Norman Rockwell painting. *If Norman Rockwell painted Christmas in West Bengal.*

She hadn't answered her mother. Would she like them to come? Wasn't that exactly what she wanted? For them to come and steep her in safety and love and to heal her fears.

"Yes!" Melinda said at last. "Yes, really? I would love that! It'll be so expensive last-minute, I'm sorry."

It was settled. They'd fly out this weekend, and stay into January to celebrate Swami Vivekananda Jayanti, a holiday in honor of the holy swami who had introduced meditation and Hinduism to the Western world.

"Dad and I follow your blog," her mother was saying, "and we love it. We watch how your beautiful self comes through in it, and that gives us comfort. I hope it's as fulfilling for you as it seems from this side of the computer screen."

"You read my blog?" Melinda should buy a Lotto ticket.

"Oh, yes," her mother said. "We love it. We take turns reading it to each other every week. It's really fun. Sometimes we recognize recipes from when you were growing up, and sometimes it's all new and we cook along with you."

Holy cannoli! This is a love-in. Melinda clutched a throw pillow to her torso in lieu of a group hug.

"I don't know what to say . . ."

"It's okay, baby. You did great. You're doing great. We're going to come be with you, and we'll talk more about this man of yours. We'll get it sorted out, don't worry. Now, do you want to tell Mafi or should we? I know you two haven't spoken much, but he misses you and would be there in a heartbeat if you asked."

Melinda's head was swimming.

Her chest squeezed with fear, then released. *Oh.* Her mother wasn't trying to expose Melinda's week of sordid undoing. Her mother was visiting a state where both of her children lived and Christmas was coming and she wanted to invite her son. How had Melinda missed this family reunion?

"I will," Melinda said. Suddenly she wanted to. She didn't want to jinx things, but the conversation had gone so well with her mother that she dared to hope for a renewed connection with her brother.

Yes. She'd call him. Tomorrow.

After his mother had died, Grant hadn't been one for Christmas. Not that while she was alive he'd been decking the halls. Every year, he'd enjoyed the time with family, and every year he had, at the first opportunity, gotten back to work. Since she'd been gone, he was comfortable adopting the more overt role of family Grinch, and purposefully did nothing celebratory the whole Christmas season. He dodged gatherings, vetoed parties, and nixed mixers and countdowns. This year, however, he finally had an inkling of what coupled people might do, and the recognition rankled.

"Dad," Grant called from behind his computer where he drafted the next month's schedule.

"Yeah," said Buck from the doorway to the office and Grant jumped.

"Christ," he said.

"You lookin' to put Him back in the season?" his dad shot back, deadpan.

Grant refused to laugh. "What are you doing hovering there?"

"I wanted a front row seat to you pissing your life away."

"I'm not pissing my life away. I have a great life. We have a great life." Grant didn't know exactly why he was arguing or what he was defending, but it was important, whatever it was.

"We're biding our time until death comes and bags our asses," his dad said, but then belied his jab by taking a swig of some kind of freshly-pressed green beverage.

"How can you drink that stuff in the dead of winter?" Grant asked. "It's too cold for something so bitter."

"You want to argue with me about vegetal enzymes, or did you have something relevant to say?"

Grant's father had no time for anxiety, which was inconvenient, because Grant's anxiety felt like it was going to take a while.

"I just hate this season. Want to get out of Dodge for a while?"

Buck snorted into his glass and shot the juice's fluffy green foam into his whitening eyebrows.

"Contemplating a cruise, are we? Where do you want to go? Jamaica? Might not be far enough away to escape your tomfoolery. Oh wait, I know—Egypt. Then you can sail right down your favorite river—*denial.*" He turned away chortling at his own joke.

"Wait!" Grant stifled the urge to combat the insinuation.

Buck's head swiveled toward Grant but his body was still bound for the hallway. "Make it worth my while."

Dammit.

"You've got juice in your eyebrows."

"I'm leaving," his father said from the hallway.

Grant leapt to his feet.

"First, how do I know if I'm in love with her? And second, what's the maximum years I could get for sexual coercion?"

Buck returned to face Grant where he stood.

"I say if you were going to end up in jail you'd be there already. From what you've told me, that young lady has a good head on her shoulders and can string a couple sentences together. If she'd wanted to go to the cops, she would've by now. I'm not saying she shouldn't, I'm just saying you'd know. What you're doing is using that remote possibility as an energy suck and letting it dominate your thinking because you're scared to death of how you feel about her."

Buck took a long draw from his juice.

"If you were any other numb-nuts than my own son, I'd tell you to sleep on it. But I've been watching you for the past two weeks, and you're a train wreck. It's not the guilt. Don't waste your time wondering if it's that. You're over the moon for this woman. You've split every chunk of wood not holding up this house, and I'm afraid to leave you alone with Mom's rocking chair."

Two weeks and two days. Grant thought it best to keep his mouth shut.

"You're in love with her," Buck continued. "The question you should be asking is what to do about it. How to repair this shitty situation you find yourself in. And I'm going to tell you the answer that's going to work every time, in every situation, no matter what, so listen up."

Buck punctuated this wisdom with more juice.

"You call her. You ask her if she wants to talk about it. You tell her you want to hear what she has to say, and then you shut the hell up and *listen*." Sip. "You listen until she's done. You pay attention, so that when she's done, you can ask her pertinent questions about her experience. You don't tell her how to get over it, not unless you never want to see her again. After you two have talked about her experience, then—and only then—do you bring up *your* experience." Sip. "You apologize for where you messed up, you tell her you've learned from those mistakes, and you fess up to how you feel." Buck drained his glass. "That's the formula. You make it through that equation enough times over the next fifty years, you might achieve partial enlightenment. But don't count on it. You're still a numb-nuts."

"This man of yours," her mother had said. But was he really hers? Did he really want her? And did Melinda really want him? He'd sent her a freaking love letter. What did she want, a sky-writer?

What's wrong with modern men? she grumbled into her cabbage. She was in her kitchen again, pounding the beginnings of sauerkraut with a sturdy wooden pestle in an earthenware crock. Inspiration was rising like bread dough and her professional life continued to blossom. That morning she had kneaded and punched down real dough and left it to rise in a slightly warm oven. She'd rubbed two frying chickens with a mixture of minced garlic, ginger, coriander, salt, pepper, and paprika and set them in the fridge to marinate. Then she'd drafted and scheduled a blog for each one.

What was wrong was that he couldn't read her mind and she'd given him absolutely no reason to contact her again. Melinda shook her head. Couldn't she just focus? It took a surprising amount of elbow grease to crush the salted cabbage well enough for it to produce brine. But it felt good to strain physically. It felt good to keep herself occupied, to be free of the couch-aholic blues.

For all her productivity, she hadn't actually ventured into the world, outside of meeting Melisa for lunch over a week ago. Once or twice she'd gotten as far as grabbing her purse but hadn't made it out the door, despite Paul and Melisa having had her car towed home the week before. Something was trapping her inside. Christmastime and agoraphobia were not good bedfellows, she conceded, but it was more than that.

Her world was crumbling and she knew it.

The conference had splintered her identity so that she didn't know what was real and what was false. The madness in the mountains had cracked her sense of safety, but more so her sense of self. The phone call with her mother had shone hope on her future, but also illuminated that she was in the driver's seat of her own collision course. And maybe it was time to steer clear. It all added up to the fact that Melinda could no longer pretend that her persona was good enough for her readers, her relationships, or herself. She could no longer pretend that operating solo was fulfilling, or that her facsimile of a life left her anything but empty.

But fake it 'til you make it, right?

Faking it is what got you here, her mind retaliated. And here was alone and afraid.

Melinda set aside the pestle and dug into the wilted gallon of shredded cabbage, combing through it to expose pieces that had avoided the salt storm. A blunt instrument worked well for the majority, but nothing beat a hands-on search for the missing pieces.

Apparently the food parallel for realizing you've got to change your entire life was sauerkraut.

Melinda swirled her hands through the strands, grateful that she had something to do so as to not go plumb crazy in her isolated convalescence. Cooking had been where she'd turned in the past when she'd needed to keep busy. Cooking had been what her father had done when her mother had miscarried. Cooking was what made up the majority of her happy childhood memories. How many other families' love language was slaving away in the kitchen? She laughed quietly.

Melinda had set Bengal gram, a chickpea relative, to soak after the call with her mother, and the next day drained them of their water to let them germinate. Now they had sprouted and were ready to be cooked. She'd let her parents decide the recipe. Melinda's job was to create the bones of the meal, and Kat and Aarjav would arrange, accent, and adorn it—a power couple of presentation.

Melinda's chest warmed at the thought of cooking with her parents again. *Don't get ahead of yourself.* They weren't there yet. There was plenty of time for Mr. Sen to emotionally evacuate. Melinda paused mid-maceration. Why did she loathe her father so? She stared at the kitchen cabinets. It was a morning for revelations, might as well dig deep. *Because he left me.* He had been right there with her but he was gone the whole time. He had let her mother chew them up and spit them out, and did nothing to help.

She pounded harder. Was that fair? Was that accurate?

Not entirely, but that was how it felt. The cabbage was turning to slippery rubber and releasing its liquid. Could she allow her father to have experienced his own pain and to have made his own mistakes without believing him a demon? Or worse, a weakling? Could she forgive her father for doing the best that he could, which hadn't been enough for her, but was better than many would have done? Melinda twisted the cabbage. It was a disarming thought.

Too disarming. She wiped her hands on her apron. Time to evaluate the decor. *I'm not avoiding, you're avoiding.*

In lieu of braving the swarm of humanity teeming outside her door, Melinda had been shopping online for everything, including fresh food. Turned out it was disturbingly easy to accomplish; people would deliver anything these days. As such, a bright red poinsettia adorned the stoop and her new fake tree hosted approximately a thousand twinkly lights. Two more lush poinsettias dressed up her dining and coffee tables. Fresh garlands lined her countertops and festooned her picture windows. More greenery, in the form of a wreath, warmed her front door. Over-the-top gold-trimmed stockings dangled from brass hooks on the west wall. It wasn't quite a fireplace, but she wasn't quite expecting Santa Claus, so it would have to do.

The food was in the works. The spare bed was made. The decor was adequate, as was the sauerkraut project. It was time to call Grant.

Melinda's stomach knotted. She picked up her phone and scrolled past Grant's name to her brother's, then scrolled further.

Chicken, she thought. She called Melisa instead.

"I'm glad you called; I was cleaning on top of my refrigerator. Guess who's escaping bookkeeping duty?" Melisa laughed.

Melinda's laugh was forced.

Now what? Say something!

Melisa took pity on her and filled the silence. "How're you doing this holiday season?"

"Fine, fine, yeah, thank you."

Melinda wondered if banging her head on the wall was audible over the phone.

Melisa tried again. "Do you have any plans with fam—"

"I can't leave the house," Melinda blurted out. "I can't figure it out. I'm not scared of anyone, I'm not scared of being alone . . . It's nothing like that. It's just that I feel so . . . naked?" She twisted her fingers through her hair. "That's absolutely the wrong thing to say but it's the word that comes to mind. Did you feel this way? Why do I feel this way?"

Melisa said nothing.

"It's just . . . I can't stop thinking about him," Melinda continued. "I can hear him repeating all the things he said to me at the cabin. He's saying them all to me here. And I say the same things back to him. And I'm so . . . exposed."

Melisa waited.

"Okay that's it. Do you have to go? I should go—"

"It's okay," Melisa entered the fray at last. "It's okay. You're okay. This is totally normal. *You* are normal. Maybe you don't feel a threat to your life, but you feel a threat to your ego, and that's essentially the same thing. You were incredibly vulnerable with Grant up there and it makes perfect sense that you'd feel the repercussions of that. Okay? Does that make sense?"

"Okay," Melinda said. "Yes. It does." And it did, and the tension she'd been feeling in her shoulders floated away like a gossamer scarf. "Okay. Yeah, that makes sense."

And then unfortunately it made so much sense, that Melinda had nothing else to say.

"Um, so do you have plans with family?"

Melisa laughed. "Heavens, no. Spare me that tornado, please. Melinda, go back to whatever you were doing. I'm fine. It's okay to call me in your moment of panic, and then it's okay to get back to your life. Leave your house, if you want to. Or don't. I'm here whenever you need me."

And so Melinda thanked her new friend, hung up, and held the phone in her hand.

"Let's keep this party going," she said. *Who's next?*

She hit a number and the phone rang, and rang, and rang again.

"You've reached Max Sen," her brother's recorded voice said. Melinda grimaced. She'd been on a roll there. What should she do? He'd see the missed call, so if she didn't leave a voicemail it would be awkward. Which meant she needed to leave a message. And say what? *Hey, sorry I alienated you, I've been caught up in my own drama and didn't have time to be a decent human being, want to come for Christmas?* Couldn't hurt.

The tone beeped. She was on.

"Hey Max," she said. "Hey, I know it's been a really long time, and I'm sorry. I shouldn't have done that. To you. Um . . . I called Mom, and she and Dad are flying in today. Crazy, right?" She laughed awkwardly. "So, uh, want to stop by? We could do a family thing? Bring back the Bengali Bling?" She unearthed a term they'd coined as kids to describe their family's over-the-top treatment of Christmas. "Give me a call. Let me know." Then, "*Ami tomake bhalobasi.*" She hung up. *I love you.*

Melinda laid the phone on the counter with a mixture of relief and sadness. She picked up her mallet to resume the assault on the cabbage and the phone rang.

"Max!" she answered, joy overflowing.

"Beloved *Didi*," he answered, and she heard his smile. He had called her sister.

She walked to the couch. "Did you get my message? Mom and Dad are coming. Do you want to . . ." She couldn't finish the sentence. How could she? *Do you want to be my brother again? Forgive me? Give me advice about this guy that took me*

238

prisoner and I might kinda love him but I'm so confused I can't leave my house?

"Would you like to join us? For Christmas?" she finished, and cringed. What was he, her office assistant?

"*Didi*, you suck at this." Melinda settled on the cushions and let her eyes play on the rocks outside. "Mom called me yesterday, thinking you would've already contacted me. You're behind the curve."

"It's you busybodies," she shot back. "Always have to be planning something, can't just let someone take her time."

He snorted. "You taking your time means I haven't seen you in two years. I'm collecting *Mata ji* and *Pita ji* from the airport today at two." She started. She hadn't even thought about how her mother and father would get to her house from the airport; she just knew that she wasn't ready to drive there herself.

"Thank you," she said.

"You know you can count on me to pick up your slack," he said. Melinda stilled. "Then we're all descending upon you," he continued, "so get your chutney going. But we have plenty of time now for you to come clean about this guy who's sniffing around. Grunt, was it? Tell me about him. Ma says we're not allowed to have him killed."

Melinda wrapped a tamarind-and-turmeric-colored throw around her shoulders and grinned.

"His name is *Grant*." She aimed for righteous indignation and fell completely short. "And no, we can't have him killed. He hasn't done anything wrong." She caught herself. How could she mean that? He kidnapped her! He tortured her! *Remember*, she thought. *Forgiveness is not wrong, and he tortured no one.* Look at that, she was growing as a person. He hadn't done anything wrong, and that included having feelings for her, reaching out to her, or waiting to hear from her. "But we might have to do something, because he knows too much."

Max laughed and Melinda smiled. She had forgotten how much she loved to hear her brother laugh.

"*Didi*," he said. "Mom says you're gaga over him."

"Oh great." Melinda's eyes rolled skyward.

"She told me some crazy story where you guys ended up stranded at a cabin during that huge blizzard a couple weeks ago. He saved your life, yeah? You okay? I wanted to call after I heard, but she told me to let you do you."

Melinda exhaled. Is that what her brother had been doing? Letting her do her? And what had she been doing? Assuming the worst of him. She shook her head—back to the phone call. Was that the picture her mother had painted of her encounter with Grant? Not too bad. She could work with that.

She filled in Max on the details—the Kaar decoy, the blizzard, the power outage. The walk in the snow, the head wound. That she had had . . . significant interactions with Grant and was maybe accidentally totally in love with him. She heard herself say as much to Max and caught her breath but hurried on. Grant had poured his heart out. Melinda had opened up but then just as quickly shut down, and hadn't replied. Melinda had gone underground.

"So yeah," she finished. "Yeah, I think he's kind of great, *Bhai*." Her chest hurt. She loved her little brother so much. "I know he's great. No 'kind of' about it. But what do I do?"

"Well, hell," said Max. "We gotta rope this guy in, don't we? I'm on it. Let me think."

"Think?" Melinda said, confused. "Rope him in? What?"

"Lina." Melinda's chest warmed at his use of her nickname. "Too much time has passed. You left the guy hanging. And speaking of leaving someone hanging, *Didi*, what the bloody hell? You think you're going to disappear on me for two years,

240

and then just leave me a message and we're all good? Where the hell did you go? What the hell did I do?"

Melinda's stomach sank so low it hit her toes.

"Max . . ."

"Seriously, Lina, was I that bad of a cellmate that you absolved any knowledge of knowing me? I haven't even gotten a birthday card!"

"It's not like you called me, either!"

"It's not like you gave me the option! You didn't even tell me you'd gotten a condo. I found out from Mom last spring after a mailer I sent you bounced back from your place downtown."

"Mailer?"

"Yeah, a mailer. An invitation. My band opened at Red Rocks and I wanted you to be there."

Now Melinda's stomach hurt. This was the opposite of the conversation she'd had with her mother. Her brother was looking for accountability and, unlike her mother, Melinda was ducking for cover. She'd abandoned her brother when each had been the only close family the other had had. He'd reached out to her and she hadn't even bothered to send him a forwarding address.

"Max," she said. "I was just . . . falling apart. But I didn't know I was falling apart. I thought I was independent. I thought I was focusing on my career. I had to focus on my career. Hawking oven timers takes a while to add up to a mortgage."

Silence answered her. *Okay, that was weak.* She sighed.

"The truth is that it was easier to blame it on you," she admitted. "I had already blamed Mom and Dad for everything that happened in Bellingham, so when we both ended up here, you pretty much became the scapegoat for things that didn't go my way."

She wondered if he'd hung up.

"Yeah. Yeah, that's about how it felt," Max said finally and the pain in his voice seared her heart. Anger shielded sadness.

"I'm sorry," she said, the phone pressed hard to her ear, her knees wedged beneath her. "I'm so sorry. I didn't know what to do. I didn't know that I was so broken."

Max sighed. "It's okay, Lina. I get it. I haven't exactly been the perfect brother, either. The first half of my twenties could stand a serious shoeshine."

Melinda sniffed, heart in her throat. Could he forgive her?

"But look," he said. "It doesn't matter how perfect this guy is, you gotta make a grand gesture if you want him to remember your name. And since I'm coming to your soiree, I want to make sure he's worth the effort. Plus, it's Christmas, and we're Bengali. Go big or go home. It'll make for a good blog."

Relief washed through Melinda's limbs and cooled her anxious core.

"Wait, what?" she asked. "Are you reading my blog now, too?"

"Of course, *Didi*. What kind of brother would I be if I neglected Lina's daily wisdom?"

Melinda was speechless. What next, Grandma Zaara would call her for seasoning tips?

"Okay. I know what we're going to do," Max said. "Put your salt away, Betty Crocker, there's a new cook in the kitchen."

CHAPTER EIGHT

In a conflict between the heart and the brain, follow your heart.
Swami Vivekananda

Grant and his father waited at a bar at the Denver West shopping center on Christmas Eve. Buck watched the news without sound and Grant watched the door, his cider untouched in front of him while his fingers tapped his impatience on the bar.

Melisa was on her way and carried with her a message from Melinda—a message that she wanted to share with Grant. And since Grant's father had learned of the meeting and insisted on driving down with him, she'd be sharing it with Buck as well.

Grant's stomach threatened to burn a hole straight through him. Was she asking him to turn himself in? Was she asking him not to contact her again? Would Melisa bring legal papers with her? Grant closed his eyes.

"Rant, go change your shirt."

Grant's eyes flew open. "What?"

Buck extended a folded flannel shirt. "You've been splitting and stacking in that shirt for a week and it looks and smells it. I don't know how you can put that thing on after you've showered. You're about to meet a woman who's vouching for you to the woman you love. Dress like it."

"I changed the shirt under it!"

"To allow that shirt's smell to dominate. We get it. We smell it. Change it."

It was useless to argue with his father, and Grant knew that Buck might have a point. Willing Melisa not to arrive in his absence, he stomped off to the restroom and changed the offending flannel for the one his father had handed him. He finger-combed his hair, watched it spring immediately out of place, and strode back to the bar for more life tips.

He slid onto his barstool. "Well? Better?" From the corner of his eye he saw Buck's nod. Unfortunately his father was often correct.

"How's the well, Dad?" he asked.

"Oh Lord. Save it, Rant," Buck said, eyes on the television. "I'm not a cat. You can't distract me with a feather." He jutted his chin toward the screen. "Gonna be windy later, looks like."

"I was thinking the well might've suffered with that big storm and I haven't even checked on it." Grant knew not to give up the farce or his goose was cooked.

"You're pathetic," his dad said, nursing his iced tea. And he was right. But was it too much to ask to read the letter Grant anticipated from Melinda in private? Apparently it was.

"Better tell your friend we can't hang around too late," Buck said. "Won't be safe on the road. Gusts up to forty miles per hour across the Front Range."

Grant didn't really mind his father's presence. He'd end up telling Buck everything anyway. For as prickly as his dad pretended to be, Grant couldn't have asked for a better parent or friend. He had Grant's back no matter the situation, had listened through years of predestined relationship failures, and had supported Grant's business notions with emotional and financial support at the first inquiry. Grant looked at his father. How could someone so outwardly grizzly be capable of so much compassion? Especially after the sudden loss of the love of his life. Grant shuddered. It was unfathomable.

The door swung open and daylight outlined a young man with dark hair. Grant turned back to his drink. The man, maybe ten years younger than Grant, approached the bar.

"Grant Samson?"

Grant and his father turned as one. "Yes?" they both said.

"Dad," Grant said, exasperated.

"Hey. Name's John. I'm your Kaar. Your friend Melisa had something come up and wants me to bring you to her."

"Us," said Buck.

Grant was confused. "So what did you say? Melisa had a what?"

"An issue with a client," the driver said.

"Why didn't she just reschedule?"

"She knew you really wanted this meeting. She said there might be someone else joining you." Grant's pulse quickened.

"Why did she think she needed to send a Kaar? We could have driven."

"I'm a friend of hers and I was over this way already. She felt bad about missing your appointment," John said. "Plus she said you were kind of wacko lately and she didn't want you driving."

This earned a burst of laughter from Buck, a sheepish chuckle from John, and a scowl from Grant.

"That's a bit excessive," Grant muttered.

"She also said something about you appreciating the irony of a Kaar," John said with a question in his voice.

Buck laughed again and Grant rubbed a hand across his face. He knew when he was had.

"Okay, okay, I get it," he said. "I'm the captive now. *We're* the captives now. Hope you're glad you came, Dad."

"Wouldn't have missed it," said Buck. "I appreciate a plot twist. Let's not keep the lady waiting."

John's phone pinged and he pulled it from his pocket. "She made it out of the pool, got the client home, south of Boulder. She expects to be able to meet us at some café near there in about thirty minutes. We should get there around then. Sound good? You both ready?"

"Yep," Buck answered and slipped from his seat to button his tan Carhartt jacket and pat down his pockets. He checked his phone.

"Since when are you carrying a phone with you?" Grant zipped his jacket and tossed a few bucks on the bar as tip.

"I always bring it when I come down below," Buck answered. He flipped up his coat collar against the chill. "Gotta see if anyone's swipe-worthy in the big city."

Grant choked. "What did you just say?"

"There are a lot of apps these days, Rant. A lot of options. Not everyone needs to be trapped in a bar or a snowbound cabin to meet someone." Buck grabbed a handled paper bag from below the bar and followed John to the door.

"*Meet someone?*" Grant wondered if he'd actually squeaked this time. He trailed after his father like a dazed puppy. "Since when are you trying to *meet someone?*"

"Since when do you care?" his dad asked as he tugged open the tavern door and waved their driver through. "Just because you're scared to make a move doesn't mean I am." He strolled toward John and the car.

Grant stood open-mouthed for ten full seconds before checking his own coat pockets—phone, keys, wallet—and following John to a navy Subaru.

When he reached the car, he found his father in the front seat chatting with John. John was laughing. Grant slid into the back seat with an almost comical knot in his stomach. There was some kind of karmic justice happening here. *Actually, karmic justice would be if John took the corner too hard and I was ejected from the back seat.*

"Ready?" asked John.

Both Samson men nodded, and John reversed the Outback to exit the parking lot. Fortunately the roads had remained clear despite the abundance of melting and blowing snow. Warmer temperatures had helped, as had road traffic that maintained enough friction on the road to keep ice from building. They made their way to I-70 and took the on-ramp away from Denver.

Small talk normally drove Grant batty, but today the silence was worse. His mind was working overtime, spinning with scenarios and conversations in which he was arrested, subpoenaed, charged, and incarcerated, or with Grant begging Melisa for Melinda's address, Grant humiliating himself outside Melinda's bedroom window, Melinda's restraining order against him, *Melisa's* restraining order against him. Frankly, he wasn't sure which option he dreaded more—Melinda throwing him in jail or hating the sight of him.

He needed to get out of his head.

Odds were she would tell him to keep his distance. It couldn't be too much worse than that, right? Not that what he had done was okay. He couldn't believe he let things go as far as they did. If she needed to talk to somebody about it, she should. *If she would just—Dammit.*

On Sixth Avenue, John flicked the turn signal and pulled onto a side street.

"There's a café here?" Grant's head swiveled left and right. "There's no way this far south is considered 'outside Boulder.'"

"Rant, there's so much urban sprawl, Salida could be considered 'outside Boulder,'" Buck drawled.

"Good one, Dad." Grant's eyes narrowed. They were heading west. Something was very off. He pulled out his phone and dialed Melisa.

"Grant?" she answered immediately. "Are you on your way?"

"Yeah. I think we're turning down a street where you might be."

"Good," she said. She sounded strained. "My client had a serious regression into childhood trauma today and I had to transfer her to a place she felt safe, so we went to her place. Her husband showed up and I left, so I didn't have to stay in Boulder. You're coming to my place."

All's fair in love and Watsu. "Uh, okay, sure. I think we're here. I'll see you in a sec."

"Thanks," Melisa said, relief audible in her voice. "John knows which apartment it is. I'll owe you a favor."

Now *that* he could get behind. Grant imagined the details about Melinda he'd wrangle from her.

John pulled the car into a parking spot in an apartment complex. He turned the engine off and caught Grant's eye in the rearview mirror.

Grant's brow furrowed. "You ever do this for her before?"

"I've driven her and her friends," John said. "We have mutual friends. But I've never been involved with anything like this."

"That makes two of us," Grant said.

The three men opened doors and stood on mostly dry asphalt. As one, they turned to face the row of apartments.

"Where are we headed?" Buck asked.

John scanned the row of tasteful conjoined buildings with muted green staircases.

"There." John led the way across the parking lot and below

one of the nondescript stairwells to a tan door. He raised his hand to knock but turned to the two men behind him. "Ready for this?"

"No way in hell," said Grant.

"Can't wait," said Buck. Grant gave his father a hard stare. There was no need for attitude.

John knocked and they waited, and Grant held his breath tightly enough for all three of them. After a moment, light footsteps approached the door. The knob turned. The door opened.

Melinda's stomach was in knots. Her hair was smoothed to the point of becoming a swim cap. Why had she trusted her brother with this harebrained scheme? Why had she not reached out to Grant herself and prevented Much Ado à la Max Sen? *What's the food parallel for way-too-late regret? A hangover.* Not as clever as she would have liked, but painfully accurate.

Two bottles of wine simmered in a saucepan with cloves, cardamom, cinnamon sticks, bay leaves, sliced orange, nutmeg, and sugar. There was her mother, sunk into Melinda's low leather couch and stringing popcorn and cranberries into a garland. There was her father grading papers beside her. Katrina's feet rested on his lap.

The two of them in the same house. At the same time. Melinda couldn't remember a time since before adolescence when family had felt like this.

"*Pita ji*," she called from the kitchen, and her father peered at her above the rim of his glasses.

"*Meye?*" he called back. *Daughter.* His accent was so much better than hers. It made her feel real and connected to him, no matter the years they'd spent distant. It made her feel connected to the culture that she'd never known in person. Reuniting with her father opened a world she thought had been closed to her.

"Where is my *payesh*?" She raised her eyebrows, a smile on her lips.

"Where is my patience, *Meye*?" he called back, all severity and prudishness. His hand swirled the air. "These tests will not grade themselves. And then where would my students be? Cut adrift in the sea of uncertain numerals."

Her mother laughed beside him.

"You've been done for ages, Aarjav. You're doing the crossword and we both know it. Go make the rice pudding before she takes matters into her own hands and uses honey instead of sugar."

"Refined sugar is terrible for you!" Melinda scolded her mother. Their banter warmed her spirit, not to mention eased her nerves.

"Oh?" Her mother didn't look up from her garland. "And what about that spiced wine, hmm? What's in that?"

"Coconut sugar!" Melinda shot back and waited for their laughter.

"Heaven preserve us," her mother said, skewering a cranberry.

"Right," said her father. He tossed his portfolio of papers and contraband newspaper onto the coffee table. "I'd better get in there before she cancels dinner and suggests takeout."

"Big talk," Melinda said as she tapped her wooden spoon on the side of the stockpot and rested it on a dish. "I remember the year we scrapped the home-cooked meal and ordered pizza."

"Yes," said her father as he walked only a little bit stiffly toward the kitchen. "To this day I can't even mention dry turkey or over-salted potatoes without backlash."

A cranberry flew over the kitchen island and hit her father

in the back. Melinda giggled and her father grumbled in Hindi about people accepting their mistakes and moving on. Melinda pulled ingredients for the *payesh* onto the countertop: short-grain rice, bay leaf, coconut milk, coconut oil, coconut sugar, cardamom.

Her father measured rice into a bowl, topped it with water, and swirled the grains with his fingers. Melinda poured coconut milk into the saucepan and turned the heat to medium. She measured the sugar and her father ground cardamom with a mortar and pestle.

"Is your mulled wine done?" He inhaled the steam rising from the stockpot.

"It is, *Pita ji*," she answered. "Should we sample?" she asked and selected two robin's-egg blue teacups from the cupboard.

"Definitely." He ladled the drink into the cups. "Only because it would be wise not to serve your Swedish mother unsavory glögg."

Melinda smiled and clinked cups with her father.

"I love you, Dad."

"And I you, beloved one."

She smiled. "Thanks, Dad."

"Of course, *Meye*," he said. "I might be a numbers man, but I also know the value of a sweet moment." Melinda smiled and her father returned to grinding cardamom. They'd had so many sweet moments in her youth. Why had she forsaken them?

"Dad?" Something in her tone stilled his hand and he turned to face her.

Now what did she say?

Now be brave.

"I'm sorry," she said.

"For Heaven's sake, why, *Meye*?"

"Because I forgot . . . you."

251

Her father was watching her, hearing her, being with her.

"What do you mean, my dear?"

"I thought you weren't there for me. I forgot who you were. Who you are. How you are. The way you love us."

To his credit, Aarjav Sen was not afraid of big or strange feelings. No one married to Melinda's mother could shrink in the face of emotion; it would find him like a heart-seeking missile.

"*Meye*, I did not know how to be what you needed me to be, and so I know that I became nothing." Melinda's heart constricted. "But human beings are meant to dance in and out of the nothingness, and I hope to one day be something to you again. I'm sorry, too, for not being the father you needed. I should have said so long ago." His smile was gentle and without condemnation.

Is that what he'd felt all that time? That she thought of him as nothing? And she thought that he must be right. She had thought of his steadfast presence as nothing for her whole life. *Crap.* Why hadn't she seen that before? Why had she been locked inside the prison of her own perspective? She stared into her mug.

Her father set aside his drink and folded her into his arms. For several luxurious minutes Melinda held on for dear life. Then she righted herself and smiled at her father with a lump in her throat.

Where is Max? Melinda returned to her drink. He should be here for this. If her brother would just get back from his errand, and hopefully before it was time to eat. Or before the wind picked up and blew him off the road.

A knock sounded at the door. *Nice timing, little bro*, Melinda thought. Her father turned to the rice and gestured that she go while he continued with the *payesh*. Melinda wiped her hands on her apron and ducked out of the kitchen to hurry toward the door.

Melisa beat her to it.

"Thank you for coming," Melinda heard her say and Melinda's hands clenched inside her apron pocket. She'd had more time than he to prepare for this moment. Her hair was brushed, her lashes thickened, her black wrap dress formfitting but still family-appropriate and comfortable. Her *jutti* slippers were festive—black and gold and encrusted with sparkly baubles. Her mouth was painted a deep mauve, blotted several times, just in case it might have a chance to smear onto someone else's mouth. Not that she was getting her hopes up.

Melisa stepped aside and then there he was, a head taller than her brother, eyebrows knit together. *He's angry. Oh, God, he's angry.* Of course he was angry! Why had she listened to her brother? Or her mother? Or anyone? Why hadn't she left well enough alone? Why had she even gone to that stupid conference in the first place?

Grant froze where he was, eyes wide. She knew Max had been feeding him lies about a meeting and Melisa's distraught client to get him in the car. Melinda assumed Max had stolen a moment to clue in Grant's father, who had to be the grinning man behind Grant.

Grant's gaze pinned her where she stood, disallowing her another step forward, doubling down on the knot in her stomach. Her toes curled in her slippers and her breath all but disappeared. He held her hostage and the rest of the room was suspended along with her. Then he blinked and squared his shoulders.

"John, was it?" Grant turned to the Kaar driver who'd led them here. "Something tells me you're related to this clan in here." He nodded to the man and woman who had to be Melinda's parents, who'd stood and stepped forward, respectively, when Grant and his father had arrived.

Max, for that's who he must be, turned to face Grant and extended his hand.

"It's Mafi," said Max. "Or Max. Up to you. I decided at some point in my youth that Max sounded less like Mafia." Max smiled at him with only a slight reservation. "But after my stint with kidnapping, I'm going back to Mafi." Grant grinned and shook Max's hand.

"I owe you one for that bit of subterfuge," he said. Maybe humor would help.

"Fair enough," said Max. "Or we could count it toward Lina's credit and then we don't have to string you up by your toes."

Grant grimaced. Too soon. *Noted.*

"It's fine, it's fine," Max laughed, then leaned closer. "Rest assured: if I didn't like you, you'd never have made it here."

Grant's smile froze. Obviously some dialogue had been had about the circumstances of his meeting Melinda—not too in depth, or he'd have been driven off a cliff. But still, he knew he had some serious ground to cover with everyone in the room. And, wonderful, his father was here to witness it all. *Nothing like bringing your own peanut gallery.*

More like combining peanut galleries. Grant eyed Melisa, Melinda's parents, and Max. Max, who hadn't departed after his gentle threat, and instead had taken a post several feet away where he could stare baldly at Grant while smiling in a way that did nothing to suggest benevolence. He willed Melinda to speak. He was drowning here.

Melisa stepped in front of Grant.

"I hope you're not angry with us," she said as she hugged him. "We thought a bit of a surprise was just what the doctor ordered. I've been haunting Melinda these past two weeks, keeping my eye on her at every opportunity and in general making a nuisance of myself. You'll see Paul later—we've invited ourselves for dinner. We're both waiting for this woman to see reason and take legal action, and we want to be there when she makes up her mind."

Grant laughed lightly. Why hadn't they let him in on the fun? He would have loved to have kept his eye on her at every opportunity.

Melinda stood rooted to the spot beside a light brown couch, elegant in a simple black dress with a red apron cinched around her waist. Her feet were clad in fancy slippers but bare besides. When his gaze reached her face he saw uncertain eyes, slightly flared nostrils, and lips that almost trembled.

Grant barely felt his footsteps as he crossed the floor to stand before her.

"Hi," she blinked at him. "Um. Welcome."

Was he? He might very well be, it seemed, but he wasn't taking any chances.

"Thank you," he said, relieved to hear his voice's solid timbre and not a mouse's squeak.

Her face tilted to search his and he ached to kiss her. *Not yet, not yet.* No pawing in front of her parents. Parents! Her parents were there. Oops.

"Is this your mother and father?" he asked without looking at them. His eyes drank in every detail of her. It had been an eternity since he'd seen her. Was she tired? Happy? Furious? Why hadn't he known her long enough to recognize the signs of each and every sentiment? That needed to change.

Melinda started. "Yes! Mom, *Pita*, would you like to

meet Grant?"

The spell broke and Grant felt more than saw two satellite figures move toward them. Grant extended his hand first to the man who approached him. "Mr. Sen."

"Grant," said Melinda's father, "please call me Aarjav. It is very nice to meet you. I understand you make hard cider?"

"Uh, yes, yes we do," Grant answered, surprised; this was not the probing question he'd expected. "I wish I had a bottle to share with you all."

"Got you covered, Rant," Buck called from his post near the door. "I brought three. Just in case." So his father had known. Was everyone in on this madness?

But all he said was, "Oh, great. Well, hopefully you'll enjoy it, Mr. Sen." No way was Grant on "Aarjav" terms with Melinda's father yet. "Thanks, Dad," he called to his father. *Thanks a lot.*

Buck nodded, a ruthless grin on his face. Grant was floundering and his dad was making popcorn.

"I look forward to trying it," Aarjav said, "and to hearing more about the production process. I'm very interested in the heirloom varietals I'm told you use. Perhaps Malina has told you that I'm an accounting professor, and that we are very boring?" He raised his hand to intercept Grant's objections. "We are, we are. It is my deepest regret." Melinda's father stopped speaking to allow for his daughter's laughter. "But we are also secretly very interesting. Has she told you that the sums and totals of even non-numeric things like apples intrigue me? No? Well, they do. So please tell all when we have a chance to speak further."

Grant agreed, then turned to face Melinda in surprise. She had talked about him? Told her father about him? How much? She gave him a small smile.

"Hello, Grant," floated a smooth voice at his side. "I'm Malina's mother, Katrina. And I'm not going to shake your

256

hand, young man, so don't even try it." Katrina wrapped both arms around him and hugged. She pulled back, and Grant could see where Melinda got her candid facial expressions. Katrina's face was warm, open, and direct. There was no coyness, no reservation, just straightforward curiosity.

Grant flashed back to sessions with his therapist, Bernard—the trust they'd built over time, the way Bernard didn't pull any punches. He'd have to watch himself with this whole family. They would talk circles around him.

"Mafi, take our guest's coat. He looks ready to bolt," Katrina said. Max stepped dutifully forward, collecting their coats, and hanging them by the door.

"Thank you, Max. Mafi. Max." *This is going well.* "And it is a delight to meet you, Mrs. Sen," Grant stumbled along. "Thank you for the hug. We Samson men aren't up to date on our hug quota, I'm sure. But who is this Malina or Lina you're all talking about? My guess is that you mean Melinda?" He turned to face her just as she blushed.

"Yes." Melinda joined the conversation at last. "Perhaps the biggest irony of this case of mistaken identities is that my Hindi name—my real name—is Malina. Like Mafi, at some point in my childhood it became easier on the teachers, or the other kids, or me, to anglicize my name. And thus Melinda was born." She ducked her head. "Just think, if I'd never changed it, maybe we wouldn't be here at all."

A chill ran down his spine. "Don't even say that," he said before he thought twice about it. Melinda's head lifted and she smiled cautiously. *At least I'm getting smiles.* From her place at his side, Katrina squeezed his arm.

"Malina is very glad you're here, Grant," Katrina smiled up at him. "We all are. So don't act any differently than you would at home. Malina has told you how I make my living, I assume?"

257

Grant nodded. "Then you'll know that I can't psychoanalyze you properly unless you're quite candid about who you are. So please don't sugarcoat anything for us. And please call me Kat, or I'll start a rumor that you're afraid of red-nosed reindeer."

Grant joined his father and the others in laughter.

But was Melinda really glad he was there? Grant couldn't let it rest. She was wearing a dress, that was a good sign. And makeup, that counted for something, right? But it was a holiday, of course she looked nice. She had smiled at him; everyone had smiled at him. But Max had smiled at him too and Grant wasn't convinced Max wasn't interested in tossing him in a snowdrift.

"Take her seriously," Max said from his latest perch against a wall where he spied on Grant. "Don't let that therapeutic voice fool you. Whatever secrets you think you're hiding, she'll get them out of you."

"Max!" Melinda hissed.

"He can take it, Lina," Max said, eyes on Grant. "Why don't you spare Dr. Sen the effort and tell us, Grant, do all of your relationships begin this way? Or just the short-term ones?"

Melinda could have smacked her brother across the face. What was he trying to do? Why was he being so antagonistic? Hadn't he helped her lure Grant here in the first place?

"Silver lining, if you need alter egos for a bank robbery, you've got Malina and Gerald," Max said, to Melinda's relief. Was Max only teasing? "Now that this cowboy's been sized up, can I have a drink please? And can I get one for my new friend, here?" he asked. "Lina makes a mean masala spiced wine, Buck. It gets you nice and cozy before it knocks you on your keister."

"Mafi!" her mother said.

"You don't have the market cornered on witticisms, Katrina," Max said. Her mom darted to his side to swat his arm and wrap him in an effusive hug. Melinda's heart squeezed as Max didn't shy back, allowing their mother to embrace him, then return the gesture in kind.

How could Melinda have shut out these amazing people for so long? Her head spun.

Max led Buck, her parents and Melisa into the kitchen to procure everyone's beverages of choice, and Melinda made a mental note to thank him later. Had he meant to leave her and Grant alone together? And what was with his cagey commentary? She had a few things to ask him when they spoke later.

Grant stayed by her side with his hand hovering at her elbow. "Will you take me on a tour?" He offered his arm.

Melinda's eyes drifted up his shirt to his face. He seemed happy to be there—was he angry that she had tricked him? She scanned his face. His eyes were crinkly at the corners. *Oh.* Because he was smiling at her. Melinda took a steadying breath. She placed one hand on his arm, surprised that she both needed and wanted the support.

Looks like there's a bear in my condo.

"Um, sure," she managed. "You've seen the, uh, grand foyer," she began, and he grinned. The others faded into the background as Melinda led Grant around her condo, stopping first at the windows.

"I was hooked on this view the moment I first saw it." He nodded his agreement. "You can see halfway to the top of the park when it's clear." They negotiated the coffee table. "These are my couches," she said with a grandiose sweep of her hand, and he laughed.

"Do you have an office?" he asked. "Or do you end up

writing out here?"

"How'd you know?" she laughed. "I do have an office. It's upstairs, next to . . ." *Don't say bedroom don't say bedroom don't say bedroom.* "The bedroom. My bedroom. My office is next to my bedroom." *Smooth.* "Anyway, sometimes I can manage to write there, if I'm feeling particularly grown-up. Mostly I use it as a yoga studio," she said. "I take my laptop down here, make myself some tea, and channel my kitchen. The office is too far away! How am I supposed to get culinarily inspired all the way upstairs?"

Grant chuckled.

Was she babbling? She was babbling. Time to move on.

"My TV is my super fancy room divider," she gestured as they walked farther. "And here's the dining table where I keep my junk mail." Grant laughed. Was he falling for this? Did he think she was stable? Good, she needed time to collect herself. She'd known he was coming, and even so, seeing him had completely thrown her. Touching him was slowly melting her brain into fondue.

"I know you're just buying time until we get to the kitchen." Now it was her turn to laugh.

"Is it that obvious?" she asked. "Okay, well then, forget this stuff; let's get to the point." Her dawdling had worked, however. Her brother had had time to provide drinks for all, and the small party had moved to the living room couches. Melinda led the way to her culinary studio and waited for him to take it in.

"This place puts Paul's cabin to shame." Grant appeared to catch himself for having brought up a touchy topic. "I mean . . . I'm sorry," he finished. The relief she felt at his awkwardness was probably inappropriate, but she felt it, nonetheless.

"It's okay. And I agree—he didn't even have a hood for his

range," she scoffed. "Amateur."

Grant grinned at her, relief in his eyes as well. "Total amateur. Okay, walk me through it, drawer by drawer. I know you want to."

Melinda was radiant. She was radiant every day and every minute he had known her. But now, in her element, talking about wire versus bamboo whisks, she very nearly glowed. He tried to listen, but he was so distracted by her fingers as they stroked the knife handles, by her mouth as she expounded on the importance of ceramic bowls for kneading bread, by the way she plucked one bare foot from its slipper to prop it against the opposite knee. How could he listen at a time like this?

Before he knew it, much too soon, Melinda's tour of her creative space was over. *Now what?* He wasn't ready to share her yet. Oblivious to his reticence, she led him from the kitchen to join the others. Together they walked toward Katrina, Aarjav, and Buck on couches, and Max and Melisa where they sat on large square floor cushions. Her hand rested on his arm, but in the face of the onlookers she pulled it away. *Dammit.* He wanted more time.

Kat was watching him. He could feel it. He caught her eye and tried to wipe all longing for her daughter from his face. All he needed was a maternal shutdown, or worse, for his father to reveal Grant's high school yearbook and take everyone on a Samsonian flashback. But Kat surprised him.

"Mafi." She smiled at her son where he sat at her feet. "I haven't toured Christmas lights in ages. What do you say you take your old mom out for a drive to see if Denver does lights better than Bellingham?"

"This oughta be good," Buck chimed in. "Of course it does. I'm going, too." He stood and ambled toward the door. Kat and Max followed suit.

"Dad, what are you talking about? You hate Christmas li—" Buck cut him a look. Shut up. Roger that, but why?

"Ah, lovely idea." Aarjav rubbed his palms together before adjusting his glasses and standing. "What fun. I'll go along as well. *Dhana*, when did we last do this?"

"Not for years, my love." Kat took the hand he extended. Both of them walked to the front door and slipped into their coats.

"May I join you?" asked Melisa as she rose from her spot on the floor. "I've got a minivan. We'll all fit. Plus I only had one sip of that delicious drink and I'm fine to drive."

"Excellent." Katrina draped a scarf around her neck. "I had rather a bit more."

"Dibs on the back seat," Max said as he laced up his boots.

"Same here." Buck clapped Max on the back. "This'll be fun. And good to go before the winds kick up."

Fun? Grant was so confused as to be worried. What was wrong with his father?

Melinda looked around. "I know I put my boots around here somewhere." She hunted behind the coffee table.

"Malina, love," said her mother. "Someone must stay here and guard the roast. Would you be a dear and do that for us?" She slid her hands into her gloves. "And, Grant, I know it's too soon for me to be making demands of you, but would you mind keeping her company? I worry about both of my children, of course, but mostly Malina with her do-or-die cooking. Plus, she's got a lot to finish in there and could use the help. She won't accept it from us. *Control issues.*" The last phrase was stage-whispered at Grant specifically, and he laughed.

When Katrina looked away he narrowed his eyes. They were being set up. Abandoned in the most generous way. Grant nodded and agreed. Of course he agreed. He hoped they'd stay out all night.

With minimal bustle, the group paraded out the door, promising to be back by dinner.

The remaining silence was the loudest thing Grant had heard all day.

He turned to Melinda. Was there a rock in her stomach as well? Why was he brought here? Was he here because she wanted him here or because she needed closure? He searched her face. She looked the way he felt: nervous, guilty, and a little scared. But why would she feel that way? She hadn't done anything wrong.

She fiddled with the strings of her apron. Her eyes searched her condo for a place to land. Her hands tucked and re-tucked her hair behind her ears. Grant had to come up with something fast.

"Can I help with dinner?" Unless that was why she was nervous and scared—because she remembered what he was like in the kitchen.

"Sure." She appeared to steady herself. "The roast is already in the oven. It needs another hour and then we'll let it rest. We've got to make a salad, bake the bread, cook the *bhapa aloo*, which is like a mustardy potato dish, the rice, the *doi maach*—a fish curry—and the Bengal gram. Uh, chickpeas, basically. Plus some steamed vegetables. It should be pretty straightforward. My dad started a dessert, but we could make something else, too."

"You can't be serious."

She cocked her head at him. All right, she was.

"It'll be easier now that everyone's gone." Was that excitement he caught in her eyes? She must have thought that all sounded like a walk in the park. Whereas he thought it sounded like being at a wild game park—where he was the game.

"Why didn't I go with them?" Grant lamented, and she grabbed him by the arm. His arm tingled.

"Chicken!" she admonished.

"Don't tell me we have to roast a chicken?" he groaned, and was rewarded with her stepping behind him and using both hands to push him toward the kitchen. He loved how authoritative she became in the kitchen.

"Almost all of my spices and sauces are prepped." She steered him into her lair. "Kat and Aarjav were all over that the second they crossed the threshold. I started the dough earlier, and braided it before you got here, so it'll be ready to go in the oven after the roast, which is coming out soon."

Now it was his turn to tilt his head. "Braided? Does it want to play with dollies?"

Melinda laughed and Grant dared to feel relieved. "We make a braided bread that's kind of like challah. It's rich and yeasty and amazing." She took a deep breath and scanned her kitchen. "Don't worry about the bread, Mountain Man. I barely trust you to boil the water. Let me find you an apron. Can't get that pretty lumberjack outfit messy."

Melinda floated in the most pleasant déjà vu ever. Wind swayed the trees outside, but blessedly warm water ran from the taps. She and her mountain man danced around each other, creating food in her very own kitchen. Fresh food stocked her refrigerator to the gills. She had every cooking implement known to womankind. Mulled wine warmed her palate and spirit. And Grant looked darn near edible in his jeans, flannel, and dainty purple apron that barely reached mid-thigh. Okay, the apron didn't make him look edible, but it did make her smile.

The roast filled the air with its heavenly scent. New potatoes parboiled on the stove and the Bengal gram simmered in the pressure cooker. Together Grant and Melinda had sautéed spices and dried coconut in ghee, set them aside, and would add them to the chickpeas later to make the *cholar dal*. Fish for the *doi maach* rested on the countertop. She planned to buck tradition and poach rather than fry it, and then cross her fingers that her father wouldn't mind the difference. Its sauce warmed at the back of the range. Her father's rice pudding was setting in the fridge.

Grant had started rice for the *doi maach* under her instruction and was manfully resisting the urge to lift the lid to check its progress. Melinda blushed. Why was she blushing? Oh. She blushed again—she was intimately acquainted with his restraint.

Melinda's parents had combined the ingredients for *panch phoron* yesterday and now she stirred the combination of nigella, black mustard, fenugreek, fennel, and cumin seeds into an oversized sauté pan coated with hot mustard oil.

Grant padded across the floor in his socks and turned off the potato water at her direction. He slid in close to warm her back as the spices sizzled in front of her. She braced herself against the headiness of his presence and stirred her sauté.

"Are you trying to intimidate me, Mountain Man?"

"I'm trying to anything you, Blogger," he breathed into her ear, and Melinda's core melted.

Beeping interrupted her intoxication.

"Was that your phone?" She sprinkled dried red peppers into the pan.

"I think it was." Grant collected the device from his coat pocket.

"Everything okay?" Melinda tilted her head to one side as she drained the half-cooked potatoes of their steaming water. Grant didn't immediately answer, and she turned to see him staring at the screen.

"They think they're so clever," he said to himself.

"What?" Melinda slipped the potatoes into the seasoned pan to brown.

"Hey Rant," Grant read, and Melinda giggled. "We gave Katrina a tour of the lights but the wind started so we're hiding at Melisa's. Paul is feeding us drinks. Fancy pad, but he's a good one. I like him. Keep the food warm until seven. We'll show up in time to eat."

"They're giving us time together, aren't they?" Melinda twisted at loose tendrils of hair, which had to be a frizzy disaster with all the steam.

"Yeah, that and time to make them a feast fit for a king," he said, but she knew from his smirk that he was happy.

"It's four-thirty now. We'll make it," she said. "Grab the bread from above the oven, and trade it for the roast. There are trivets against that wall there." She gestured with a wooden spoon. "You can put the roast on them. We'll let it rest until dinner." She directed him to raise the oven's temperature and put the bread in. For a moment she attended the potatoes and then continued. "Reach into that cabinet and pull out those two steamers. Yes, those metal pots with the holey inserts. Plus their lids."

She paused to tug her apron into place and glanced at his face. Grant took the time to grin more slowly than necessary at her, but then filled the lower basins partway with water. Was she being bossy? Maybe, but food was food.

"One of these is for the *bhapa aloo* packets," she continued, "which are made from banana leaves, so that'll be fun. The other is for broccoli. Which do you want to be in charge of?"

Grant stared at her, deadpan.

"Okay, okay," she laughed. "I'll do the banana leaf part." She coated the browned potatoes to perfection, using the seasonings her parents had prepared, then ladled them onto softened banana leaves, securing them into multiple packets with toothpicks.

Grant watched from her elbow.

"Cool, right?"

"Any food you get to stab is good by me," he replied.

Melinda laughed. "Get ready for your own excitement." She grabbed a cleaver from the magnetic strip on the wall and held it aloft.

His eyes widened in a show of fear. "Is this how it ends?"

She laughed again. "It's only fair. You gave me a gun, I'll give you a knife. What do you think?"

His eyes crinkled deeply as he grinned at her.

"I think I'm liable to julienne my own finger, and you know it."

"Hey, I'm just impressed you know that word. But if you could avoid making me drive you to the ER, I'd appreciate it. I don't leave the house much these days."

She stilled. Why had she said that? They had been having a nice, flirtatious time, doing the thing she loved most in the world. She hadn't meant to say it and hadn't meant it in the way that he would take it.

"I mean," she began. "I didn't mean . . ." *Keep digging that hole.*

Grant exhaled. "Melinda—No, Malina . . ." Grant couldn't spit out a sentence either. "What do you want me to call you?"

She thought about it. "I'm fine with all of it," she said finally. "Melinda, Malina, Lina. Everyone has a name for me that's personal to them, so I guess you could just choose your

267

favorite and stick with that." She shrugged one shoulder. Not much help.

"Okay then," he said, undaunted. "I'll try Malina." He smiled. "I like that one. It's like Melinda, but it has a flair to it that reminds me of you. You've got a flair to you." He reached for her hand and pressed her palm to his. His long fingers wove with hers, each touchpoint a caress.

"Malina." He rolled her name around on his tongue. "Malina, I hate the reasons you feel the need to hide at home." He closed his fingers around hers and lowered their joined hands between them. "And I hated not being with you every second after Paul and Melisa came for us. I wanted to be with you. I wanted to go *with* you." Grant looked at their hands. Couldn't he meet her eyes anymore?

"But I couldn't force myself on you, not again, not after the way we met, not after what an ass I was. But I guessed that you were going it alone, and possibly, uh, uninterested in being around other people." He squeezed her fingers. "And I'm endlessly sorry for that." He pinched the bridge of his nose.

"I'm not going to ask for your forgiveness," he continued. "It's not my right, and it's not my goal. My goal has just been to see you, to be with you in the same space, and offer you my shame and my regret. And to go away forever, if that's what you want from me. Please. Tell me what you want from me." He rubbed his jaw.

The rugged stubble was back, she noted, and her skin flushed at the memory of his rough face against hers.

"Dammit," he startled her from her memory. "I meant to ask you what you wanted to say. And I went on a rant again. That's why my dad gave me that nickname. *Rant.* Unfortunately, it fits."

Melinda took a shaky breath. Familiar numbness stroked

the edges of her awareness and she felt the pull to shut down and flee. But her family had been with her for two days and it had mended her soul. She felt free. Plus, Katrina's benignly probing questions had spurred some deep realizations. Now Melinda felt the numbness approaching her, but she didn't have to engage with it. She was ready for it, ready to allow it to move straight through her. Her mind was online. Her senses were alive, urging her to stay present.

"Grant," she began. "I know you want to apologize to me for not believing me and for, well, kidnapping me. And that's okay. You should apologize." He smiled, like she'd wanted him to, but she saw the tension in his jaw, too.

"That was horrible. And horrifying." She took another deep breath. "But I also need to apologize to you."

Grant's eyebrows slid upward.

"We went through something together . . ." Her fingers twisted her hair. Maybe she could comb out some vulnerability? "We connected. And you reached out to me. You wrote me." She bit her lip. "And I just froze, I guess. Like I've done every other time I've been scared of getting too close to someone or something. That letter you wrote—"

Why wouldn't the words come? She'd very nearly practiced what she wanted to say in the mirror. *That letter changed me. Say it!* "I've never received anything like it. I've never felt the way I did when I read it." She watched his face. So far no sign that he was headed for the door. That was good, right?

"Meeting you changed my life, too." Melinda referenced the words he'd penned her. "Not just because of the way it started. I think that's the way we were destined to meet: in a way that would break us down so we could build back up again." Her hair had to resemble a tumbleweed by now.

"I should speak for myself," she said. "I think it was a way *I* needed to be met. I was so complacent in my life and with my cozy digital world, it took a battering ram to break it all down. You took on that role, cosmically. Or something. And you took it seriously, and you've taken me seriously. I don't really know how to thank you for that."

Grant's jaw set a bit tighter.

"No," she hurried to say. "I'm not giving you the brush-off. I'm trying to tell you that meeting you changed my life because . . . I've fallen for you. And I've never felt this before." She was gaining momentum now. The words had finally come, and with them power and ownership. "I thought I had, and what I had was sweet, but it was small-time. Completely safe."

Grant's eyes widened but he held his tongue.

"This is an entirely different experience," she went on. "I haven't been able to leave my house because my family is here, and yes, because I'm a little overwhelmed by the thought of crowds, but also because I haven't spoken with you or seen you. I'm a new person now, and you helped make that possible. I want to leave my house with *you* now. I want to return to my house with *you* now. I wanted to process it all *with you* because we went through that experience together and came out different people afterward. People who cared about each other." Did he understand? "I thought I'd been hiding out, but actually, I've been waiting. For you."

She had said it. She had said a lot. But was it enough? What would he think? What would he say? Her eyes searched his for a flicker of reciprocation. There was something. What was it? Why did he look . . . angry?

"Are you about to lock me in my car?" She took a miniature step back.

"Does this mean you're not going to bring me up on charges?"

"Charges?"

"Assault. Coercion. Anything. What I did was so wrong." His eyes were boring into hers again.

She laughed but let it die when he didn't join her in mirth.

"What are you talking about, Grant? Were you not in the same room with me? I started it, both times! Did I not seem like I was enjoying myself?" Did he think every element of their encounters was fake?

"No!" he said. "You seemed perfect. But maybe . . . maybe you did that because you were trying to save your skin. From a monster. From me." Grant looked like he was about to vomit. "You brought me here today, but I don't know why. I know I sound crazy. I just hope you can understand how sorry I am for what I did."

"Grant, do you really think I could profess my love for someone I feared? I know some people can, but I'm not one of them. No, I'm not bringing you up on charges. I wanted to be with you. I *want* to be with you."

Grant said nothing.

Melinda held her breath, then gasped as Grant dropped to the floor in front of her. He wrapped both arms around her waist and crossed them against her back. His forehead pressed hard against the silk of her dress.

"Grant?"

He didn't move.

"Grant? Talk to me. Was it too much? I understand if you're—"

Melinda squeaked as her legs were swept from beneath her. She caught air for a split second and then landed solidly in Grant's arms.

Grant clutched Malina to his chest, one arm beneath her knees, the other around her torso. If he kissed her now he'd topple over. *Romantic hero stuff sure is awkward. No one tells you this.*

Malina's eyes were huge. His would be, too, he supposed, if someone swept his legs from beneath him and bear-hugged him in the kitchen. Time to make his intentions clear.

Grant settled Malina on his lap and stroked her cheek with the pad of his thumb. Her face turned almost imperceptibly in toward his caress and he felt like beating his chest in victory. *Tone it down. Plenty of time to go caveman.*

"Malina," he said. "I've thought of you and nothing but you for the last twenty days and six hours." Something sparkled in her eyes and hope soared in his chest. "I love you. I'm fascinated by you. I think you're incredible. I can't stand to be away from you. All I've done is imagine what it would be like if you showed up at my house, or if I showed up at yours. Or if we lived in the same house." He drew in a deep breath.

Time to say it.

"Or if you were my wife. Malina, would you consider becoming my wife?"

For once his mind seemed to agree with him and miraculously stayed silent.

"But . . . you barely know me." His heart sank.

Sure, she was right, but this was no time for entertaining the truth.

"Yes," he said. "But I also truly know you."

Tears sprang to her eyes; a good sign, right?

"Do you feel this thing between us like I feel it?" he asked.

272

"Please tell me you do." Oh good, now he was begging.

But she nodded and he didn't hesitate.

"Then be with me," he said. Grant held her with a tenth of the ardor he actually felt, trying not to scare her. "Be with me. At my home, or your home, or at a new home. Write in an office of your choosing. We'll build you a bigger kitchen, and you can install a ropes course leading up to the oven."

By now she was laughing as well as crying, and Grant was smiling. Hope inflated his chest like a hot air balloon. Soon enough he would launch into space.

"I don't know how else to say it, Mal," he said, "but you'll be safe with me. I said it before, and I don't know why, but I want to say it again. All I want to do is keep you safe. You won't need your walls with me, I promise. We can dismantle them together, brick by brick—"

She cut him off with a finger to his lips, clearly tired of his endless ramble of a proposal. Tears sparkled in her incredible eyes.

"But will you?" He pulled away.

"I . . . I will." This time he did throw back his head and crow with joy.

It had been nearly three weeks, plus a lifetime, since their last kiss, and he tried and failed to hold back. Malina's mouth was heady, and Grant drank her like the sweet and spicy wine she'd prepared. He savored the softness of her lips, the smell of her skin, the sublime sensation of her body against his. One hand supported her back as she sat on his knees, and the other buried itself in the recesses of her hair, reveling in the silky strands.

"Malina," he breathed against her mouth.

"Yes," she whispered back. "Yes, I've missed you . . ."

How had things come to this? How had he gotten so lucky? Grant had awoken that morning humming with the faint hope that Melisa would pay a short visit and tell him the woman of his dreams might not hate him. Now he sat on her kitchen floor, of all places, near exploding with bliss.

Had he really proposed? Had she really said yes? Was she really kissing him with, of all things, love? Grant shook himself mentally. What time was it? He broke the kiss to gild her face with the backs of his fingers.

"Is it time to move already?" she asked, eyes closed, and he laughed. What was it about her reticence that he loved so much? *She's a sexy curmudgeon with a heart of gold, that's what.* He kissed her cheek.

"You want to feed some people with me?" he asked.

That got her attention. Malina's head jerked upright. Her fingers slid down his biceps and gripped him with what was sadly not sexual fervor. Wouldn't be a great moment for her parents to walk in.

Melinda leapt to her feet, twisted her hair into a low bun, skewered it with a chopstick—where had that come from?— and marched to the stove. Grant stood slowly, useless until she directed him.

"Can you get those pots steaming?" She gestured at the two pots and their contents. "And can you get me the broth from the fridge? It's in the large mason jar on the top shelf."

She added the broth he handed her to a shallow sauté pan, then jumped sideways to shift wine from inside the fridge to the counter, and wine from the counter to the fridge. What had she called the process of splitting and saving wood? *A do-si-do.* She danced her own version here.

"We might not have enough time to put everything in serving dishes," she said as she salted the broth and trained loose strands of hair behind her ears. "It's okay, I've had a buffet Christmas before. It'll be fine. Mom won't care."

She nodded toward some cucumbers. "Can you get to work

274

on the salad? Slice those and mince the parsley. We'll skip pressing them." *Pressing what?* "I'd rather use the time to marinate them."

Grant started on his tasks with the certainty that his work wasn't going to meet any expectations anytime soon.

"So . . . is this your mom's favorite recipe?" He sliced the first cucumber at a snail's pace.

Melinda laughed. "Don't stress. It's a Swedish dish passed down from ages ago that reminds her of her grandma. It's tasty but not complicated. And Mom's very forgiving." Malina lifted the banana leaf packets into the steamers and covered them with their stainless steel lids.

"Does Max cook too?" Grant hoped his fear of contributing a lackluster dish wasn't audible.

"Max?" She pulled light blue plates from a cabinet. "Oh yeah, he loves to cook. He makes a mean *Jaynagarer Moa*. Speaking of which, we don't have enough dessert."

"They have to be on their way back from Paul's about now," Grant said, "Want me to text and ask them to get something?" He stopped slicing for a moment. "Are Paul and Melisa staying for dinner?"

"Yes, she and I have become friends." She slipped the fish into the broth. "We're a motley crew, but why not? It's Christmas. And yeah, that would be great," she added. "Maybe from that Indian place on Kipling?"

Grant traded his paring knife for his phone and tapped a text to his father. "You've got pies in the freezer? Plural? Why am I telling them to stop for more?"

"Keep chopping, Mountain Man." She darted to the freezer to remove three pie-shaped parcels from its depths. "Of course I have pies. I make a pie a week and I can't eat them all, now, can I? We love dessert in our family. I could take down a whole pie by myself. In fact, that sounds great." She withdrew a fourth pie from the freezer.

Grant's guffaw was embarrassing, but she had surprised him. *Where does she put it?* He returned to his task. Malina shuffled items on the stovetop to allow the frozen pies a burner each, so they could thaw with the help of the oven below.

Slice. Where would they live?

Slice. How often would they see her parents?

Slice. Did she want children? Grant stilled the knife.

"So, uh," he began as he poured the mountain of cucumber slices into the waiting bowl. "Do you like kids? Do you want kids? Either way is good for me. No pressure. I'm thirty-eight."

Smooth. Great job proposing lifelong fidelity to someone who didn't know your age.

Malina switched off the burner for the fish and faced him a moment before the room was plunged into darkness.

"Oh my gosh," Melinda gasped into the blackness. "Why is this a thing for us?"

"The wind must've taken something out," Grant said. "Do you have flashlights?"

"Somewhere," she said. "But I know for sure where my candles are. Let's go to the sitting area; I've got candles on the coffee table and a lighter in the drawer. But hang on, the rice is done."

Oops, it smelled like the rice was overdone. *What's the life parallel for burned Christmas rice? Burned bridges.* Maybe it wasn't too late to reconstruct them. Melinda turned off the saucepan's gas and moved it to a cold burner. She lifted the lid to add a little cool water and soften the grains at the bottom of the pan. Maybe no one would notice a few rock-hard pebbles on their plate.

Then she led the way out of the kitchen and through the gap between her couch and television. She kneeled on a floor cushion beside the coffee table and searched for the drawer where she kept the long-handled lighter. She lit the first pillar candle and suddenly her condo wasn't destitute, it was classy. Grant's face flickered into view as he sat cross-legged beside her.

What had he just asked? If she wanted kids. *What?* Melinda lit the second candle and more of her home floated into view. She pressed her hand to her overworked heart. First it was the stress of the day as she prepared for dinner, coupled with the heart-wrenching excitement of being around her family for the first time in years; then Grant's arrival; then the group's departure and the time with him. The amazing conversation that led to—was it real?—his proposal of marriage. And then the power had added its two cents by abandoning them. Melinda smiled to herself as she lit the final candle. All that was missing was a broken futon.

Oh. That's what Grant meant when he asked about kids. They'd used condoms in the mountains, but there was no guarantee. *Whoo.* This was a doozy.

Melinda twisted her necklace and imagined children. She was starting to understand why Chandi hadn't torn Grant limb from limb. Looks like she owed the goddess a favor. As she thought about the directions she wanted her life to go—deep, wide, layered, vibrant—she realized that the complexity and intensity of bringing children into her world didn't scare her at all, and in fact, the thought appealed to her.

"Um." How to return from flashlights to offspring?

"I think I do," she said. "I think I do want children. I think I'd actually love to have children. With you. I would love to have children with you." Could she look at him? What if he didn't want kids? What if he wouldn't want her anymore now that she said that? What if she was already pregnant and he didn't want kids and—

Grant lifted her chin to press his kiss to her lips.

"Oh," she breathed, and twined her arms around his neck.

"Malina." He reset his forehead on hers as her heart threatened to burst. "It would be my greatest joy to have a child with you. Let's get to work on that right away."

"Oh," she said again as his arms encircled her and he deepened the kiss. How was a girl to cope?

As it turned out, she wouldn't have time to cope, because at that moment their family and friends burst into the house, chattering and stomping their boots. Laying eyes on Grant and Melinda in their celebratory embrace, the group—Katrina, Aarjav, Buck, Max, Paul, and Melisa—fell immediately silent.

"Well, well, Samson," Max said, eyes locked on Grant where he cradled Melinda. All three candles jumped as the two of them righted themselves.

Melinda averted her gaze from their audience but could feel her mother's eyes from across the room. Judgment? Disappointment? She raised her head to read her mother's face and marveled that even after years apart, her mother could read her like a book.

"Do you have anything you'd like to share with us, Malina?" her mother asked and Melinda grinned, eyes suddenly swimming with tears.

"I do, *Mata ji*," she said. "I do. Grant has asked me . . ." Words failed, again. "Grant has asked me to be his wife," she said.

"And what did you say, *Didi*?" Max asked, his smile so wide Melinda's heart ached.

"I said yes, *Bhai*." She ran to the embrace of her family.

Grant wanted his mom. He wanted her there to envelop him in a hug, to kiss his face and tell him she was proud of him and his choice. He wished with all his being that she could meet Malina. He dashed away tears, relieved that all eyes were on Malina in that moment, and that the lights were still out.

"She's raising a glass to you both," Buck said behind him, and Grant turned in surprise. Where had his father come from? And how did he know what Grant was thinking? Buck pounded Grant on the back and then, to Grant's shock, wrapped him in a bruising hug. "Proud of you, son. Your mom is too. You made a great decision today. I can't wait to get to know your young lady better."

"Does it bother you that *I* don't know her better?" Grant asked. "I mean, are you going to tell me to wait to get to know her better first?"

"Best way to find out if it's a good fit together is to fit together." His father released Grant from the hug and gripped him by the upper arms. "I've counseled you on dozens of ideas and ventures over the years, and your instincts are spot on. If they weren't, everything you touched wouldn't turn to gold."

"Dad . . ." Grant was lost for words.

"Don't ruin it by talking, Rant," Buck said. "You guys do anything but get frisky while we were out? I'm feeling peckish."

Grant had the best father in the world.

"I can't take credit for any of it, but there's a veritable banquet coming our way as soon as all this hugging is over."

Buck chuckled. "Let's get on with it, then. I gotta replenish after all this excitement. First the tour de Christmas lights, then the bullet elevator ride up to Paul's penthouse, then you pull this on us. Tell me there's something I can eat."

"Well, I did make a cucumber salad." Grant was rewarded with his father's snort of laughter.

"Sounds like you two are as hungry as I am," Katrina said as she emerged from the shadows. "I'm so happy for you, Grant." She reached up to hug him for the second time that day. "I'm so happy, and I'm also famished. I definitely shouldn't have had that cocktail at Paul and Melisa's but that shaker looked so fun. Malina," she called. "How can I help with the food, honey? Time to sober up your mother."

Malina floated toward them, toward him, and he captured her waist in the hook of his arm and twirled her into their own private world.

"The troops are hungry," he smiled down at her. "Are we ready?"

"As we'll ever be." She beamed up at him with such luminescence that he couldn't help but sweep her into his arms for a kiss.

"Could you stop with that?" Max called from his conversation with Aarjav, Paul, and Melisa by the door. "Some of us would like to keep our appetites."

Malina laughed free of the kiss. "Go get our guests a plate, mongrel," she chided her brother from behind Grant's shoulder.

In spite of her directive, Malina herself took a candle from the coffee table and led the way for all into her kitchen. She pointed Buck and her parents toward the stack of plates by the stove.

"It's buffet style, everyone. Mom, Grant made the *pressgurka* all by himself."

"Should I worry about what you're saying to my future mother-in-law?" Grant wasn't sure what strange word Malina had said, but he didn't want Katrina thinking he had anything to do with it.

"It's the cucumber salad of my youth, Grant." Kat smiled at him in the candlelight. "And I thank you for your efforts. I'm sure it will be delicious."

While they loaded their plates, Malina fetched more candles, and by the time everyone had assembled their meal and returned to the living room, the coffee table had been adorned with a mountain range of tapers, hurricanes, and pillar candles. The room glowed with flickering light.

"This is exquisite," said Melisa from her cushion on the floor.

Paul nodded. "Melinda," he said. "We owe you much gratitude for your grace and now we are indebted to you for this abundant meal as well. Though my offer to sue me still stands."

This was met with a round of laughter as well as a few *hear, hears.*

"I'd like to offer a toast," Aarjav announced, and everyone raised a glass. "To Malina and Grant. May your marriage be as exciting, though not as frightening, as the way your union began. Enjoy the adventure, dear ones. To Grant and Malina!"

"To Grant and Malina!"

EPILOGUE

All differences in this world are of degree, and not of kind,
because oneness is the secret of everything.
Swami Vivekananda

Melinda closed her laptop and rubbed her belly. Supposedly there was something—someone—the size of a cantaloupe in there. Melinda hoped they liked curry because that's what she craved today. Green curry, to be exact. She stood from her nest on the couch and stretched her fingers high toward her father-in-law's exposed-beam ceiling.

The energy that had graced her second trimester had faded and now even cooking was less and less attractive. Melinda was incredibly lucky to have Grant's dad as well as Paul and Melisa in the picture as her first and second trimesters had dawned and closed. She'd had very little nausea, and for this she was grateful, because those pregnancy-inspired food blogs waited for no woman. Now, most of the way through her third trimester, the fatigue was getting to her. "Buns in the Oven," "I'm Exhausted But Starving Nachos," and "Ain't Nobody's Business But My Okra" were scheduled for three weeks hence.